"Did you really believe I could kill a man?"

She hadn't expected him to deny it. Automatically a defensiveness came over her. "I—"

"No." He held up his hand as a signal for her to stop. "Don't answer that."

He started to turn away but she caught his arm. Looking up into his face, she allowed her sincerity to show. "I could never believe you would purposely harm anyone. I just thought, considering the rumors, that you and Mr. Strope had quarreled and the gun had gone off accidentally."

"You mean that, don't you," he said incredulously. His hand came up to touch her cheek.

ABOUT THE AUTHOR

Betsy Page is a well-known name to readers
of Mills & Boon romances and their
American counterparts at Harlequin
Romance and Presents. *The Perfect Frame* is
her first venture into romantic suspense.
Betsy Page lives with her husband and three
sons in Wilmington, Delaware.

Books by Betsy Page

HARLEQUIN ROMANCE

2627—THE BONDED HEART
2704—DARK-NIGHT ENCOUNTER
2730—THE WYOMIAN

HARLEQUIN PRESENTS

965—THE ARRANGEMENT

The Perfect Frame

Betsy Page

Harlequin Books

TORONTO • NEW YORK • LONDON
AMSTERDAM • PARIS • SYDNEY • HAMBURG
STOCKHOLM • ATHENS • TOKYO • MILAN

To Jane and Bob—just for the fun of it

Harlequin Intrigue edition published June 1991

ISBN 0-373-22164-9

THE PERFECT FRAME

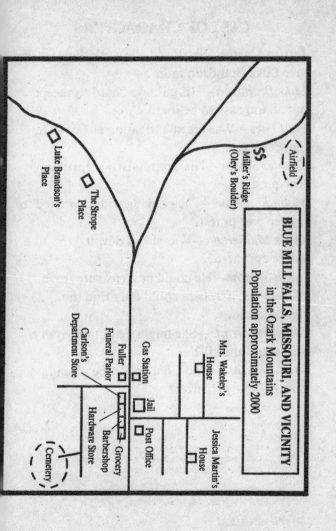

BLUE MILL FALLS, MISSOURI, AND VICINITY

in the Ozark Mountains

Population approximately 2000

Airfield

$$

Miller's Ridge
(Oley's Boulder)

Luke Brandson's
Place

The Strope
Place

Mrs. Wakeley's
House

Jessica Martin's
House

Gas Station

Jail

Post Office

Fuller
Funeral Parlor

Grocery

Barbershop

Hardware Store

Carlson's
Department Store

(Cemetery)

CAST OF CHARACTERS

Jessica Martin—She loved her work, but did she love Luke Brandson more?

Luke Brandson—His guilt was hard to accept, but all too easy to believe.

Paul Pace—Was his investigation as fair as he made it seem?

Charles Strope—His death raised surprisingly few questions.

Melinda Strope—The grieving widow wanted to lay the past to rest.

Lydia Matherson—Was she as devoted to Luke as she appeared?

Mark Smythe—He could be a treasure trove of answers, if Jessica could only find the right questions.

Margaret Demis—She might lie out of loyalty, but would she kill?

Max Johnson—Had Charles Strope given him one too many chances?

Chapter One

The phone by the bedside rang shrilly. Fumbling for the receiver, Jessica focused her sleep-fogged eyes on the clock beside it. It was 2:52 a.m.

"Sorry to wake you," Sheriff Paul Pace's harsh voice came over the line. "But the time has come for you to put all that college expertise and big-city training to work. I'm over at the Brandson place. We have a real questionable death on our hands here."

A questionable death—at Luke's place! Jessica's heart caught in her throat. "I'll be right there," she heard herself saying and wondered how she had managed to sound so calm.

Without further conversation, the sheriff hung up.

For a long moment after the line was disconnected, Jessica held the receiver in a white-knuckled hand. Move! her brain ordered her body. In the next instant she was out of the bed and pulling on the tan uniform that came with the job of deputy in this small Missouri town.

Her bedroom door opened as she was pulling on her boots. "What's going on?" her mother demanded, yawning and belting her robe. As Jessica took her holster out of the closet and buckled it around her waist, her mother's expression became fearful. "Where are you going? It's the middle of the night."

"I'm not sixteen any longer, Mom," Jessica replied absently, too preoccupied to get angry.

Molly shook her head as she combed her sleep-tangled hair back from her face. "I wish you were. I'd burn all of those mystery novels you used to read and stock the house with nothing but cookbooks, secretary manuals, and home decorating magazines."

Jessica had heard all of this before. Brushing past her mother, she started down the stairs.

Molly followed. "You haven't answered my question. Where are you going?"

"Sheriff Pace called." Jessica answered tersely, grabbing her uniform jacket from the hall closet. "It's police business out at Luke's place. I'll tell you about it when I get home."

Jessica paused and kissed her mother on the cheek, then hurried out into the cool March night. She couldn't tell Molly what had happened. Not yet. Not until she knew for sure that Luke was dead. She would have to think of a way to break that news gently. Luke was the same age as her brother, Dan, and he had been like a second son to Jessica's mother, a part of the family. Luke had always been a close friend of her brother's and when he lost both of his parents in a car crash barely a year after Jessica and Dan's father died, their mutual loss had bonded them even closer. Now, with Dan living in California, Luke had taken advantage of the five-year difference in their ages and become her self-appointed big brother. He could be even more irritating than her real one.

Her hands tightened on the wheel of her car as old memories assailed her.

There had been one truly humiliating evening at a local barn dance when her date had gotten drunk. Dan had a date that night and hadn't been paying any attention to his kid sister. But Luke had come alone and, although he wasn't obvious about it, Jessica had felt his eyes on her and her date most of the evening. When it came time to leave and she was trying to coax her date out of his car keys so she could drive them home, Luke was suddenly at her side. He had taken her date home and then her.

"And how did you plan to get home?" he'd demanded darkly.

"I was going to insist on driving," she'd informed him.

"And what if he hadn't let you take the keys?" he'd asked coldly.

She'd glared at him. "Then I would have walked home."

The scowl on his face deepened. "It's nearly midnight!"

She knew he was right, but she didn't have to like it. "You don't have any right to interfere in my life," she'd responded without thinking.

"I don't have a kid sister of my own and as Dan's best friend, I feel responsible for you when he's not around," he'd replied gruffly.

She'd had no snappy answer to that, and he'd maintained his position as surrogate brother ever since.

The truth was that after his parents' deaths Luke didn't have any close family. There had been no brothers or sisters, and his closest living relative was an uncle who owned a farm in the next county. Still, one older brother was all she could handle. But that didn't mean she wanted to lose Luke.

Breathe! It was a command she had to force her mind to pass on to her lungs as she pulled into the drive at the Brandson place. Life with Luke around had been difficult, but the thought of life without him suddenly seemed impossible. Luke couldn't be dead.

Parking beside the custom-built truck Luke drove with such pride, she climbed out of her own car and walked past two other cars, to the one patrol car owned by the Blue Mill Falls police force. Opening the truck with the extra key she carried, she found the official evidence collecting kit that spent most of its existence collecting dust. Carrying it with her, she mounted the steps to the porch of the two-story, white frame farm house, her back becoming more rigid with each forward movement.

At the door she came to an abrupt halt. Luke's image filled her mind. Tall, over six feet, and muscular from doing hard labor all his life, he'd always seemed indestructible. He had ruggedly handsome features with dark brown eyes that turned near ebony when he was angry and thick dark brown hair he wore cut in a medium length, traditional style. Just one of the "good ol' boys," she mused.

Her jaw suddenly hardened with resolve. He wasn't old. He was only thirty-two and, beneath his rough exterior, a good person. It was her job to find out what had happened here and, if someone was responsible, to see that they were punished. She reached out for the doorknob and turned it.

Luke's dusty Stetson hat hung on a wooden peg in the small entranceway. Tenderly she touched the brim of the hat. A muscle in her jaw twitched as she pulled her hand away. She entered the living room.

Standing beside the fireplace in his usual attire of faded jeans and a broadcloth shirt was Luke. He was facing the sheriff, his jaw set in that arrogant line she knew so well. Relief flooded through her. She wanted to laugh and cry at the same time. But as Luke swung around to face her, his eyes narrowed in disapproval.

"What's she doing here?" he growled.

"She's my deputy. The one with all the education and experience, remember?" Paul Pace replied dryly. A widower in his mid-fifties, standing just over five feet, ten inches in height with a slightly chunky build, he had been sheriff in Blue Mill Falls for the past twenty-two years. It was a small town, nestled in the Ozark mountains, with a population of around two thousand. The men here still felt protective toward their women and when the town council had voted to place a female in the position of his deputy, he had voiced certain reservations. The fact that most of the people in town had known Jessica all of her life was probably the only saving grace about the whole situation.

"In fact," Sheriff Pace continued, "if my memory serves me right and it generally does, it was you and Mildred Harper who were the two council members most insistent that Deputy Martin, here, was the best-qualified applicant."

The scowl on Luke's face deepened. "We hired her to hand out parking tickets and make certain none of the high school kids got out of hand at the local basketball games. It's not her job to view dead bodies."

Jessica met Luke's concerned scowl with a scowl of her own. "I don't recall any restrictions of that sort in my job description." She turned toward the sheriff and continued in a businesslike tone, "What do you want me to do?"

"The doc..." With a nod of his head, Paul indicated the third man in the room, "has pronounced the victim dead." Dr. Jonathan Clark was a lanky gray-haired man in his late sixties. He had helped bring a large portion of the population of Blue Mill Falls into this world, including both Jessica and Luke. "Doc says he probably died instantly. I've taken pictures of the room from all angles and marked the position of the body. Now I want you to collect the evidence. This could be a very touchy case and I don't want any mistakes made.''

Both the sheriff and the doctor glanced toward Luke who remained stiffly stoic. A wave of anxiety swept over Jessica. ''Where's the body?''

''In the study.'' The sheriff indicated the closed door across the hall with another nod of his head.

Starting to move in that direction, Jessica suddenly found her way blocked by Luke's large bulk. ''Do you have to go in there?''

''If you didn't think I could handle this job, why did you talk the rest of the council into giving it to me?'' she demanded, her nerves still on edge from the fear that it had been his body she had been called to view.

''For your mother's peace of mind. Mine, too,'' he admitted grudgingly. ''Neither of us felt comfortable with you on that big-city police force.''

It was that arrogant protectiveness that infuriated her. As if she couldn't take care of herself. ''The two of you watch too much television. Fortunately I'm perfectly capable of handling my job.''

''I know you're capable of handling your job,'' Luke responded. ''I just don't like the idea of you dealing with dead bodies.''

''If I'd gone into nursing, would you have approved of my dealing with dead bodes then?'' she asked tersely.

''Nursing is different,'' he retorted.

''If you two don't mind,'' Sheriff Pace cut into the exchange. ''As much as the doc and I enjoy watching the two of you face off against each other, we've got a little matter of a dead body to take care of. Councilman, step aside and let my deputy do her job.''

Now it was an official order. For a moment Luke looked as if he was going to challenge it. Then, with an angry stiffening of his jaw, he obeyed.

Opening the study door, Jessica stepped inside. This was not her first encounter with a dead body. Still, the smell and sight of violent death was not something she thought she would ever get used to. It took a strong effort to control her features in order to avoid allowing the men watching from the doorway to guess that she suddenly felt very queasy.

Knowing the victim was an added shock. It was Charles Strope. He was lying approximately in the middle of the study floor on his back, his stocky five-foot, eleven-inch frame looking curiously relaxed. As owner of the local bank, in addition to various other properties, he was, without question, the town's wealthiest citizen. He was also Luke's closest neighbor, and there had been rumors that Luke was having an affair with the dead man's wife. Until now Jessica hadn't believed them. She hadn't wanted to believe them.

The man's face held a startled expression that was disturbing. But then, death came as a surprise to many people.

A darkening red pool stained the rug to the right of the body. Within its perimeter lay a blood-smeared gun. It was a round-bellied, forty-five revolver similar to the type generally considered part of a cowboy of the Old West's attire. In spite of the blood that coated it, she could see that the barrel was ornately carved and the handles were made of mother of pearl. It was obviously an expensive collector's item.

Everyone in town knew Charles Strope was a gun collector, and Jessica wondered if this gun was one of his. Had he succumbed to the rumors and come gunning for Luke? The sheriff hadn't said anything about suspects, or the

question of murder versus self-defense. There was however a grimness in his manner that caused a knot of apprehension to form in her stomach. She knew Luke would
never kill anyone on purpose.

Just collect the evidence, she ordered herself. You can
figure out what happened later.

Maintaining her businesslike demeanor, she turned her
attention to the three men standing in the doorway.
"Someone turned the body over."

"I did," Luke volunteered tersely. "I turned him over to
see how badly he was hurt. That's how my gloves got the
blood on them."

That explains the gloves lying on the floor to the left of
the body, she thought and frowned, considering what else
that information meant. "Did you move anything else?"
she asked.

"No," came his firm response.

"Are you certain?" Her gaze met his with a dark intensity. She didn't like the way the evidence was shaping up.
Although she didn't believe Luke would ever have shot
Charles Strope intentionally, there were others who might,
and from the increasing grimness on the sheriff's face, she
guessed he might be one of them.

"Yes, I'm certain," he replied in a low growl, his gaze
never wavering.

"What phone did you use to call the sheriff?" she persisted, her instincts warning her to be especially careful
about collecting the verbal as well as physical evidence in
this case.

Luke's gaze burned into hers, as if he were trying to read
the meaning behind her questions. "I called the sheriff
from the phone in the hall."

Breaking the disquieting eye contact, she shifted her attention to the doctor. "The sheriff said you examined the

body. Did you move him in any way or touch anything else in the room?''

"It was pretty obvious he was dead when I arrived but I felt for his pulse and unbuttoned the top buttons of his vest and shirt to check the wound. My guess is that the bullet went directly through the heart.'' He shrugged toward the sheriff. "Paul had cautioned me not to disturb any evidence so I didn't touch anything else. Once I determined there was no life left in the body, I left the room.'' His manner was that of one professional addressing another, and for that she was grateful. She only wished that he was the rule in Blue Mill Falls instead of the exception.

Her eyes traveled back to Luke, and this time she noticed a small smear of blood on his shirt. That would have to be collected as evidence when she was done checking the room. Without touching anything, she straightened and walked slowly around the room, noting the positions of various objects and looking for any signs of disturbance.

Fully conscious of the men's eyes on her the entire time, she was again grateful that this was not the first time she had been involved in investigating the scene of a death. That first time she'd had to run from the room to be sick. This time, while she felt nauseous, she was able to steel herself against it. She knew that on the surface she appeared in control.

Finally, when she was satisfied she had seen all there was to see, she opened the evidence-collecting kit and took out a large bag. She carefully inserted a metal rod down the barrel of the revolver and lifted it into the bag. With the same care she placed the gloves in another bag and sealed it. Looking up, she met Luke's steady gaze and felt a wave of betrayal sweep over her. "I'm sorry,'' she said stiffly, "but I'll need that shirt, too.''

Luke's expression remained shuttered, and he said nothing as he unbuttoned the garment and handed it to her to be enclosed in yet another evidence bag.

"Luke—" Her professional mask slipped as she began to form an apology.

"You're only doing your job," he interrupted. Then, turning away as if he found the whole situation distasteful, he stalked down the hall. Sheriff Pace followed him.

Hearing their footsteps going up the stairs, she forced herself to return to the body. Carefully she began removing the contents of the victim's pockets, placing them in individual bags. She heard Luke and the sheriff come back down the stairs.

Dr. Clark went into the living room to call Harry Fuller, the local mortician, and Luke was permitted to join him there while Paul Pace returned to watch his deputy work. Admiration for the way she was conducting herself mingled with a twinge of disappointment. Paul had hoped that the prospect of actually having to deal with a corpse might unnerve her enough to cause her to reconsider her desire for a career in law enforcement. However, she was handling the situation better than many men he knew would have.

Having already removed Charles Strope's wallet and keys from his suit coat pockets, Jessica now extracted the ornate gold pocket watch he wore at the end of a heavy gold chain draped across the front of his vest. Vividly she recalled how pompous the fifty-four-year-old banker could look when he pulled out that watch in the middle of a conversation and flipped it open. It gave the unquestioning impression that he had much better things to do than speak with whomever was currently occupying his time. Well he wouldn't be silently insulting anyone anymore, she mused, as she opened the timepiece and noted that the crystal was broken and the hands had stopped at precisely two-seventeen.

Pausing for a moment, she relayed this information to the sheriff, then continued her search of the body. Finally finishing this unsavory task, she stood and stretched her taut back muscles.

The night breeze fluttered the curtains and chilled the sweat on Jessica's forehead.

There were no signs of a struggle in the room and, considering the rumors concerning Luke and Melinda Strope, this did not look good for Luke. The fact that Charles Strope was a very influential man didn't help, either. Even if the death had been an accident, the district attorney might decide to charge Luke with manslaughter.

A knock sounded on the front door. "That'd be Harry," the sheriff said, going out to meet the mortician.

"We'll take the body over to Harry's place," Dr. Clark was saying as he, Sheriff Pace, Luke and the mortician returned to the study door a couple of minutes later. "I'll do the autopsy there. But it looks pretty straightforward—one bullet through the heart."

The long-practiced, sympathetic expression that came so naturally to Harry Fuller's face when dealing with death suddenly became a critical frown as he became aware of Jessica's presence. He turned toward the sheriff accusingly. "Did you have to call little Jessica out here?"

"She's the most qualified person I have to deal with this sort of thing," Paul pointed out, keeping his tone neutral. He was tempted to add that the town had insisted she be hired and that with only himself and one deputy to enforce the law, he couldn't afford to treat Jessica with a deference that would restrict her ability to perform her duties.

"Please be certain to touch nothing but the body," Jessica interjected in an official tone, before the mortician could continue his criticism of the sheriff's actions. Then, brushing past the men, she walked down the hall and out the back door. The crisp clean air felt good in her lungs as she concentrated on stopping the churning in her stomach.

"Are you all right?" Luke's gruff tones broke the dark stillness surrounding her.

Startled, she turned to find him standing directly behind her. "Yes, of course I am," she replied stiffly.

"There's nothing to be ashamed of if your stomach feels a little queasy," he said with a frown. "I didn't feel so good myself. The sheriff said I could come out for some air, so long as I stayed where you could see me."

He didn't look good, she thought as the moonlight accented the lines of strain on his rough-featured face. "I suppose the two of you were fighting over you having an affair with his wife." She knew she had been blunt, but her nerves were too on edge to find a more subtle way of approaching what was foremost in her mind.

The lines deepened. "We didn't fight, and I'm not having an affair with his wife."

A frown of confusion wrinkled her brow. "What happened, then?"

Luke shook his head. "If you're asking me how he was shot, I don't know. I found him in my study when I got home."

The confusion on her face increased. "You found him already dead?"

"Did you really believe I could kill a man?" he demanded.

She hadn't expected him to deny it. Automatically a defensiveness came over her. "I—"

"No." He held up his hand as a signal for her to stop. "Don't answer that."

He started to turn away but she caught his arm. Looking up into his face, she allowed her sincerity to show. "I could never believe that you would purposely harm anyone. I just thought, considering the rumors floating around, that you and Mr. Strope had quarreled and the gun had gone off accidentally."

"You mean that, don't you?" he said incredulously. His hand came up to touch her cheek. "Jess . . ."

"You finished outside, Jessica?" the sheriff interrupted from the back door. "The doc and Harry are on their way back to town, and I'd like to get Luke's story on tape for the official record." A barely discernible edge in his voice suggested that he didn't believe whatever Luke had told him so far.

Luke's hand fell back to his side and, without further words, he turned and walked back into the house.

The feel of Luke's work-callused hand lingered on Jessica's skin as she followed him. She'd had a terrible crush on Luke when she was a teenager. But it was nothing but pure fantasy. You were supposed to have gotten him out of your system years ago, she chided herself. He's never thought of you as anything other than an adopted little sister. Forcing these disconcerting thoughts about Luke from her mind, she concentrated on the more immediate problem—if Luke was telling the truth, how did Charles Strope die, and why did he die in Luke's study?

In the living room the sheriff had set up a tape recorder on the coffee table. He stated the time and date into the machine then asked Luke to recount, in as much detail as possible, the sequence of events surrounding his discovery of the body.

Jessica watched Luke as he stood by the fireplace. There was a tautness about him that reminded her of a wild animal who knew it was in danger.

"I came home..." he began levelly.

"At about what time?" Paul Pace interrupted.

"I'm not certain." Luke shifted uncomfortably, obviously knowing his story wouldn't sound good. "I left Henry's place around two, I think. It probably took me fifteen minutes to drive home."

"Henry Hargrove?" the sheriff questioned.

"Yes," came the clipped response.

"And I suppose a few of the other boys were there, too?" Paul asked.

Luke nodded.

"I'll need their names. One of them might be able to be more accurate about the time of your departure."

"Frank Lawson, Sam Jordan, Bob Philes, Steve Lewis," Luke recited evenly.

He made no mention of what the men had been doing. The sheriff, being an old-timer knew already, and Jessica knew because her brother, Dan, had been a participant in the regular Tuesday-night poker group before he had moved away. Admittedly gambling was illegal in this state except for bingo games and the state-run lottery, but, on the other hand, a man's home was his castle and it required something a great deal more serious than a friendly gathering of old buddies playing a few hands of cards to bring an invasion of the law. However, since this was an official statement Luke was making and would be entered into a police file, it was best if the evening's activities remained anonymous.

"You say you returned home a little after two?" the sheriff asked, directing the question to the discovery of Strope's body.

"Sometime after two," Luke confirmed, his voice holding a stiff edge.

"What happened then?" Paul prodded.

Luke ran a hand through his hair in an agitated manner. "I saw Charles Strope's car parked in front of my house. I couldn't imagine why he was here, especially at that time of night. The car looked empty but I was going over to take a closer look when I heard what sounded like a shot from inside the house. It took me a minute or so to unlock the front door. When I got it open, I saw the light was on in the study. I went directly in there and found Strope lying on the floor. I turned him over and saw that he'd been shot. He looked dead. I felt for a pulse but couldn't find one. Then I called you and, on your instructions, called the doctor. After that I took a look around the house but didn't find anyone. In the kitchen I noticed that the bolt on the back door was not thrown. I know I threw it before I left. So I guessed whoever had shot Strope had gone out that way. I looked around outside, but in the dark, with the barns to hide in and the woods to run to, I figured it would be impossible to find someone who didn't want to be found. So I came back inside and waited for you."

"Did you hear a car or any other type of vehicle drive away?" Jessica asked.

"No," came his firm reply.

"There are rumors going around that you and Strope's wife have been seeing each other?" Paul Pace's intonation made this statement a question.

"We haven't and I'd like to find the person who started that lie," Luke insisted angrily.

"Then why was Strope here?" the sheriff demanded, clearly attempting to press Luke into confessing the truth.

If Jessica hadn't been so worried about Luke's chances of convincing the sheriff he hadn't shot Charles Strope, she would have been amused by Paul's attempt to intimidate the rancher-farmer. She'd never known Luke to be intimidated by anyone or anything.

Luke was regarding the sheriff coolly. "Like I said before, I have no idea. Even before the rumors started, he and I weren't on the best of terms. We found it better to avoid each other as much as possible."

"Was the gun lying by the body one of yours?" Jessica asked.

He met her gaze levelly. "No. I've never seen it before."

Paul Pace leaned forward and switched off the machine. "I guess that will do for now. Don't plan any trips. I'll probably have a few more questions for you later."

Inwardly Jessica flinched while outwardly maintaining a professional pose. She definitely didn't like the underlying note of challenge in the sheriff's voice.

"Don't worry. I'll be here," Luke responded.

"Good." Paul nodded. Putting his tan Stetson on his head, he turned toward Jessica. "Guess it's time to tell the widow." The sound of his voice and look on his face made it obvious he didn't relish this responsibility.

"I'll come with you," Jessica volunteered. "But I need to seal the study first. Considering what Luke has told us, I'll have to fingerprint the entire room, and I don't want anyone in there before I do it."

The sheriff nodded his agreement. He didn't like hysterical women, and if Mrs. Strope went to pieces, Jessica might be able to take care of her. "I'll take another look around outside until you're ready to go."

Luke's study door had an old-fashioned lock. He gave the key to Jessica, and she locked the room and pocketed the key. Going out to the car, she found a door seal. When attached, it would not be impossible to bypass but she would know if it had been tampered with.

Luke stood behind her as she fastened the seal into place. The urge to apologize was again strong. But she controlled it. She was only doing her job. Besides, this was for his good. Maybe she could find a set of fingerprints that didn't belong in that room.

"Be certain to tell Kate to leave this alone," she instructed him tersely. Kate Langely was Luke's housekeeper. She came in on a daily basis except weekends to cook and clean. She was a widow in her early fifties with no children, and the arrangement worked well for both her and Luke.

"Kate's sister is having an operation. She's in Ohio to look after her," he replied coldly. "I'm the only one who's going to be here."

Finishing her task, she straightened and turned to face him. She wanted to tell him not to worry, but that would be a lie. The way things looked now, he had a lot to worry about.

"You finished?" Paul asked, coming back into the house at that moment.

Jessica nodded and picked up her equipment to follow him outside.

"We'll take the squad car and I'll drop you off back here when we're finished," he said as she opened the truck and put all the evidence she'd collected inside.

Climbing into the passenger seat, she glanced back toward the house and saw Luke watching from the doorway. Abruptly he turned and went back inside.

Starting the engine, the sheriff too glanced toward the house. "It was two-twenty-five according to my watch when he called me."

"Luke admitted to being on the spot when the shot was fired," she reminded him, trying to keep her voice businesslike.

Paul raised a questioning eyebrow. "You believe his story?"

"I've never known him to lie," she replied honestly.

"I don't like to think that he would," Paul admitted. "But even if he's telling the truth about not having an affair with Strope's wife, it's my guess Strope believed the rumors. He was a jealous man. Didn't like anyone even looking at what he considered his. It'd be much easier to believe Strope went after Luke and Luke acted in self-defense, than that someone lured Strope out here to kill him."

"I know," Jessica conceded. Her chin tightened with resolve. "But I still think Luke is telling the truth about finding the body. There's got to be some explanation."

Still watching her, Paul frowned. "I didn't think the two of you got along."

Jessica shrugged. "We don't, but that doesn't mean I don't have some respect for the man."

Guiding the car onto the main road, Paul's voice took on a sage tone. "Anyone in trouble is likely to lie if they consider the personal risk in telling the truth to be too great. Luke Brandson is not the type of man who could stand being locked up."

Jessica frowned worriedly. It seemed as if the sheriff might have already made up his mind about this case. And she didn't like to think he might be right. Silently she promised herself that she would do everything in her power to clear Luke. Because my brother and mother would want me to, she stipulated, and because it's the right thing to do. No matter how bad things looked, she wasn't ready to believe the Luke Brandson she knew would kill a man and then flat out lie about it. And the sheriff couldn't believe it completely either, or they'd have had to bring Luke in.

Chapter Two

A little more than a mile of pastures and woods separated the Strope place from Luke's. Pulling into the circular drive of the stately two-story home, they saw lights on both upstairs and down.

Before the sheriff had turned off the engine, the front door was flung open by Melinda Strope. The woman was Charles Strope's second wife and twenty-two years his junior. Her features were delicate and finely cut. Large deep blue eyes completed a face that anyone would have had to judge as beautiful. She was thin to the point of being willowy. That, coupled with the pale complexion that went with her naturally blond hair, produced an effect of refined frailty.

She and Charles had met when he was in New York on a business trip. He had extended his stay by two weeks and returned home with her as his bride. It was, as far as anyone in town could recall, the only impulsive act of the man's life.

Jessica had heard that Melinda had been met with suspicion upon her arrival in Blue Mill Falls. There were a great many who had thought she was a fortune hunter. But when it was learned she had money of her own, that talk had died a swift death.

Since her marriage, two years ago, Melinda's deep involvement with her church and the local historical society had gained her the respect and admiration of the majority of the townspeople. Of course, the recent rumors concerning her and Luke Brandson had done some damage. Still, those who claimed to know her best stood loyally by her, denouncing the stories as absurd.

Tonight, as Melinda stood in the doorway of her home, dressed in a floor-length, pale pink robe, her hair hanging loosely down to her waist, she looked even more fragile than usual. Glancing toward the sheriff, Jessica saw the strong male protectiveness that suddenly etched itself into his features.

"I was hoping you would be Charles," Melinda stammered, chewing nervously on her bottom lip as Jessica and Sheriff Pace approached. When they were directly in front of her, the liquid blue eyes focused on Paul. "I've been so worried ever since he stormed out of here. Something terrible has happened, hasn't it?" Tears began to flow slowly. The woman looked exhausted.

"I'm afraid so." The sheriff's voice was soothing. "I think it would be best if you sit down."

Taking her cue, Jessica slipped an arm around Melinda's waist and gently guided her back into the house and into the living room. Seating her on the couch, she stood nearby.

"I hate to be the bearer of bad news." Paul coughed uneasily as Melinda looked up to meet his steady gaze. Instinctively he removed his hat. "But it is my duty to inform you that your husband is dead."

Shock registered on Melinda's features. She buried her face in her hands and her tears began to come in torrents. "I just knew something dreadful had happened," she sobbed, her whole body shaking with the force of her grief.

"I should never have allowed him to leave. He was so angry. I've been worried sick that he would drive so recklessly he would have an accident."

Again Paul coughed uneasily. Crying women unnerved him. They were the part of his job he hated most. Taking out his handkerchief, he handed it to the new widow before continuing. "He didn't die in a car accident."

"Thank you," she sniffed, accepting the large white piece of cloth and dabbing at her eyes, while she struggled to control the weeping. Finally she again met the sheriff's gaze. "If it wasn't a car accident, then how did he... how did he... die?"

"He was shot." He would have preferred not to have been so blunt, but he didn't know how else to say it.

"Shot!" Melinda's blue eyes widened in horror. "But how? Why? Where?"

"We don't have all the answers." Studying her reaction closely, Paul added, "It happened over at the Brandson place."

Melinda Strope's naturally pale complexion went paper white. "Are you telling me that Luke Brandson shot him?" she demanded.

"Like I said, we don't know for certain what happened," Paul replied.

Scarlet patches appeared on her cheeks, and she wrung the handkerchief with nervous agitation. "I suppose this means there will be a terrible scandal even though I've done nothing wrong."

"Something like this does stir up gossip," he admitted sympathetically.

"Gossip." She pronounced the word as if it was poison. "That's what's to blame for this whole thing. Charles believed the gossip about Luke Brandson and me," she said tersely, confirming the suspicions the sheriff had expressed earlier to Jessica. "I told him it was all lies, but he hasn't been quite the same since Chuck died last year. He wouldn't even listen to me."

"The loss of a man's only child can be very hard to accept," the sheriff offered consolingly. "Sometimes it takes a while before he can think straight again."

"Yes, I know," Melinda conceded, beginning to sob once again. "And Chuck was such a fine boy. Barely seventeen. It doesn't seem right that he should have died so senselessly."

Continuing to remain a silent bystander, Jessica studied the woman skeptically. She'd heard from her mother that Chuck and his stepmother had been enemies. However, Molly had said that everyone agreed, to Melinda's credit, she had tried hard to get along with the boy. It had been Chuck's continued adoration of his dead mother that had prevented them from living peacefully with each other.

"Alcohol and drugs don't mix. Combine that with driving and you have a deadly situation," Paul Pace said, shaking his head sadly. Telling Charles Strope that his only son had destroyed both his car and himself on a telephone pole had been one of the most trying experiences of Paul's career. Strope had nearly gone wild.

Melinda moaned softly. "To have lost both of them in so short a time."

Stiffly seating himself across from her, Paul self-consciously removed a small tape recorder from his jacket pocket. "I realize this isn't easy for you, but could you tell me what you know of your husband's activities this evening?"

"I can barely think." Melinda raised a delicate, long-fingered hand to her forehead. "Couldn't this wait?"

"I'm afraid not," Paul replied apologetically. "It would be best if you could tell me now. We will go over this again later, but I need to gather as much information as possible while it's fresh in your mind."

Breathing a heavy sigh, Melinda wiped at her tears. Her shoulders straightened as she made an obvious effort to steel herself against a further outburst. Then, meeting the sheriff's gaze, she said stiffly, "I'll try. Where do you want me to start?"

"Start with when he came home for dinner," Paul replied, turning on the recorder.

"He arrived here at six sharp," she began. Tears again brimmed in her eyes. "You know my husband. He's such a precise man. The Time and Standards people could set their clocks by him."

Recalling the broken pocket watch, Jessica frowned.

"I had his cocktail ready for him," Melinda continued, an introspective look coming into her eyes as she concentrated on recalling the events precisely. "He was in a bad humor but I've gotten used to that. As I said before, he has not been the same man I married since the death of his son. He tends—" She paused and shakily corrected herself. "He tended to be moody and lose his temper easily." A hand went to her mouth. "I'm afraid that is what happened tonight."

"Please go on," the sheriff coaxed.

Melinda's chin quivered and she studied her hands, which lay in her lap still holding tightly to the handkerchief. "He said something about seeing Luke Brandson in town with Lydia Matherson today. Then he started taunting me about how it was too bad I wasn't free to monopolize all of my lover's time." Her face flushed red and her eyes darkened to a midnight blue. "I told him for the hundredth time that Luke Brandson is not, nor ever has been, my lover. But he merely laughed." She spread her hands in a helpless gesture. "Five months ago he was accusing me of having an affair with Reverend Jonis because I was spending so much time at the church working on the Christmas bazaar. I honestly haven't known what to do. I've tried to get him to see a doctor but he refused."

Continuing to maintain his sympathetic demeanor, Sheriff Pace studied Melinda more closely. "I never heard anything about you and the reverend. But these rumors about you and Luke are pretty far spread. Do you have any idea what or who started them?"

"As to the *who,* I have no idea," she replied. "Some vicious-minded busybody, I suppose." Her chin trembled. "As to the *what,* it had to be the perfectly innocent business trips I've made to Luke's place. I went to see him about a horse. He has an exceptionally fine gray gelding I was thinking of purchasing for Charles's birthday. But if I had known the gossip it would cause, or how ridiculously Charles would react, I would have settled for buying my husband a tie."

"You were saying he was taunting you about Luke while he drank his cocktail," the sheriff said, guiding the conversation back to the events of the evening. "What happened after that?"

"We went in to dinner. I wasn't hungry after what had passed between us." Melinda frowned self-consciously as she lifted her eyes to meet the sheriff's gaze. "I was certain Margaret had overheard and, although the woman is a prize cook and housekeeper, she does have a penchant for gossip. During the meal Charles and I barely spoke."

Again a prolonged silence threatened, and the sheriff had to coax Melinda to continue. "What happened after the meal?"

Taking a deep breath, she again lowered her gaze to her hands. "Charles left to go back to the bank. He has always worked long hours. But during the past few months, he has become a true workaholic. He spends most of his evenings at the bank. I didn't feel like being alone so I called Jane Jordan and invited myself over to her house. We're trying to organize a picnic for the residents of the Olsen Home. Some of those old folks don't get out at all. Since it was Tuesday night, I knew her husband wouldn't be home and thought she wouldn't mind having some company.''

"And what time did you return here?" the sheriff asked.

"I arrived back here near eleven o'clock. Charles was in our bedroom pacing around like an angry bear. I've never seen him so worked up. He demanded to know where I had been. When I told him, he called me a liar. As embarrassing as it would have been, I told him to call Jane, but he refused." Melinda's eyes flashed with self-righteous indignation. "He actually accused me of convincing Jane to lie for me. Then he stormed out of the room. He went down to his study. I thought he'd have a drink or two and sleep on the couch down there. But a little while later I heard the front door slam. I tried to put the row out of my mind and go to sleep, but I couldn't. I've been so worried I even woke Margaret to ask her what I should do. But she wasn't any help. She told me to go back to bed and forget about him." Melinda paused to draw a terse breath. "But I just couldn't. As angry as he has made me lately, I still love the man. So I've been pacing around ever since then, waiting for him to return. This time I was going to insist that he see a doctor." Tears again filled her eyes. "Only now it's too late."

"Would you happen to know if your husband owned a pearl-handled revolver?" the sheriff asked before the new flood of tears could overflow.

"He does have one in his collection." Melinda's nose wrinkled in distaste. "Guns." She shuddered. "I can't abide the things. They make me nervous, but you people out here appear to have practically teethed on them." She suddenly flushed with embarrassment. "I don't mean that as an insult. It's very brave of both of you to be able to handle one of those things. It's just that I've always been afraid of guns. If I ever picked one up, I would probably shoot myself."

"No offense taken," Paul assured her. "Would you mind showing us where Charles kept his weapons?"

"Of course." Rising shakily, she led them out of the living room and down the hall to her husband's study.

Charles Strope's gun case, a large, glass-fronted, mahogany cupboard, was well stocked. Hanging from a peg near the center was an empty holster.

"The pearl-handled pistol is missing," Melinda said, frowning at the empty leather gun belt.

"Do you recall when you last saw it?" Paul asked.

Melinda's frown deepened. "I saw it in there after I returned from Jane's house tonight. I don't normally pay much attention to Charles's guns but when I got back to the house I was still tense. I wanted something to read to help me relax, so I came in here before I went upstairs." She indicated the well-stocked bookshelves lining one wall. "I happened to pick up a Zane Gray novel, and the pearl handle on that gun caught my eye. It was just like the guns the cowboys in Western movies always used, only more ornate. I recall thinking that it belonged in a Zane Gray novel and not in a banker's study." Then, catching the glance between the sheriff and his deputy, she paled. "Was it...do you...do you think it was that gun that was used to shoot my husband?"

"It does look that way," Paul admitted as he tested the door of the gun case and found it to be locked.

"Charles always kept it locked," Melinda said staring at the empty holster.

Paul frowned musingly. "It doesn't look like it's been tampered with." Returning his attention to the widow, he said, "Are you certain you saw that gun in here this evening?"

"Yes," Melinda said, nodding to add strength to her word.

The sheriff drew a terse breath. "Then I think it's safe to assume that your husband carried it with him when he left the house the second time."

"I just can't believe any of this." Still staring at the empty holster, Melinda sank into a chair. "I knew he had come in here before he went out. But I thought he just wanted a drink. I feel so responsible. I should have come down here and tried to reason with him. I should have insisted that he see a doctor. But a woman can only take so much. I have my pride, too." Tears again began to flow.

Catching the look in the sheriff's eyes that said the sooner he was out of this house, the better he would like it, Jessica moved toward the study door. "I'll go find Margaret. I think she has a room off the kitchen."

"No, please don't bother her tonight," Melinda pleaded, holding up a retraining hand. "I've already disturbed her once."

"You shouldn't be alone," Jessica replied without breaking stride. Leaving the study, she headed toward the back of the house. Finding the kitchen was easy. Finding Margaret's room took her two tries.

The first door she knocked on turned out to be a walk-in pantry. After knocking on the second door leading off the kitchen, she waited for a moment. When she again received no response, she tried the knob. It was unlocked. The room was dark, but light from the kitchen enabled her to discern a twin-size bed with a large shape occupying the greater portion of it. A mild snoring sound was coming from the shape.

Switching on the light, Jessica saw Margaret snuggled under the covers, her head practically buried in the pillow. The sudden brightness caused the sleeper to throw an arm over the exposed portion of her face, but did nothing to bring her to a level of coherent consciousness. Approaching the bed, Jessica shook the housekeeper gently. "Margaret, Mrs. Strope needs you," she said coaxingly.

The woman only moaned and buried her face deeper into her pillow.

Margaret could most definitely be defined as a sound sleeper, Jessica decided, shaking the housekeeper harder. It took another couple of minutes of shaking and coaxing to finally waken Margaret enough to explain what had happened.

"Mr. Strope dead?" Margaret muttered in disbelief as she sat on the edge of the bed rubbing her eyes in an attempt to unfog her sleep-clogged mind.

"Yes, and Mrs. Strope should not be left alone. You need to take care of her," Jessica said insistently. Keeping her voice patient was a challenge. After what Melinda Strope had said, Jessica was more worried than ever about Luke.

Still groggy, Margaret forced herself to rise. Going into the small adjoining bathroom, she splashed water on her face.

It was a somewhat homely face. Margaret was a large woman in her middle thirties with frizzy brunette hair. She had worked for Melinda Strope before Melinda's marriage to Charles and had come to Blue Mill Falls with her. There had been some resentment in the community when Charles had dismissed Hanna Burns, the woman who had cooked and cleaned for him and his family for years, to make a place for Margaret. But Hanna had been getting on in years and had been talking of retiring anyway. Also, in an unusually generous gesture, Charles had given the older woman a very handsome cash gift for her many years of service. Now, according to Molly, other than a day cleaning lady who came in twice a week, Margaret took care of all of her employer's needs alone.

Margaret was not as reticent about her past as Melinda. It was known in town that she had married young. She claimed her husband had beaten her regularly and she had finally left him, gotten a divorce and sworn never to involve herself with a man again. As far as anyone knew, she'd kept this resolve.

"Mrs. Strope is very upset," Jessica said again, watching the woman dry her face then run a brush through her hair. "Would you like me to call Dr. Clark?"

"No. She's a bit high-strung but I can take care of her." Now fully awake, Margaret pulled on a heavy quilted robe and shoved her feet into a pair of worn slippers. "She's tougher than she looks. She'd have to be to put up with what that husband of hers has been dishing out lately. If you ask me he's been unbalanced since his son's death. You wouldn't believe the accusations he's made." The housekeeper paused to shake her head admonishingly. "Why just tonight he had her reduced to tears before dinner, and she wasn't able to eat a bite. Then she couldn't sleep after she got home from the Jordans."

"How do you know that?" Jessica asked, playing dumb.

"Because she woke me up at a few minutes past two to ask me what she should do," Margaret replied with a snort of impatience. "She said something about Mr. Strope still being out. I told her to forget about him and go to bed. I don't like speaking ill of the dead, but at least he won't be upsetting her constantly anymore. Men ain't worth the trouble they put women through."

"Jessica, where the devil are you?" Paul interrupted from the kitchen door.

"We're coming," she called back, wishing he had given her more time to lead the woman into relating some specific details of Strope's recent behavior. Maybe there was someone besides Luke who Strope had taken a strong dislike to recently. But that still wouldn't explain how the man had died in Luke's study.

Returning with Margaret to the Strope study, they found the new widow staring into the empty hearth, her complexion ashen. It was as if the real horror of it all had finally sunk in.

"Perhaps I should call the doctor," Jessica suggested again.

"No, I'll be fine," Melinda refused in a voice that sounded unnaturally calm. "Margaret is here with me now."

"I'll be in touch with you later this morning to complete a few formalities," the sheriff said stiffly. "But right now I think you should rest. I know this has been a terrible shock."

Melinda nodded and, allowing Margaret to help her, left the room.

"Damn, I hate this part of the job," Paul muttered as he led the way back to the squad car.

Jessica felt too drained to respond. Part of it was having to deal with the grieving widow, but mostly it was from the fact that everything Melinda Strope had said had made Luke look even more guilty. "What are you going to do?" she asked the sheriff worriedly as they drove away from the Strope home.

Paul glanced toward her. "You asking if I'm going to arrest Luke for murder?"

"I still say he wouldn't have shot Charles Strope in cold blood," she replied.

"I tend to agree with you," Paul conceded. "If he'd told a different story, I would have believed self-defense. It was Strope's gun. It's clear he brought it with him. At the most, the D.A. could have charged Luke with manslaughter. But for Luke to claim he doesn't know anything about anything makes it look as if he's trying to cover up something."

"I know," Jessica admitted tightly, forcing herself to face the truth. The evidence against Luke was growing stronger by the moment. And she knew the sheriff was right about human nature. Even a normally honest person might lie if he was frightened enough of the consequences of telling the truth. Her jaw tensed. "But I still want to believe him."

Paul gave her an encouraging glance. "Hope you're right. Known that boy since he was a baby." But he didn't look hopeful, and Jessica felt a chill run along her spine.

Chapter Three

The sun was coming up as the sheriff drove Jessica back to Luke's place. The sky was clear, promising a crisp, bright day, but it did nothing to lift Jessica's spirits. She saw the indecisiveness on the sheriff's face. He was a fair man and did not like to rush his decisions. But he couldn't disregard the evidence against Luke.

Parking the car, Paul frowned toward the house. "There's a couple of things I want to check out before I leave you," he said.

Following him up to the front door, she watched as he slid his hand along the edge of the wood. "Doesn't look tampered with to me. You agree?"

"Yes." Her voice was stiff as she realized the direction of his thoughts.

He knocked. There was no answer. "Luke must be doing chores," he said. Next he tried the knob. It was unlocked. "You go inside, in case this doesn't work," he directed Jessica. Taking out his wallet, he found a credit card. "Saw this done on television once," he muttered self-consciously. Stepping inside, Jessica watched him lock the door and then close it. He tried the knob to satisfy himself it was closed then she heard him working the plastic card between the door and the jamb. It took a couple of minutes, but to Jessica's relief, he managed to open the door. Joining her in the entrance hall, he surveyed his handiwork. There was no trace of what he'd done. "But if that bolt was thrown, this little trick wouldn't have worked," he said, nodding toward the heavy dead bolt set into the door above the feeble knob lock.

Jessica nodded and mentally crossed her fingers, hoping Luke hadn't thrown that bolt when he left the house the night before.

Motioning for her to precede him, the sheriff stepped back on the porch and pulled the door closed. Then he turned his attention to the windows. All of the ones facing the front had screens which showed no evidence of tampering. Next, they checked the screens on the rest of the windows around the first floor. All appeared to be in good condition.

They had inspected the back door for any signs of tampering and, having negative results, the sheriff was again trying his card trick when Luke's voice sounded from behind them.

"I was under the impression that breaking and entering was against the law," he said.

Startled, Jessica turned to find Luke staring at them coldly.

"Just working out a few loose ends," Paul said nonchalantly, opening the door to take a closer look at the dead bolt above the knob. It was a twin of the one on the front door. "You ever throw these bolts?"

"Whenever I leave the place at night," Luke replied, continuing to watch them levelly.

"You throw them last night when you left?" Paul questioned.

"Yeah," Luke said without hesitation.

Paul's frown deepened. "Then you want to tell me how Strope got into your study?"

Only the slightest twitch of Luke's jaw gave any evidence that the sheriff's question had affected him. "I don't know. I wasn't here."

"There's no signs of tampering on any of the windows," Paul continued. "With these bolts thrown, either Strope had a key or the person who shot him had a key."

"Maybe I forgot to throw one of the bolts," Luke said doubtfully.

"Maybe," Paul conceded. "You think about it." Turning to Jessica, he said, "See you back at the office."

An uncomfortable silence descended between Jessica and Luke as the sheriff left them. She wanted to say something encouraging but there wasn't anything to say. The knuckles of her hand whitened on the handle of the evidence-collecting kit she was carrying. "I should be going inside and getting started with the fingerprinting," she said at last.

A humorless smile curled Luke's lips. "Don't you think it's a bit careless of the sheriff to leave you here alone with a murderer?"

Jessica's back stiffened as she looked hard into his weather-toughened features. "He's known you all your life. He doesn't think you did it on purpose."

A challenge flickered in his eyes. "And what do you think, Jess?"

"I want to believe your story," she answered honestly. "But that means that either a unique string of coincidences occurred, or the murderer somehow bypassed your bolts, and was not only able to maneuver Charles Strope here at an advantageous time but also managed to have him bring his gun along."

The humorless smile vanished. "You don't paint a very encouraging picture."

Unable to resist, she reached out and touched his arm. "You look tired, Luke. Why don't you get some sleep?"

He scowled bitterly. "And waste my few remaining hours as a free man?"

"If you prefer, I'll ask the sheriff to request someone from the state police laboratory to come and do the fingerprinting," she offered. "Their people are probably more experienced than me."

"No. I trust you." His manner and tone added the unsaid, "even if you don't trust me."

She let her hand fall away and entered the house. Once inside, she went directly to the study. Her objective police training told her that Luke was probably guilty despite his denials. Still, a part of her refused to accept that.

Applying herself to her task, she worked diligently. If Luke was telling the truth, there were two possible contingencies. The first was that Strope's death was due to a string of coincidences. Perhaps Luke had forgotten to throw the bolts and someone had entered to rob him. Then Strope came along looking for Luke, found the door unlocked and went in and discovered the thieves. They panicked and shot him, possibly with his own gun, possibly with another—only examination of the bullet would tell—and fled the scene without taking anything. In that case there might even be some fingerprints, especially if the thieves were amateurs.

The second possibility was that someone had carefully and meticulously framed Luke. In that case, the killer would not have been so stupid as to leave his fingerprints around to incriminate himself. Still, Jessica intended to check everything in sight.

Suddenly a whirring sound interrupted the stillness. Glancing up, she watched as two wooden dancers emerged from the doors of a large ornate clock hanging on the wall

and did a little dance to the German folk tune being plinked
out by the music box inside.

"It was my father's," Luke said from the doorway.

Jessica jumped slightly. She'd been concentrating so hard
on her work, she hadn't heard him coming down the hall.
"Don't you find it distracting?" she asked.

"You don't even notice it after a while," he replied.

Like not noticing when an adopted kid sister grows from
a girl into a woman, she thought tersely, then scowled at
herself. Now was not the time for such thoughts.

The ringing of the phone interrupted the heavy silence
that had fallen between them. Leaving the doorway, Luke
went into the living room to answer it. A couple of minutes later he reappeared. "It's your mother," he informed
Jessica.

Having finished fingerprinting the phone in the study,
she picked up the receiver.

"What in the world are you still doing out there?" Molly
demanded. "I couldn't believe it when I woke up this
morning and discovered you hadn't come home."

"I'm busy right now, Mom," Jessica hedged, not feeling up to a conversation with her mother at the moment.
"I'll tell you about everything when I get home."

"I want to know right now!" Molly insisted. "Luke was
extremely evasive. And I can tell from the sound of your
voice that whatever is happening or has happened is serious."

Luke had returned to the doorway and was watching her
with a shuttered expression. "I'll tell you about it when I
get home," Jessica repeated and hung up before Molly
could persist in her questioning.

"What's wrong, Jess?" Luke demanded. "You need
more time to think of a subtle way to tell her you think I'm
a murderer?"

"I don't think you're a murderer," she replied stiffly.

He smiled cynically. "But you do think I killed Strope, don't you?"

"I don't know what to think," she replied honestly. The "coincidence" theory required a great deal of imagination and leeway, and the "framed" theory meant that this quiet, safe little town in which she had spent her childhood housed a cold-blooded murderer.

For a long moment Luke stared hard at her, as if trying to read her thoughts. Then, turning abruptly, he stalked off down the hall.

She wanted to run after him and tell him that she believed him. But there was the question of her professionalism. It was her duty to discover what had happened here without allowing her personal feelings to interfere.

Jaw set determinedly, she returned to her task. An hour later she stood and stretched her arms above her head. She had fingerprinted every likely looking object in the room, and her back ached. Glancing around at her handiwork, she frowned. Kate was going to throw a fit. The study looked as if someone had showered it with baby powder.

Hearing a car pull into the drive, Jessica wandered over to the window and looked out. She couldn't see who was arriving. The windows of the study were on the back side of the house, facing the barns and corrals. Barely breathing, she wondered if the sheriff had returned to arrest Luke. She heard a car door slam. A few moments later she drew a steadying breath as she saw Slim Morely, Luke's only full time hand, walking toward the barns. Slim lived on a small farm a few miles down the road with his wife and six children. His farm didn't pay enough to support his family so he worked for Luke as well as taking care of his own property.

Jessica shivered as a sudden brisk breeze whiffed around her. Glancing down she saw that the window was open. Not much ... barely an inch. Vaguely she recalled feeling that same breeze earlier and noticing the curtains swaying while she was examining the body. It probably didn't mean anything. The screen beyond the window was firmly in place. She'd been with the sheriff when he'd checked it from the outside. Still the weather had been cold and it seemed a bit unusual for Luke to have left the window open. Willing to grab at any straw to help him, she eagerly dusted the frame but found nothing.

Perturbed with herself for nearly having overlooked the window, she glanced around the room to make certain there was nothing else she had missed. Satisfied that she could now say she had done a thorough job, she placed the collection of prints in her case and, after closing it, went in search of Luke.

He was stretched out on the sofa in the living room, lying on his back with his hands folded over his belt buckle. He hadn't removed his boots. His feet, crossed at the ankles, were propped up on one of the arms. The throw pillows formed a cushion for his neck while his head rested on the other arm. His eyes were closed and his breathing was regular.

Standing quietly, she studied him. He wasn't every woman's idea of handsome but she'd always considered him attractive. That was the problem. Again she recalled the teenage crush she'd had on him that he'd never noticed. She was just "Dan's sister". She had assured herself that time had erased the childish infatuation but now she was forced to admit that she had merely been suppressing it; she was strongly attracted to him in a very womanly sense. *And he probably still thinks of me as nothing more than a nuisance, if he thinks of me at all,* she mused. *Grow* up, she ordered herself. You're too old to be affected by past teenage crushes.

She needed to wake him. There were a few questions she wanted answered and she still had to get a set of his fingerprints. But even asleep, he looked tired. I'll let him sleep for another half an hour, she decided. Taking the afghan from the rocking chair, she was going to throw it over him when his eyes opened. "You finished?" he growled.

"Yes," she replied tightly. She had never liked having him angry with her. And this time she had the feeling that there might be no truce. "I'm afraid I left a mess in the study. But tell Kate to stay out of there for now. I'm going to reseal the room in case the evidence I collected turns up something I'll need to investigate further. Is there anything in there you'll be needing during the next few days?"

"Other than all my business papers, absolutely nothing," Luke replied sarcastically.

Jessica's temper broke. "I'm only trying to take all the precautions I can to ensure that you are fairly treated," she snapped. She didn't intend to say more but she hated having him feel as if she was his enemy. "I know we haven't always gotten along, but I am trying to do all I can to help you."

Luke raked a hand through his hair in an agitated manner as he shifted himself into a sitting position. "Sorry," he apologized gruffly. "I'm tired. Kate always complains about how grouchy I get when I haven't slept." He rose to his feet. "I'll be needing my checkbook and a couple of other things."

She wished she could keep this unexpected truce between them, but she had a job to do. "I'll need to note what you take," she said stiffly, bracing herself for renewed hostility.

Instead he just shrugged. "Guess it's your job."

But Jessica could feel the barrier between them again and it hurt.

As he opened the desk drawer and began selecting the books and papers he would be needing, she again walked over and looked out the window. "Yesterday was pretty cold. I'm surprised you left this window open."

Frowning, he glanced toward her. "I didn't leave that window or any window open."

Jessica regarded the window contemplatively. "It was ajar when I arrived this morning." A thought suddenly struck her. "Maybe Kate left it open to air out the room."

Luke shook his head. "Kate wasn't here yesterday, and I know for a fact that it was closed when I left last night."

"Well, it's open now," she said again.

Interest sparked in Luke's eyes as he moved to join her. Opening the window further they both examined the screen.

"It wasn't tampered with," Jessica announced resignedly after several minutes.

The tired frown returned to Luke's face, and he went back to his desk and finished collecting the papers he wanted without saying anything.

A few minutes later he left the room and Jessica resealed the door. She guessed he would be glad when she was gone, but she still had business to complete with him. She followed him into the kitchen and watched him finish setting up a pot of coffee. Shoving her hands into the pockets of her slacks, she coughed a little self-consciously to gain his attention.

"You finished now?" he questioned grimly.

"Almost." Nervously she moistened her lips. "I was wondering if you would give me a tour of the house. You could tell me if anything is out of order."

"Sure," he said, with an indifferent shrug. "I went around with Paul, but I can do the same for you." He led her through the downstairs and then the upstairs. There were four bedrooms and two baths on the upper level and, for the first time, she realized how really large this house was. It must have seemed very empty to a boy of nineteen left suddenly on his own.

As if he was following her train of thought, Luke said in cold tones, "This place was built for a large family. Too bad my mother was only able to have one child."

"Maybe you should consider having a family of your own," she suggested, then flushed when she realized what she'd said. Even more unnerving was the intensity of the desire that filled her as she suddenly pictured herself in the role of his wife. Stop it! she ordered herself. She was here to help him. Behaving like a schoolgirl wasn't going to do that.

"I've thought about it," he admitted gruffly. "But now it looks as if it may be too late."

And even if he did marry, it wouldn't be you, she told herself firmly. She struggled to cover her inner turmoil, to find the strength to reassure him. "You haven't been tried. You haven't even been arrested."

The scowl on Luke's face deepened. "I'm not a fool, Jess, and I refuse to kid myself. I know it's only a matter of time before Sheriff Pace comes back with handcuffs for me."

As much as she wanted to, she couldn't refute what he said. Even his position as a town councilman couldn't protect him much longer. A heavy silence accompanied the remainder of her inspection of the house. To Jessica's disappointment, they found nothing out of the ordinary. "There is one more matter that needs taking care of," she said with an edge of self-consciousness as they returned to the kitchen. "I'll need to take both your and Slim's finger-prints. They'll have to be sorted out from any others I found in the study."

"Sure," he replied hollowly. "Guess if someone is going to have to take my fingerprints, I'd rather it was you."

I'd rather not be doing this at all, she thought worriedly, *but it may be the only thing that can keep you out of jail.*

She waited patiently as he went to the back door and called out to the farm hand to come inside. She took Slim's prints first, then let the man return to his work. Taking Luke's prints was harder than she'd expected. Finishing as quickly as possible, she stored the prints in her case. "I'll need Kate's sister's address and phone number," she said apologetically. "If you don't have them, maybe you could tell me who would. I'll have to call Kate and explain what has happened. Then I'll arrange for someone from the local police department there to take her prints and send them to me."

"I hate involving Kate in this," Luke said as he wrote out the requested information.

"So do I, but it's necessary," she replied. As he handed her the address, her gaze met his. "I'm sorry any of this had to happen," she added sincerely.

The brown of his eyes softened, and for a moment she felt herself being drawn into their warm depths, then his gaze became shuttered again. "Yeah, me too," he said gruffly.

Jessica had the strongest desire to put her arms around him and tell him that she would stand by him no matter what. But that would only embarrass them both and jeop-ardize her ability to work toward proving his innocence. Avoiding his gaze, she turned a page in her notebook. She had one last question to ask. The answer was vital if she was going to be able to help Luke, but a part of her was afraid to hear the answer. "Who besides you has keys to this house?"

"Kate and I are the only ones with keys. The spares are locked in my safe in the study," he replied.

Jessica breathed a sigh of relief. Even knowing that she and Luke had no future together, she hadn't wanted to hear that he'd given some woman other than Kate the keys to his home, and the fewer spare sets of keys that were about, the easier it would be to find out who could have gotten one. She forced herself to continue. "Have you ever loaned your keys to anyone for any length of time? Maybe when you were going to be away and someone needed to pick up something at the house?" Actually it was the thought of Lydia Matherson coming over to fix him dinner that formed in her mind. Jessica didn't believe the rumors about Luke and Melinda Strope, but everyone in town knew the high school history teacher had set her cap for Luke. A hard lump formed in Jessica's stomach as she waited for the answer. It had nothing to do with the resolution of the case.

"No," he replied after a few moments' thought. "Not that I can recall."

Her momentary relief was fast overshadowed by the knowledge that it was beginning to look more and more impossible for anyone but Luke to have killed Charles Strope. Checking that the evidence-collection case was securely shut, she said tightly, "I guess that takes care of everything for now."

But as she turned to leave, he caught her by the arm and swung her around. "I want to know if you think I'm guilty," he demanded.

"If you tell me you're innocent, then I'll believe you," she heard herself saying and knew it was true. No matter what the apparent facts of the case were, she trusted that Luke would never lie to her.

"I've already told you that," he growled, tightening his grip on her arm.

"I need to hear it once more," she said tersely. "When there are no other witnesses. When it's just you and me."

"You think having witnesses will make a difference in my story?" he demanded acidly. "Damn it, Jess, either you believe in me or you don't, and it's obvious that you don't."

"Luke." His name came out almost as a plea.

Abruptly he released her. "Get out!"

She knew that look on his face. It would do no good to try to talk to him now. She understood his anger. Leaving the kitchen, she started down the hall toward the front door.

Suddenly the kitchen door opened so hard it hit the wall with a loud bang. Heavy footsteps approached her rapidly. Turning, she met Luke's gaze, black with anger.

"I did not kill Charles Strope," he ground out through clenched teeth, then he turned and stalked back into the kitchen.

Setting the case she was carrying on the floor, she followed him. He was standing, looking out the back door, his back rigid. When he turned to look at her there was arrogant defiance engraved on his features.

She met the blackness in his eyes levelly. "I believe you."

"For how long?" he threw back cynically.

Once again her nerves reached the brittle edge. "Do you want my help or not?"

A bitter half smile curled one corner of his mouth. "Is this what you call helping?"

Her jaw hardened. She started to turn to leave but paused as another thought crossed her mind. "Melinda Strope said she came over here to ask about buying a horse. She seems to feel that is how the rumors about you two might have gotten started.''

''She did come by a couple of times to look over a gray gelding. Said something about considering it for a present for her husband,'' Luke admitted. He added flatly, ''Selling horses is one of my chief means of making a living.''

Jessica tossed him a disgruntled frown. He was obviously in no mood to be forthcoming. ''Get some sleep,'' she suggested tersely. ''Maybe that will improve your disposition. We'll talk again later.''

The ringing of the phone interrupted the rebuttal Luke was about to make. Thinking it might be the sheriff, Jessica waited for him to answer it, but it wasn't Paul Pace.

''I appreciate your faith in me, Lydia,'' Luke said after a moment. ''At a time like this a man needs to know his friends believe in him.'' Glancing toward Jessica, he added, ''Without reservations.''

Not waiting to hear any more, Jessica left. Pulling out of Luke's drive onto the main road, she bit her lip to keep it from trembling with rage. It was easy for Lydia Matherson to have given Luke her complete support without question. She hadn't spent the morning examining a dead body and gathering information that all pointed to Luke as the killer.

But Jessica wasn't questioning Luke's guilt or innocence any longer. She had meant what she had said. Luke had told her he was innocent and she now believed him without reservation. She knew it wasn't a professional attitude. But it was born out of her gut instincts. And she knew she'd have to trust her instincts to lead her to the proper path for what seemed to be turning into a case that could make or break her career in this town.

Chapter Four

Returning to the jail, Jessica was greeted by Harriet Forde, the dispatcher, secretary and all-round Girl Friday to the sheriff. Harriet was obviously curious but she asked no questions. This was precisely the reason the slightly plump, middle-aged woman had kept her job for fifteen years. She knew when not to pry, and she never gossiped about what she heard at work. "You wouldn't believe how busy this phone has been," she said with a shake of her head. "Half the town wants to confirm that there has been a killing, and the other half wants to know who the sheriff is going to arrest."

"Just keep them all guessing," Jessica responded. The attempt at humor failed miserably when she could not force herself to produce even the smallest smile or comradely wink.

Immediately Harriet's expression was one of motherly concern. "Are you all right? Looking at dead bodies isn't a pleasant way to start the day."

"I'm fine, just a little tired," Jessica assured her. Opening the case she was carrying, she extracted the collection of fingerprints. "Could you see that these get to the state lab as soon as possible?" She felt a sudden wave of nausea as she noticed Charles Strope's prints on top of the stack.

She'd stopped by the mortuary on her way to the jail to take them. It had been one of her least favorite activities of the morning. "I need to know which of the prints I collected in the murder room and from the doors match the identified ones, and which prints there are no matches for."

"You're in luck. They can still go out with the rest of the stuff the sheriff gave me," Harriet said with an encouraging smile as she accepted the stack of papers and pulled out a large manila envelope. In more businesslike tones, she added, "The sheriff said he wanted to see you as soon as you came in."

Nodding, Jessica knocked on the door of the only private office in the place and waited until Paul Pace gave his usual bark of acknowledgement.

"You find anything else of interest?" he asked as she entered and lowered herself into one of the wooden chairs across from his desk.

"I won't know until the state lab people check out the fingerprints," she replied. "I sent along Luke's, Charles Strope's and Slim's. Kate Langely is in Ohio. I'll call and arrange for her prints to be taken and sent to the lab, as well. Then it will be up to the experts to tell us if there are any unidentifiable prints in the lot. They already have yours, mine and Doc Clark's on file."

Tilting his chair back so that it was balanced against the wall on the two back legs, Paul Pace shoved his hands into his pockets. "I don't like saying this but from where I sit right now, this case looks pretty clear cut. I don't suppose Luke changed any part of his story?"

"No." She hesitated for a moment then added, "I know it looks bad for him but I honestly believe he's telling the truth. And, when I was out there I noticed that one of the windows in the study was unlocked and open."

Interest showed on the sheriff's face. "Thought I checked out all the screens. You telling me someone could have gotten in that way?"

"No," Jessica admitted. "It's just that Luke says he didn't open that window."

A sternness came over the sheriff's features. "I know how you feel. I'd like to believe Luke's story myself. But we're lawmen, Jessica. We have to deal with the facts and right now all of the facts point to Luke Brandson's guilt. The death occurred in his study. By his own admission the house was double locked and even if one of the bolts hadn't been thrown, Charles Strope is not the type of man to break into another man's house. Not to mention the fact that there was no sign of forced entry."

"But if Luke was mistaken and one of the door bolts hadn't been set, the intruder could have used a plastic credit card. That wouldn't have left any signs," Jessica pointed out sharply.

Rewarding her with a fatherly scowl, Paul continued, "And we know Strope went gunning for Brandson. He'd been drinking and was in a rage. Seems most likely to me that Luke was forced to defend himself."

"But if that was the case, he would have told us it was self-defense," Jessica insisted.

"Not if the rumors about him and the widow have any basis in truth," Paul pointed out matter-of-factly. "Even if they don't, they could cause trouble. It'd be reasonable for Luke to be afraid we wouldn't believe the death was pure self-defense. And, the smallest shred of evidence that the rumors were true could give the district attorney enough ammunition to go for a charge of manslaughter, maybe even murder. Strope was too influential a man in these parts for his death to go unchallenged."

"I suppose," she admitted. Her jaw tensed with resolve. "But I still think Luke is telling the truth."

"Then you better hope the gun carries more than Strope's fingerprints and doesn't carry Luke's." The sheriff lowered the front legs of his chair back to the floor. "In the meantime, you call Kate Langely and set things up with the Ohio police to get her fingerprints taken, then go have some lunch. I want to give Mrs. Strope a couple more hours before I question her again, and while I'm talking to her, I want you to talk to Margaret Demis. She doesn't like men, and she might tell you things she wouldn't say if I was around. Then we'll both talk to Max Johnson. I wouldn't want to be accused of running a sloppy investigation."

Jessica nodded and left. Max Johnson. The image of the bearded, forty-four-year-old horse trainer loomed strong in her mind. About two years earlier, soon after his marriage to Melinda, Strope had bought a couple of thoroughbred colts. At the same time he had hired Max Johnson. Talk had it that Johnson had been working for one of the top stables in the country until he developed a strong taste for liquor. Then his career had taken a quick downhill turn, especially after a prize foal had died in a freak accident while under Max's care. He had claimed to be reformed and looking for a second chance. Strope wasn't normally a man who was willing to deal with life's losers, but Johnson undeniably knew horses and came cheap. Strope had offered him the small apartment built onto the end of his stables. Max kept pretty much to himself, spending most of his time with the horses.

Occasionally Jessica had seen him on a Saturday night, hanging around the pool hall, but he'd never caused any trouble. Still, she didn't feel comfortable around him. Maybe it was the way the big man looked at her, as if appraising her like an animal he was considering purchasing.

Setting thoughts of Max aside for the moment, Jessica dialed the Ohio number Luke had given her. After explaining to Kate in vague detail what had happened, she got the woman's consent to have her fingerprints taken. Next Jessica asked her about her keys. When Kate left the phone to check her purse, Jessica mentally crossed her fingers, hoping that Kate would find her set was missing. But they weren't. Kate was also insistent that they had never been out of her possession. "I'm more responsible about Luke's keys than about my own," she stated firmly.

Thanking Kate for her cooperation, Jessica hung up. So much for the theory that someone has stolen Kate's keys and used them, she mused tiredly. Depressed and still suffering from the effects of dealing with a dead body and missing most of a night's sleep, she couldn't stand the thought of lunch. She did, however, drive home.

The garage that went with the house was a separate structure and had been converted into Jessica's mother's beauty salon. Every piece of gossip worth knowing, and a great deal that wasn't, eventually filtered through her mother's establishment. Maybe, just maybe, Molly had heard something that might help Luke's case. Jessica knew she was grabbing at straws, but right now she was willing to settle for anything she could use to help Luke.

Molly was settling a customer under a dryer when Jessica arrived. Assuring the woman she would be back in twenty minutes, Molly took her daughter by the arm and guided her out of the salon and into the house. "Do you have any idea how humiliating it is to learn from a customer that your daughter has been investigating a murder?" Molly looked more angry than distressed. "And what is this foolishness about Luke maybe being the murderer? If I have to put up with a daughter who wants to be Wyatt Earp, I should, at the very least, have the satisfaction of knowing what is going on in town before everyone else.''

Jessica sank down into a chair at the kitchen table. "It wasn't something I felt like discussing over the phone," she said tiredly.

Molly's indignation was immediately replaced by motherly concern. "And I don't suppose you've eaten anything, either," she said with a shake of her head.

As she headed for the refrigerator, Jessica held up her hand. "Please, the thought of food is nauseating to me at the moment."

"Some orange juice then," Molly prescribed, already pouring.

Taking a tentative sip of the juice, Jessica had to admit that the cold liquid did taste good and soothed her stomach.

Molly sat down opposite her. "Now will you, please, tell me what is going on? People are saying that Luke might have killed Charles Strope."

"Mr. Strope's body was found at Luke's place," Jessica explained levelly. "He'd been shot apparently with one of his own guns. Luke claims he didn't do it. He says he had been over at Henry Hargrove's place until two this morning, and that he had just gotten home when he heard a shot. He went into the house and found Strope dead on the study floor."

Molly looked hard at her daughter. "Since Luke's parents died, he's been closer to us, me and Dan, anyway, than anyone. I know the two of you haven't always gotten along, but I know Luke like a son and he's not a murderer."

"I know all that, Mom." Jessica stared into her glass. "It just doesn't look very good for him right now."

Molly frowned. "I suppose the rumors about him and Melinda Strope aren't helping."

Jessica shook her head. "No, they aren't."

Molly's expression hardened. "Well, I don't believe them. Luke's not the kind of man to fool around with a married woman."

"The problem is that Charles Strope did believe the rumors," Jessica said tightly, worry wrinkling her brow. "According to his wife, he went off the deep end last evening, and the evidence seems to imply that he went gunning for Luke."

"Then the killing could have been an accident. The gun could have gone off while Luke was defending himself," Molly speculated hopefully, then she frowned in confusion. "But that's not what Luke says happened?"

Jessica nodded. Lifting her head to face her mother, she said apologetically, "I'm counting on you not to discuss whatever I tell you with anyone."

"You certainly do know how to make a person's life difficult," Molly said grimacing. "But I won't. However, I do intend to tell everyone that I believe Luke is completely innocent."

"That you have my permission to do," Jessica conceded, adding, "Now I need your help. Do you know of anyone who might have wanted to see Charles Strope dead? Is there someone he might have made a bad business deal with, for instance, or a foreclosure that caused particularly bad feelings?"

"Killing someone is pretty strong revenge," Molly mused. "I admit Charles was a hard businessman, and made quite a few enemies, but the only one I can think of who might go to an extreme to get even would be Hank Kirkland."

Jessica frowned, trying to place the name. "Who is Hank Kirkland?"

"He owned that little liquor store just across the county line," Molly elaborated.

Recognition sparked in Jessica's mind. "I remember that place."

"Well, I certainly hope you weren't one of his customers," Molly said with a reproving grimace.

"I'm female," Jessica reminded her. "In this town, if anyone brought liquor to take on a date it was the male. At least that was the way it was when I was in high school."

"I wish you had been that conscious of your gender when you settled on a career," her mother muttered.

Jessica rewarded her with a scowl. "Could we get back to Kirkland? What did he have against Charles Strope?"

"Charles Strope ran him out of business," Molly explained. "You weren't here when Charles's son Chuck died. You can't imagine how Charles behaved. He ranted and raved about revenge and harassed Paul Pace daily, insisting that the sheriff find out where his son had purchased the liquor and drugs and arrest the people responsible for providing such things to minors. In the end Paul never could trace the drugs. But he did trace the purchase of the liquor to Kirkland's place. The man was arrested and fined for selling to a minor, and that was it as far as the law was concerned. But Charles wanted more. He bought the land directly across the highway from Kirkland's place and built another liquor store. He sold everything at cost until Kirkland went bankrupt. I think even Hank Kirkland might not have taken it so hard if Charles had closed down his store and sold it after that, but he didn't. He merely hiked the prices up to the going rate and ended up with a very profitable business out of his act of revenge."

"Where is Kirkland now?" Jessica asked.

"I heard he went to Texas and opened up a bar." Glancing toward the wall clock, Molly gave a shriek. "I have to run. I want Linda's hair dried but not cooked." In the next instant she was up and gone.

Jessica took a couple of sips of the juice, then, unable to wait any longer, drove back to the jail.

"I've already talked to him," the sheriff informed her, when she asked him about Hank Kirkland. "He was tending bar at his place in Texas and has several regular customers who will vouch for him."

Jessica could not suppress a disgruntled frown. She had known Kirkland was probably a long shot but she had hoped he could be counted as a suspect, at least long enough for her to find something more concrete to clear Luke. "What about someone at the bank? Or maybe Strope wasn't working late. Maybe he was so suspicious of his wife because he was having an affair himself. Maybe while he was waiting for Luke, the irate husband caught up with him."

"You're grasping at thin air," the sheriff cautioned. "I was over at the bank this morning. Strope was definitely working late last night. He left several letters on the dictaphone for his secretary, and he'd read through some complicated papers and signed them."

"Maybe he discovered someone was embezzling money," Jessica suggested, unwilling to give up too easily.

"The bank had its yearly audit last month and the books were perfect," Paul replied.

He has to have overlooked something, Jessica thought frantically. "Would you mind if I did a little snooping on my own?" she asked.

A flash of anger in Paul Pace's eyes warned her that he didn't like having his competence questioned. And he had earned the right to be angry. He was good at his job. But Luke's future was at stake.

She schooled her face into an expression of enthusiasm. "I would really like to cover all of the bases myself, just for the experience." She hated making herself look like an amateur, but if she was going to be able to discover anything that would help Luke she would have to be continuously treading on the sheriff's heels, and she didn't want him to become offended and stalemate her investigation.

For a moment he studied her. Then he shrugged. "Go ahead," he said with an air of fatherly tolerance.

Before he could change his mind, she left.

CYNTHIA WILSON, a curvaceous redhead in her late twenties, was Charles Strope's private secretary. For a brief moment, Jessica toyed with the idea that Cynthia and Charles might have been having an affair. But according to the town gossip, Cynthia was happily married, and Jessica knew for a fact that the redhead had outstanding secretarial skills—the top in her class in both typing and accounting. "The sheriff has already been here," she said as she opened the door of Charles Strope's office and stood to one side to allow Jessica to enter.

"I know," Jessica replied, throwing the woman a carefully schooled, self-conscious smile. "But he wants me to learn as much as possible about investigating a murder, so I'm supposed to take a look around, too."

Only a year older than Jessica, and one of the locals with whom she had attended school, Cynthia eyed her curiously. "I really will never understand why you would want to spend your days chasing criminals."

Jessica had heard dozens of variations on this since she'd decided on a career in law enforcement in her home town. She'd taught herself to respond with a sense of humor. "My mother keeps hoping it's just a phase I'm going through," she replied with a friendly smile.

"Well, I know I wouldn't want to have to deal with some of our Saturday-night drunks down by the pool hall," the redhead said with a grimace as she continued to watch Jessica from the doorway.

Jessica refrained from mentioning that the Saturday-night drunks had been a great deal easier to handle than the domestic brawls she'd witnessed. Instead she concentrated on leafing through the papers stacked neatly on Charles Strope's desk. "Your boss certainly kept you busy," she said in easy conversational tones, hoping to get Cynthia talking about her job and about her boss.

"Yes." The redhead frowned thoughtfully, holding her carefully manicured hand out in front of her to examine the quality of the workmanship. "I suppose I should feel more mournful about Mr. Strope's passing but he wasn't an easy man to get along with. Especially the past year or so. He's been working extra late and leaving letters on the dictaphone, then expecting me to have them done when he got in as if I was a day late in my work."

"I never realized a bank president had so much to do," Jessica remarked absently, continuing to sift through the papers, her mind only half concentrating on the secretary's complaints.

"Oh, it wasn't just this bank that kept him busy." Cynthia stepped fully into the office and, closing the door, said in a conspiratorial tone, "The people in this town didn't realize it but Charles Strope had loads of other investments. He even owned partnerships in a couple of banks in St. Louis and Kansas City and some apartment complexes."

This caught Jessica's attention. "No kidding?" she said, putting a gossipy edge on her voice to encourage further elaboration.

"While he was alive, I'd have lost my job if I mentioned any of this to anyone." In spite of the fact that the door was closed, Cynthia lowered her voice even more. "But now that he's dead I suppose it will come out anyway. Mrs. Strope is going to be a very rich widow."

Jessica filed that information away in the back of her mind as she quickly leafed through the desk calendar. "I suppose Frank Lawson handled all of Mr. Strope's legal affairs?" she questioned, seeing the lawyer's name neatly penned in.

"As far as I know," the secretary confirmed.

"I notice Mr. Strope had scheduled an appointment with Mr. Lawson today," Jessica mused thoughtfully.

"Wednesday at two," Cynthia confirmed. "It was probably more about that foundation business."

Jessica gave the woman a questioning glance. "Foundation business?"

"He's been thinking of setting up a foundation to deal with drug and alcohol abuse among the youth in this state," Cynthia elaborated. "Since Chuck died, Mr. Strope's been almost a fanatic on the subject of teenagers drinking and using drugs. Then, a few months ago he came up with this foundation idea. He's been keeping it pretty hush-hush until the details were all worked out."

"I had heard his son's death had affected him strongly," Jessica said sympathetically.

"It certainly did." The redhead nodded to add emphasis to her words, then added in disapproving tones, "And then to have his wife take up with Luke Brandson. I suppose he had reason to be angry all of the time. Still, he made my life miserable some days."

"Well, he won't be doing that anymore," Jessica replied, adding tersely, "And so far it's only rumor that Luke was having an affair with Melinda Strope. There isn't any proof."

The redhead's jaw tightened defensively. "Well, Mr. Strope sure believed those rumors," she said haughtily.

Jessica took a calming breath. It wouldn't do to leave the secretary feeling insulted. She might need Cynthia's cooperation later. "It's my job to remain open-minded," she said with an edge of apology. "I'm only supposed to look at the proven facts."

Cynthia shrugged. "I guess so," she conceded in less hostile tones. "But it's always been my experience that where there's smoke, there's fire."

A lot of people probably feel the same way, Jessica thought worriedly. Aloud she said, "Thanks for letting me take a look around."

"It was no problem," Cynthia assured her as she opened the door and stepped aside to allow Jessica to pass. "But I don't understand why you're spending time here. Even if the rumors aren't true, from what I heard it seems pretty clear-cut that Luke Brandson shot him."

"Things are not always what they seem," Jessica replied cryptically, holding a tight rein on her temper. "Luke has a good reputation in this town, and the sheriff doesn't want to be accused of running a one-sided investigation."

"I suppose he does have to cover all the bases," the secretary conceded.

Walking back to the jail, Jessica wondered how Luke would do in a public opinion poll. She guessed that people like Cynthia Wilson, who believed the rumors about the affair, were probably convinced he was guilty. But there would be many who knew Luke better and would be willing to give him the benefit of the doubt. However, that benefit might not last too long once the more damning details of the case began to come out.

Back at the jail, she confronted the sheriff with the information she'd discovered concerning Charles Strope's plans to subsidize a foundation.

"So he was serious about that," Paul mused thoughtfully.

"You knew about it?" Jessica questioned.

"He came by to talk to me about it a few months ago," Paul explained. "Wanted to know if I felt something like that would make a difference. I told him that any effort would make a difference."

"Apparently he took what you said to heart. He had an appointment with Frank Lawson for today."

Paul regarded her skeptically. "And you think it was to draw up papers for a foundation?"

"Cynthia Wilson thinks so," Jessica replied, wanting him to know she hadn't pulled this out of thin air.

Paul continued to regard her skeptically. "You aren't suggesting that a criminal element, who didn't want a foundation of that sort established in this state, arranged for Strope's murder?" The sheriff's tone implied that he felt his deputy had been watching too much television lately.

"I was thinking," she replied, probing carefully, "that a foundation of the sort he was considering would have taken a great deal of money."

"I take it you're implying that Melinda Strope killed her husband because of greed. But, in the first place, she has money of her own. And secondly, considering her fear of guns, I find it hard to picture her shooting her husband. Jessica, you don't even know for certain if Strope was going through with the plans for the foundation. If that woman was putting on an act this morning then she's one hell of an actress."

"I thought you were supposed to be open-minded until all the facts are in," Jessica said tersely. "She has at least as good a motive as Luke. By her own admission, her husband has been making her life miserable."

Paul drew a harsh breath. "I am being open-minded. I don't have Luke behind bars yet, do I?"

"But you do think he shot Strope," she returned bluntly.

"I'll tell you what I think," Paul said with impatient anger. "I think Luke came home and found Strope waiting for him. For some reason they went into Luke's study. Maybe Luke invited him in to try to reason with him. Maybe Strope held the gun on Luke and forced Luke to let him in. Anyway, they went into the study. Strope wasn't rational. He threatened Luke. Luke tried to protect himself and the gun went off."

"If that was what happened, Luke would have said so," Jessica insisted.

"I think he panicked. He figured no one would believe the truth so he made up that ridiculous story," Paul argued.

"Then why didn't he at least say he hadn't thrown the door bolts?" Jessica pointed out curtly. "He's not stupid. He'd realize Strope would have had to find a way in."

"Because Luke's basically an honest man. He's not used to being deceitful."

"That's right," Jessica snapped. "He is an honest man. And if he said that he didn't shoot Charles Strope then I believe him."

Leaning back in his chair, Paul studied his deputy. "Never thought you'd fight for Luke Brandson so hard."

Jessica felt a flush of embarrassment spreading from her neck upward. "I'm fighting for justice," she said stiffly.

"We both are," Paul replied levelly. "If Luke's lying, he's only hurting himself by it."

"He's not lying," Jessica replied with conviction.

"I hope you can prove it," Paul said honestly. "Meanwhile I have to act on the facts I have."

Going back to her desk, Jessica considered the possibility that Melinda Strope was a very good actress. She could be. Very little was known about the woman's past. And greed had always been a sound motive for murder. Of course there was Margaret's statement that Melinda had awakened her a little after two. That would have made it impossible for Melinda to get over to Luke's place in time to kill her husband. Jessica made a mental note to get a more exact confirmation of the time, the next time she interrogated the housekeeper.

Chapter Five

"The coroner's report came in while you were out," the sheriff informed Jessica as they drove in the squad car to the Strope place. "Strope died of a single shot through the heart. The doc has set the official time of death between two and two-thirty. Also, if there was a struggle it was minimal and left no marks on the body."

Jessica remained silent. With each new piece of evidence the situation looked blacker and blacker for Luke.

Margaret Demis answered their knock. "Mrs. Strope is resting," she informed them in hushed tones. "Surely you don't have to disturb her again. She's still in quite a state of shock." Margaret glared at the sheriff accusingly. "She had to go in this morning and identify the body. Don't see why, either. You already knew who it was."

"Who is it, Margaret?" a strained female voice questioned from the interior of the house.

Glancing toward the stairs, Jessica saw Melinda Strope standing near the top. Even at this distance she could see the tear-swollen eyes looking puffy and red against the pale, drawn features and felt a nudge of guilt for her suspicions.

"It's the sheriff and his deputy." Margaret turned to face her mistress while continuing to block the doorway with her large frame. "But I'm certain they can wait to see you another time."

"No." The word came out determinedly as Melinda descended the stairs. "I want to help find out what happened to Charles."

"You should be resting," the housekeeper admonished protectively.

"I can't." A stream of tears trickled down Melinda's cheek. "Every time I close my eyes I see Charles slamming out the door and myself making no move to stop him."

"Now, you mustn't blame yourself," Margaret consoled, moving to Melinda's side to provide physical support if it should become necessary. "Mr. Strope has been in a foul temper for ages now. Anyone else would have left him long ago."

"Please, Margaret, you mustn't speak ill of the dead." Melinda shook her head feebly. "He didn't mean any of the things he said. He just wasn't himself after Chuck died."

As she spoke, the fragile blonde moved toward the living room with Jessica and the sheriff following. Seating herself on the sofa, she motioned for them to be seated also.

"I'm deeply sorry you had to go through the ordeal of identifying the body, but it's the law," Paul apologized.

"At least the doctor was able to ease my mind." Her facial muscles tightened as she fought to hold back a fresh flood of tears. "He did assure me that Charles didn't suffer." Her gaze focused on Sheriff Pace. "My husband was really a very good man."

"I've heard rumors that he was thinking of setting up a foundation to help the youth of our state," Jessica interjected watching the widow's reaction closely.

"Oh, yes." Melinda smiled gently. "I had hopes that once the plan was completed he would become his normal self once again. Ever since Chuck's death, he's been like a man struggling to find himself." She paused to dab at her eyes with a lace-edged hanky. "If only I could have given him a child. I did try. I know a new baby would never have replaced Chuck but it might have eased Charles's sense of loss."

The sheriff gave Jessica a glance. She hated missing any of what Melinda Strope had to say, but she had her orders. Rising, she said, "I think Margaret and I should go make some tea for Mrs. Strope."

"Yes, that would be nice," Melinda said.

"Are you sure you don't want me to stay here with you?" Margaret asked, watching the sheriff suspiciously.

"I'll be just fine," Melinda assured her.

Margaret glared at Paul Place. "Don't tire her," she cautioned with a threat in her voice. "It ain't right putting good, decent people through all this." Having said her piece, she stalked out of the room toward the kitchen.

As Jessica followed Margaret down the hall, she heard Melinda Strope say to the sheriff, "Margaret's such a mother hen. But she means well, and I have to admit I appreciate it. I don't have any family to turn to."

"It must be difficult for Mrs. Strope, not having any family, especially at a time like this," Jessica remarked sympathetically a couple of minutes later. She was leaning against the kitchen counter watching the housekeeper fill a kettle with water.

"Yes," Margaret replied, but said no more. After setting the kettle on the stove, she turned on the heat, then seated herself at the kitchen table.

"But she must have been well provided for," Jessica persisted. "I understand you were her housekeeper before she married Mr. Strope. Not just anyone can afford to maintain a permanent staff."

"Her parents left her a trust," Margaret offered. "It was not a fortune but enough for her to live comfortably."

This was getting her nowhere. Jessica decided to try another approach. "I understand New York is a very exciting city."

"I wouldn't know." The housekeeper's back stiffened with self-righteousness. "We led a very quiet existence. Mrs. Strope spent most of her time doing volunteer work at the hospital and helping with various charities."

Adopting a properly chastised manner, Jessica said in more respectful tones, "As pretty as she is, I'm surprised she wasn't overrun by suitors."

Margaret smiled pridefully. "Oh, there were always men calling and sending flowers. But she never paid much mind to any of them until Mr. Strope came along." Margaret's smiled turned to a frown. "For her it was love at first sight."

Jessica caught the change in the housekeeper's mood. "You sound as if you didn't approve of the match."

Margaret shrugged a shoulder. "It's no secret. Marriage isn't one of my favorite institutions. However, to be fair, I have to admit that he did treat her like a princess at first. Anything she wanted was hers. But that son of his did everything he could to make her life miserable. She went out of her way to be nice to him but he was always accusing her of being a gold digger." Indignation flashed in the housekeeper's eyes. "Can you imagine that! Her with that nice trust and him accusing her of marrying his father for the money. It was a disgrace. Then he went and got himself killed, and the poor woman still didn't have any peace. First Mr. Strope got real moody. Then there was this business of him accusing her of having affairs!" Margaret snorted with indignation.

Now that she had the housekeeper talking, Jessica didn't want to give her a chance to stop. "I understand that was what they argued about last night," she prodded.

"That's what they always argued about lately," Margaret confirmed. "He'd become insanely jealous, and for no reason. Just because she was working so hard for the church bazaar he started accusing her of having an affair with the reverend. Then when she looked into seeing about buying Mr. Strope a horse, he starts accusing her of having an affair with Luke Brandson. A lady like her wouldn't have anything to do with a rough rancher like him."

Jessica didn't like being persistent on this point, but she needed to know how certain Margaret was that Melinda had shown no interest in Luke. "You have to admit that he does have a certain masculine appeal," she said suggestively.

Margaret's gaze traveled over Jessica, coming to rest momentarily on her holstered gun before returning to her face. "To more uncultured types, perhaps," she replied coldly.

Refusing to take offense, Jessica merely smiled. "Perhaps," she agreed, glad that the housekeeper had shown no hesitation in refuting the possibility of an affair between Luke and Melinda Strope. It would be very damaging to Luke for the district attorney to have a witness like Margaret who was close to Melinda Strope suggesting that an affair was possible.

The water started boiling, and rising from her chair, Margaret began assembling a tray.

"Did Mr. Strope ever strike his wife?" Jessica questioned, watching the woman closely.

Margaret turned sharply toward her. "Not to my knowledge. If he had, I might have killed him myself."

Giving up any further pretense of two women having a simple chat, Jessica's manner became purely professional. "Before we rejoin the sheriff and Mrs. Strope, there're a few questions I need to ask you. You said they argued before dinner. What happened afterward?"

Margaret obviously resented this intrusion into her mistress's privacy, but she was resigned to it. "He went back to the bank, and Mrs. Strope went over to Jane Jordan's home."

"When did they return?" Jessica asked, opening her notebook.

"I wouldn't know," Margaret replied haughtily. "I had my cup of cocoa like I always do and went to bed."

"You heard nothing of the second argument?" Jessica coaxed.

Margaret frowned in annoyance. "I lived near an airport when I was a child. Once you've learned to sleep with planes landing and taking off over your house, nothing disturbs you."

Recalling how difficult it had been to wake the woman, Jessica had to admit that the housekeeper probably would have slept through the argument even if it had been in her bedroom. "But you did mention that Mrs. Strope woke you sometime during the night?"

"It was nineteen minutes past two exactly," Margaret replied.

"How can you be so certain of the time?" Jessica challenged, her theory regarding Melinda Strope as a suspect fading fast.

The housekeeper smiled confidently. "There's a digital clock on my radio. I saw the numbers clearly."

"Do you mind if I take a look at the clock?" Jessica requested.

"Would it matter if I did?" Margaret returned dourly, crossing the room and opening the bedroom door.

Without dignifying the question with an answer, Jessica entered the room and checked the clock against her watch. There was only a one-minute difference. "Thank you for your cooperation," she said, returning to the kitchen.

The housekeeper's eyes narrowed coldly. "If you think Mrs. Strope had anything to do with her husband's death, then you're going to discover that you're sadly mistaken."

Jessica met the woman's gaze levelly, her expression one of total innocence. "I never said she did. I'm merely trying to make a thorough investigation."

"What you're trying to do is dig up dirt on Mrs. Strope," Margaret snarled. "And there isn't any. It's my opinion you should turn in your badge and forget about being Annie Oakley. If you can't tell an innocent woman when you see one, then you're a threat to all of us."

"I see the two of you are getting along well," Paul Pace interrupted from the doorway.

"Humph!" Margaret snorted indignantly. Without giving either the sheriff or Jessica another moment's attention, she finished making the tea and carried the tray out of the kitchen.

Paul eyed his deputy judiciously. "I thought you women knew how to talk to one another without ruffling any feathers."

"That's another of your male myths put to rest," Jessica threw back with a shrug of her shoulder. "What about Max Johnson? Do we talk to him now?"

A hint of amusement escaped from behind Paul's frown. "I'm not certain I should let you talk to anyone." His expression became totally serious once again as he added, "However, I'm not forced to make that decision. Johnson isn't here. He's on a trip to Kentucky to pick up a couple of new colts. Left Saturday and won't be back until Friday.''

Jessica frowned. "That seems like a long time for the trip.''

The sheriff opened the back door and waited for her to pass through. Then, joining her, they walked together around the house to their car. "The colts were an expensive pair. He'd have to make certain he had all the proper papers. Then he'd have to drive them slowly so they didn't get excited and injure themselves in the confines of the horse trailer.'' Being a man who still believed in old-fashioned chivalry, he opened her door and waited for her to climb in. "Think I had better stop and have a final word with Luke before I make my report,'' he added as he closed the door.

There was an ominous quality in his voice that Jessica didn't like. Waiting until they were on the main road, she asked tightly, "Did Melinda Strope have anything new to say?''

"Nope,'' he replied. "What about the Demis woman? Could she add anything?''

"No. But she did confirm the fact that Melinda Strope woke her,'' Jessica admitted.

He glanced toward her. "Have any definite idea of the time?''

"Nineteen minutes past two,'' Jessica answered.

The sheriff raised an eyebrow. "Guess that eliminates the widow from your suspect list.''

"Guess so,'' she muttered.

A terse silence persisted during the remainder of the drive to Luke's place. Jessica's mood was already black and the sight of Lydia Matherson's car in the drive did nothing to help it. She told herself she didn't care if Luke was seeing the history teacher, but it felt like a lie.

Luke opened the door and led them into the living room. He looked as tired as when she had left him that morning.

Lydia was there, her strawberry blond hair hanging in loose silky waves to her shoulders. She was wearing a softly feminine shirtwaist dress unbuttoned almost to the point of indiscretion. Rising from the couch, she greeted the sheriff and his deputy with an indignant glare. "I don't understand how either of you can honestly believe Luke is a murderer."

Gently but firmly, Luke slipped an arm around Lydia's shoulders and guided her toward the hall. "Perhaps it would be best if you left."

Her eyes met his beseechingly. "Are you certain you don't want me here for moral support?"

He smiled a tired smile. "I'm sure."

Her carefully made up lips formed a pretty pout, then, sliding her hand over his shoulder, she raised up on tiptoes and placed a light kiss on his lips. "All right. I'll leave if that's what you want." And, with a second disapproving glance toward the law officers, she moved with a graceful swinging motion of her hips down the hall and out of the house.

The masculine gleam of approval in the sheriff's eyes blackened Jessica's mood further. "Nice motion," Paul remarked, whistling low as the front door closed behind Lydia. "Teachers never looked like her when I was a boy."

Luke shrugged. The dark circles under his eyes seemed to grow even darker as he faced the sheriff. "Have you come to arrest me?"

"No, just to ask a few more questions." Paul's manner was politely official.

"Then ask," Luke said with a suspicious frown.

Paul studied the younger man. "You figured out how Strope got inside your house?"

"I thought that was your job," Luke replied.

The sheriff's jaw tensed. "If Strope came gunning for you, no one could blame you for defending yourself.".

Jessica's breath locked in her lungs. The sheriff was giving Luke one final chance to change his story.

The rancher's back stiffened. "I never saw Strope alive last night."

Paul studied Luke in grim silence for a long moment. Then putting his hat back on his head, he ordered, "Don't leave town."

"I'll join you in a minute," Jessica said as the sheriff headed toward the door.

Alone in the room with Luke, Jessica watched him uncertainly. "Luke..." she began, wanting to say something encouraging but unable to think of anything.

Ignoring her, he hooked his thumbs into the pockets of his jeans and stalked over to the window to stand with his back toward her.

Approaching him, she laid her hand on his arm. She felt his muscles tense beneath her touch. Jerking free from the contact, he swung around to face her. "Do you want me to lie, Jess?" he demanded acidly. "Do you want me to confess to killing a man I didn't kill?"

She drew a shaky breath. "No," she replied, managing to keep her voice even.

"That's good," he growled, "because I'm not going to change my story for you or for anyone." Turning away from her, he again stared out the window. "It's the truth whether you believe it or not."

The fact that he couldn't stand to have her touch him caused a cold lump in her stomach. He'd let Lydia kiss him. Hot tears burned at the back of her eyes. "I'm not your enemy, Luke. And I do believe you. It's just going to be very hard to prove," she said stiffly. Then she turned and stalked out of the room.

She was in the hall when booted footsteps sounded behind her. Luke caught up with her before she reached the door, and his touch on her arm brought her to a halt. He looked hard into her face.

"It means a lot to me, knowing you're on my side," he said gruffly. "Truth is, it takes a little getting used to."

She wanted to tell him that she'd always been on his side, but she couldn't afford to be that open. "Let me know if you remember anything you think might help. Even if you remember something you don't think is important, you call me," she instructed.

"I've told you everything I know," he growled. Releasing her, he strode back into the living room.

"Luke say anything to you?" Paul asked when she joined him in the squad car.

"Only that he's telling the truth," she replied.

Paul's mouth formed a hard, set line and he said no more as they drove back to town.

"THE MAYOR and nearly all the members of the town council have called," Harriet informed them when they entered the jail. "No one wants to believe Luke is guilty but they all want some action taken. To quote our public officials, 'Blue Mill Falls is a law-abiding town.'"

Paul Pace glanced toward his deputy. "You look tired. It's nearly five and you started the day early. Go home and get some rest. One of us should be fresh for tomorrow."

Jessica didn't have to ask what he meant by this last statement. She knew. As sheriff, he occupied an apartment above the jail, and once Harriet was gone for the day, all incoming calls would be transferred to his office phone which had an extension in the apartment. A murder was bound to spark a rash of prowler reports by some of the more excitable citizenry. For him, it could prove to be a very long night.

She left without any argument. Arriving home, she noted two other cars in addition to her mother's in the enlarged driveway. Obviously Molly had a couple of late customers. Jessica breathed a sigh of relief. She needed a little time to herself.

Inside, the house was quiet, a total contrast to the turmoil churning within her. At every new turn the case against Luke was growing stronger. And then there was Lydia Matherson using this opportunity to bind herself to Luke.

Forget about Lydia and concentrate on getting Luke out of this mess, she commanded herself. Still, the shapely history teacher continued to impinge on her mind.

Upstairs in her bedroom she surveyed herself in the full-length mirror. In her stocking feet she stood five feet, six inches tall. The boots she wore with her uniform made her even taller. Because long hair got in the way, she'd had her mother cut her thick black hair into a short wavy style that required very little care but was still very feminine looking. As for her figure, she was average in build with a pleasantly full bust line and a nice curve to her hips that prevented any hint of masculinity even when she was in her uniform.

Leaning closer, she studied her facial features. She wasn't beautiful but she wasn't plain, either. It was a nice enough looking face. There were, however, lines of fatigue in evidence, and the green eyes which she considered one of her best features showed marked signs of worry.

What difference did her appearance make anyway? she chided herself. Scowling, she turned away. Luke Brandson was never going to look at her with the kind of interest she wanted to see in his eyes, and she was more concerned with proving his innocence than getting him to call her for a date.

Sitting on the side of the bed, she pulled off her boots then lay down. Almost instantly she was asleep.

"JESSICA," her mother's voice brought her back to consciousness. "I'm sorry to wake you, but I'm putting dinner on the table. Tonight's my bridge night at Susan's."

Forcing herself to get up, Jessica joined her mother at the kitchen table. Food still didn't seem to be agreeing with her, but she made an effort to eat.

"I called Luke and asked him to come to dinner but he refused. Claimed he wouldn't be good company," Molly said, studying her daughter closely. "I told him that wouldn't matter to us but he still refused. You haven't changed your mind about his being innocent or had a fight with him, have you?"

"I haven't changed my mind about his being innocent nor have we had a fight," Jessica replied tersely. "He probably just had other plans and didn't want to mention them."

"That sounds very cryptic," Molly mused. A reproving frown suddenly wrinkled her brow. "You aren't hinting that you think he might actually be seeing Melinda Strope on the sly, because I won't believe it!"

Jessica scowled at her mother. "No, of course not. I was thinking of Lydia Matherson."

Molly's mouth formed a thoughtful pout. "It's pretty obvious she's set her cap for him. A time like this, when he's probably grateful for any show of support, would be the perfect opportunity for her to get her claws into him."

The ringing of the phone on the kitchen wall behind Molly saved Jessica from any further speculation about the history teacher and Luke.

Answering on the second ring, Molly listened, frowned darkly and extended the receiver toward her daughter. "It's the sheriff. I hope there hasn't been another murder."

"I've got Luke Brandson in my office," Paul said as soon as Jessica came on the line. "And old Mrs. Wakley just called to report a prowler. I know it's nothing more than the Millers' cat but could you run over there and take a look?"

"Sure," she replied readily, glad of any excuse to escape any further discussion of Luke's female interests.

"Sure, what?" Molly demanded as Jessica hung up.

"Mrs. Wakley has reported a prowler, and I'm going over to look around and ease her mind," Jessica answered.

Following her daughter into the hall, Molly watched disapprovingly as Jessica retrieved her holster from the closet and buckled it on. "But you haven't eaten your dinner yet."

Jessica frowned indulgently as she pulled on her jacket. "It's my job."

"And not only is it downright chilly out there, but there's a storm brewing," Molly continued. "It could start raining at any moment and you could end up with pneumonia just because of some old woman's fantasies."

"All jobs have their drawbacks," Jessica returned philosophically.

Dismay mingled with angry concern on Molly's face. "You're not taking me seriously."

With a tired sigh, Jessica stopped in the midst of zipping her jacket and faced her mother squarely. "Yes, I am tak-

ing you seriously. I only wish you would take me more seriously. This is the job I want to do.''

Molly reached out and touched her daughter's cheek caressingly. "Then please be careful. I know it's only the
Millers' cat or the Thompsons' dog this time, but other
times I'm scared half to death when you leave.''

"I'm always careful," Jessica assured her.

In the next moment she was out the door and heading
toward her car. Watching her, Molly shook her head and
muttered, "I'll never get used to this . . . never!"

Parking in front of the Wakley house, Jessica caught a
glimpse of the elderly woman peeking out through the curtains of one of the living room windows. Mrs. Wakley was
eight-two and had been seeing prowlers on her property for
the past fifty years. When her husband was alive, he used
to complain that she had him out in the middle of the night
at least three times a week checking their yard because she'd
heard a noise. After his death twenty years ago, she started
calling the sheriff.

Walking up to the front door, Jessica banged the large
cast iron knocker twice. Almost instantly the door was
opened, and a little wrinkled face dominated by enormous
brown eyes peered out at her.

"You're not Sheriff Pace," the age-weakened voice informed her indignantly.

"I'm Jessica Martin—" Jessica started to introduce
herself.

"Molly Martin's daughter?" the woman interrupted
sharply. "What in the world are you doing out on a night
like this and wearing a man's uniform?" A hint of fear entered the brown eyes as if she suddenly saw this perversion
as a possible danger signal.

"I work for the sheriff," Jessica explained, keeping her
voice polite. "You called to report a prowler and I'm . . ."

"I thought Harriet was still working at the jail," Mrs. Wakley interrupted again, her tone even more suspicious than before. "When did she retire and why in the world would the sheriff send his dispatcher to search for a potentially dangerous prowler?"

"Harriet does still work at the jail," Jessica said, fighting to keep the impatience out of her voice. It had been a long day and the cold wind whipping across the porch carried an increasingly threatening smell of impending rain. "I'm the sheriff's deputy."

"That's ridiculous! A female deputy! The town council would never hire a woman." The little gray head shook violently to reinforce each negative statement.

Jessica's patience was slipping, and her tone became forcefully official. "They did and I am. You called to report a prowler and I'm here to look around."

Mrs. Wakley continued to study Jessica as if she had an eye in the middle of her forehead. "Perhaps I should call—"

The sound of a car coming to a halt and doors slamming interrupted. Glancing over her shoulder, Jessica saw Paul Pace and Luke approaching.

A triumphant gleam sparked in the elderly woman's eyes. "Here's the sheriff now. He can clear this up, young lady, and then I would suggest that you go home and have a long talk with your mother."

Stepping aside to allow the sheriff full access to the irascible old woman, Jessica frowned at Luke. "What are you two doing here?" she asked in hushed tones as Paul Pace assured Mrs. Wakley that Jessica really was his deputy.

"With a killer on the loose I didn't think it was a good idea for you to be wandering around in the dark on your own," Luke replied gruffly.

As his words sunk in, her cheeks flamed. "You didn't think I could take care of myself against the Millers' cat! You made the sheriff come out—" The rest of what she had to say stuck in her throat as her anger reached a point that made speaking coherently impossible. Clamping her lips shut, she counted to ten. Once more in control of her vocal chords, she ignored Luke as she said to the sheriff, "I'll take a look around."

"You should wait for Sheriff Pace to accompany you," Mrs. Wakley insisted. "Proper young ladies do not go wandering around alone in the dark looking for dangerous criminals."

Paul accurately read the growing anger on Jessica's face. "Now, Mrs. Wakley, you're going to catch pneumonia if you remain exposed to this cold air much longer," he interceded before his deputy could make a retort she and the sheriff might regret. "I wouldn't want you getting sick. You just close that door and we'll check around out here."

"Such a gentleman," the elderly woman cooed as she obeyed.

Jessica, however, missed this last bit of praise. Too furious to stand still, she had left the porch and was already around the corner of the house before Luke and the sheriff could move.

She didn't draw her gun. In spite of all of the searches that had been conducted on this property, no one but Mrs. Wakley had ever caught even a glimpse of the elusive prowler. Shivering against the wind, she peered into the hedges and bushes lining the yard. If a prowler was hiding in them, she guessed he would be home in bed for the rest of the week with a well-deserved cold.

A drop of icy rain hit her face and she frowned skyward. In that instant a muscular arm encircled her neck and shoulder from behind, threatening to block her windpipe.

Panic brought her heart to a standstill but her hours of self-defense training paid off. Without even thinking, she cupped her left hand over her right fist to add strength to her counterattack and drove her right elbow into her assailant's side with all the force she could muster.

There was a shocked groan of pain and the arm around her neck slackened. Taking advantage of the momentary lapse, she brought her judo training into action. In one lithe movement she flipped her attacker over her shoulder. He landed on his back with a thud. Before he could move, she had her gun drawn and aimed at him.

"Don't shoot," Paul Pace ordered, his half-amused, half-irritated tone breaking the fear-filled silence. Turning to the man on the ground, he said, "I told you she could take care of herself."

"What?" Jessica had begun to breathe once again, and as her panic cleared, she recognized her assailant.

"Luke was concerned about your ability to take care of yourself," Paul elaborated.

While the sheriff spoke, Luke was shifting his sprawled form into a sitting position. As he moved, he held his side with one hand. A grimace of pain accompanied the oaths he was muttering under his breath.

Sorry she had hurt him, but still too angry to apologize, Jessica watched him in icy silence.

"Now that you have demonstrated your ability to defend yourself to the councilman, you'd better take him over to Doc Clark's," the sheriff directed her. Turning his attention back to Luke, he held out his hand to offer the rancher assistance in returning to his feet. "And I hope this is the last time I'll hear you questioning my deputy's abilities."

"She's got a punch that could flatten a mule," Luke admitted as he accepted the sheriff's aid and rose to his feet.

Jessica continued to glare at him. "An excellent descriptive choice," she said dryly.

Paul had been watching the exchange between his deputy and the rancher with an amused grin. Suddenly he scowled. "You take Luke over to the doc's. I'd better have a word with Mrs. Wakley."

Following the line of his vision, Jessica too saw the elderly woman peering through the window and quickly holstered her gun. "Come on, cowboy!" she growled over her shoulder as she started toward her car.

"You don't have to be so angry," he muttered, climbing into the passenger seat. "I'm the one whose whole body feels as if it's been dislocated."

"You nearly scared me half to death," she retorted as she started the engine and shifted the car into gear. "Not to mention the trouble you've probably caused yourself by putting on that show for Mrs. Wakley. That woman has the imagination of a seven-year-old. There's no telling what kind of story she'll spread around about what happened."

"You've made your point." His voice took on a cold edge. "Now drop me off at the jail. I left my truck there."

She would have liked to obey him but, as angry as she was, she couldn't make herself behave so callously. "I wouldn't want to send you to Lydia in such a state of disrepair," she returned acidly. She was distressed by the sharp stab of jealousy she felt at the thought. "Besides, I always follow my boss's orders and he said to take you to the doc's," she added curtly.

"I'm going straight home... alone," he informed her. "And as for the injury, it isn't nearly as painful as being thrown from a horse, and I don't go running to the doctor every time that happens."

Ignoring his refusal, she pulled into Dr. Clark's drive. After parking, she climbed out of the driver's seat, slammed her door closed, rounded the car and jerked his door open. "Get out!"

Remaining seated, he frowned up at her as if she was the one being unreasonable. "I said I don't need to see a doctor."

Jessica saw the pain lines on his face and her stomach knotted. "And the sheriff said you did. Now get out before I drag you out!"

A dry smile tilted one corner of his mouth. "How can a man refuse so solicitous a request?"

Clamping her mouth shut, Jessica marched up to the doctor's front door and knocked purposefully. "I've got a mild emergency for you," she explained apologetically when Dr. Clark answered her knock.

His gaze traveled from her to Luke, then back to her. "A mild emergency?"

"I had a little fall," Luke growled. "I've been hurt worse working a horse." Glancing toward Jessica, his scowl deepened. "I don't need to be here."

"Then why are you here?" the doctor questioned as he motioned the duo inside.

"Because the lady has got such a convincing way about her," Luke replied wryly.

Dr. Clark raised a questioning eyebrow but received no clarification. Again his gaze traveled between Luke and Jessica. Obviously deciding it was not prudent to ask any further questions, he motioned for Luke to follow him into the examining room.

Outside in the waiting area Jessica flipped through a magazine, but the pictures blurred in front of her eyes. She'd hurt Luke. She'd jabbed him and thrown him. She might have cracked a rib. If she'd had any chance at all that he might one day look at her as a desirable woman, it was gone now. Damn! she muttered under her breath.

"He'll have a bruise but other than that he's healthier than one of his horses," Dr. Clark informed her a short while later as he entered his waiting room.

"Thanks," she replied levelly, her eyes traveling past him to Luke. The rancher said nothing as he joined them. She tried to read his expression, to tell how angry he still was with her.

"He told me what happened," Dr. Clark said, smiling broadly. "And I have to admit that I'll feel a whole lot safer with you protecting our streets, Deputy."

Jessica forced an answering smile as she quickly ushered Luke out the door and back to her car. The situation was bad enough; she didn't want it aggravated by the doctor taking a few joking jabs at Luke.

"Why were you in the sheriff's office tonight in the first place?" she asked, breaking the heavy silence between them as she shoved her key into the ignition.

"I wanted to find out how the investigation was going," he answered in clipped tones.

Glancing toward him she saw his jaw set in a hard line. To most people this expression would have caused them to believe that he was simply impatient and irritated with the world in general. But Jessica knew differently. That was the look he used when he was worried but didn't want anyone to know. Exhaustion was also etched deeply into his features. "Have you eaten?" she asked stiffly.

"I was going to go to the café after I finished talking with the sheriff," he replied, looking surprised by the question.

She figured he probably wouldn't want to sit at the same table with her, but still she said, "My mother's cooking is better than the café's. You're welcome to eat with us. She made fried chicken, and there's a cherry pie for dessert."

"I never could resist your mother's cherry pie," he replied hesitantly.

He was considering accepting. It was stupid to let it mean so much to her, but it did. "Good, then it's settled," she said in a casual tone. "We'll drive by the jail so you can pick up your truck and follow me home."

He continued to study her uncertainly. "Are you sure Molly won't mind?"

"She won't mind," Jessica assured him. "She always makes extra when she fries chicken. Fact is, she'll be furious with me if I don't bring you home to dinner," she added, as a final incentive.

"Wouldn't want to be the cause of any trouble between you and your mom," he replied.

The rest of the drive to the jail was accomplished in silence. As she drove toward home, she found herself holding her breath until she actually saw his headlights in her rearview mirror. Catching a glimpse of herself at the same moment, she frowned at the wistfulness in her green eyes. "Don't make a fool of yourself," she ordered. Her hands tightened on the wheel. "Just be the friend he needs. And keep in mind that you'll never be anything more than that to him."

"Well, as I live and breathe. If it isn't my trigger-happy daughter and the mad killer!" Molly greeted them sharply as they entered the kitchen.

"Mother!" Jessica's face paled and without thinking, she caught Luke's hand to assure him that he was still welcome.

"Sorry, Luke, I didn't mean any offense," Molly apologized grimly in the next breath. "But I've just spent a miserable half an hour on the phone with Mrs. Wakley. According to her, you tried to kill Jessica while she was searching for a prowler, and she threw you to the ground and shot you." Her attention shifted to her daughter, concern and reprimand mingling in her expression. "You didn't actually shoot at Luke, did you?"

The feel of Luke's large calloused hand wrapped around hers was causing warmth to spread upward along Jessica's arm. "No," she answered. She'd meant to sound indignant, but the way he was slowly rubbing his thumb over the back of her hand was stirring up feelings inside of her that caused the word to come out with a curious little catch. Angry with herself for being so affected by something that was nothing more than an unconscious, nervous reaction on his part, she slowly but firmly removed her hand from his. She didn't dare look up at him for fear he might read the effects of his touch on her face. Moving toward the refrigerator, she could feel him watching her. Worried he might guess how she felt, she added stiffly as she pulled a head of lettuce out of the fridge, "But I was tempted."

"Will one of you please tell me what did happen?" Molly demanded, breaking the sudden silence that had fallen over the room.

"I was worried about Jessica's ability to defend herself," Luke replied evenly. "So Paul decided to let me see what would happen if she was attacked."

"And?" Molly prompted when the silence once again threatened.

"And I need not have worried," he finished.

"Mrs. Wakley said Jessica had to take you to see Dr. Clark," Molly persisted, her gaze traveling from her daughter to Luke and back again as if seeing both of them clearly for the first time.

"He surprised me. I used a little of my self-defense training," Jessica offered tightly as she slammed the head of lettuce against the counter to loosen the core. She hated the thought that she had hurt him. But even more disconcerting was her awareness of him watching her. Think casual acquaintance, she ordered herself. But there was nothing casual about the warm hard knot in her abdomen his presence was causing.

Molly's gaze shifted to Luke. "Were you badly hurt?" she asked with concern.

"Just bruised," he replied.

Turning her attention back to her daughter, Molly watched Jessica tearing the lettuce apart. "Obviously this business has shaken the two of you up a bit," she observed with a thoughtful frown. "I assume from Jessica's actions that you're planning to stay for dinner, but neither of you has even taken your coat off."

Flushing, Jessica bit her lip and, after dropping the lettuce into the bowl, began to unzip her jacket.

"And I'm tired of seeing you in that uniform," Molly continued, focusing her full attention on her daughter. "You take Luke's coat and hang it in the hall closet, then go change while I finish this salad and reheat the chicken."

Jessica ignored the look of surprise on Molly's face when she obeyed her mother without an argument. She told herself she'd decided to change clothes because she wanted to escape from Luke's presence long enough to regain her equilibrium. But once she was in her room, she admitted to herself that the thought of changing into something a little more feminine appealed to her. It's not going to matter what you wear, she told herself as she opened her closet. He's never going to look at you the way you want him to look at you.

Sifting through the clothes in her closet, she was tempted to put on a dress. Instead she settled for a softly tailored pair of pale green trousers with a matching sweater. She didn't want Luke getting the idea she was chasing him. "That'd be sure to send him running," she mused. She did, however, take the time to brush her hair and put on some fresh lipstick.

Returning to the kitchen, she found Luke seated at the table drinking coffee while her mother removed the re-heated chicken from the oven.

"Susan is expecting me," Molly said as she set the platter of meat on the table. "So I'd better be on my way. I hope you two enjoy your meal."

Jessica flinched at the hint of matchmaking she was sure she heard in her mother's voice. But Luke didn't seem to notice.

"I always enjoy your cooking," he replied casually and was rewarded with a broad smile.

"Have a good time," Jessica said. Hoping to send her mother swiftly on her way, she added, "Susan is probably pacing the floor. I know how punctual she likes people to be."

"I will and I know," Molly replied, pulling her coat on. Pausing with her hand on the door, she glanced back at Luke. "Maybe you'll stay for a while after you've eaten and keep Jessica company. I hate leaving her alone for a whole evening."

"Weren't you supposed to be at Susan's ten minutes ago?" Jessica interjected sharply.

"Yes, I was," Molly conceded, and with a final quick goodbye she left.

Rising from his chair, Luke moved around the table and held Jessica's chair for her. "I like that outfit," he said in an easy drawl.

He's just being polite, she told herself. Still, a small pleased smile tilted the corners of her mouth. "Thanks." She barely managed to keep her tone casual as his hand brushed against her arm and currents of charged energy raced through her.

Seating himself, he glanced toward the door as he served himself a piece of chicken. "Your mom was in an unusual mood tonight," he remarked casually.

So he *had* noticed Molly's matchmaking. Jessica felt a surge of panic. He'd be uncomfortable if he guessed how she felt, and she'd be embarrassed. "You know how she is sometimes." She shrugged as if to say Molly had her moments of insanity. "I hope you won't feel obligated to stay. I'm perfectly capable of spending an evening alone."

A touch of frost entered his voice. "Is that a hint that you want me to leave as soon as I finish eating?"

"No." The word came out too swiftly and Jessica felt a flush spreading as he studied her guardedly. "I just didn't want you to feel obligated if you had something more important you wanted to do," she added quickly.

"I don't have anything else to do," he replied, turning his attention to his food.

You came really close to making a fool of yourself, she cautioned herself curtly as she, too, focused her attention on the food.

"Did your mother ever get around to teaching you to cook?" he asked, breaking the uneasy silence that had fallen over the kitchen.

"What?" She lifted her head to meet his gaze, expecting some sort of big-brother joke, but his expression was serious.

"Never mind," he muttered, again turning his attention to his food.

Jessica was acutely aware of the tension in the room, but she didn't know how to disperse it. She wished her mother hadn't been able to read her so well. At the very least, Mom could have kept her mouth shut, she thought tersely. Noticing that Luke had finished, she said with forced casualness, "Are you ready for some pie?"

His expression was grim as he studied her intently for a long moment. Then, reaching across the distance between them, he took her hand in his.

Jessica held her breath as his touch warmed her. She braced herself, waiting for him to say something about how he thought of her as a sister. Mentally she practiced a wide-eyed innocent look as if she'd never thought of him as anything other than a self-appointed big brother. Still, a part of her couldn't help hoping he might say something very different.

"Jess," he said, "I want you to do me a favor. I want you to let the sheriff handle this murder investigation on his own."

Well, he had said something different. But obviously their minds had been following two very divergent trains of thought.

He traced the line of her jaw with the tips of his fingers. "You frighten me, Jess," he continued gruffly. "You have ever since you turned sixteen and Dan and I tried to teach you to drive. Do you remember when we took you out to the pasture at my place and let you drive my old truck?"

This was not one of her favorite memories.

His touch made her feel like a woman, but his words let her know he still thought of her as a nuisance he felt obligated to look after. "I didn't hit anything," she muttered, hating the way he remembered the childish things she'd done and the way he acted as if he expected her to repeat these mistakes.

"Only because I was able to switch off the engine fast enough," he reminded her grimly.

Jerking away from his touch, she pushed her chair back from the table and rose with defiant dignity. "Well, I'm not sixteen any longer. I know what I'm doing."

Stalking out of the kitchen, she was almost to the stairs when fingers like tempered steel closed around her arm. "Jess, I'm sorry." Luke's voice was gruff as he turned her slowly toward him. "It's just that I worry about you, and I've been thinking about Strope's death all day. If I was purposely framed, then you're dealing with a cold-blooded murderer, and if the death was an accident, and Strope's being in my study an ill-fated string of coincidences, you're still dealing with someone who has killed and might kill again to protect himself from discovery. I just don't want to be responsible for anything happening to you."

The concern etched deeply into his face softened her anger, and when he drew her into his protective embrace, she did not fight him.

Holding her tenderly, he cradled her head against his shoulder with one large hand while the other spread over her back. "We don't seem to be able to be in the same room for more than a few minutes without fighting, but just this once could we call a truce?" he requested.

She had to admit that she could understand his anxiety. They were dealing with a murderer. But more than that, she knew he needed her as a friend right now, not as a deputy. "Truce," she conceded quietly, circling her arms around his waist.

As they stood silently, holding each other, the feel of his body pressed against hers stirred a longing so intense her knees weakened and her heart began to pound. Afraid she would make a fool of herself if the contact continued, she gently drew away from him.

"Why don't you go into the living room and watch some television," she suggested. "I'll bring your coffee and pie in to you, and you can relax while I clean up the kitchen."

Combing a wayward strand of hair from her cheek with his fingers, the tired lines in his face seemed to deepen even further. "Thanks, Jess," he said softly. Leaning forward he placed a light kiss of gratitude on her forehead.

Forcing a smile, she escaped into the kitchen. "Damn!" she muttered under her breath as the door closed behind her. Bracing herself against the counter, she tried to stop the trembling. She could no longer deny that she was hopelessly in love with Luke Brandson. Tired of deceiving herself, she admitted that he was the reason she had left Blue Mill Falls and the reason she had returned. Knowing he would never feel the same about her, she'd gone off to college and then taken the job in Kansas City. But putting distance between them hadn't worked. When the job in Blue Mill Falls became available, she'd applied. She'd told herself it was because she missed her hometown and she did. She'd also missed Luke. But he obviously just thought of her as the sister he had never had, and right now that was the kind of support he needed.

Taking a couple of deep breaths, she poured him a cup of coffee and cut him a piece of pie. But when she carried them into the living room, she found the television on and Luke asleep in a sitting position on the couch.

Placing a couple of throw pillows against the arm of the couch, she gently shifted him into a reclining position. When she pulled his boots off, he didn't even open his eyes. It was obvious he was totally exhausted. Setting the boots aside, she covered him with an afghan.

Gently she touched his cheek. His day's growth of beard felt rough beneath her fingertips. He snored lightly, completely unaware of her presence. "I am going to help you," she promised in a voice barely above a whisper. Unable to resist, she bent and kissed him lightly on the lips. He smiled as if suddenly entering a very happy dream, and immediately she began to wonder who he was dreaming of. Not her, anyway. Shoving the thought out of her mind, she went back into the kitchen and finished cleaning the dinner dishes.

Luke was still sleeping when she returned to the living room a little while later. Picking up a book, she tried to read, but her eyes constantly traveled to him. If only he would, just once, see her as a desirable woman.

It was close to midnight when Molly returned to find her daughter curled up in a chair with a book and Luke asleep on the couch. "I see you two have discovered a way to spend the evening together without fighting," she remarked as she entered the room.

"He was exhausted," Jessica explained in low tones. Seeing the knowing look in her mother's eyes, she wished she'd woken Luke and sent him on his way before Molly came home.

"Well, he can't spend the night on the couch," Molly said. "He'll wake up with a cramped back and a sore neck. If he's going to stay, we had better get him up to Dan's old room."

"There's no need for that," a sleepy male voice interjected. Yawning, Luke threw off the afghan and shifted into a sitting position. "Sorry I was such rotten company tonight, Jess," he apologized as he rubbed his neck and eased his sore ribs.

"Actually it wasn't so bad," she replied. "As Mom pointed out, we spent several hours in the same room without arguing."

A quirky smile curled one corner of his mouth. "I suppose we did. But now I have to be on my way."

Jessica frowned anxiously. "Are you awake enough to drive?"

Having finished pulling on his boots, he rose. "Surprisingly, I feel rested. You're better than a tranquilizer, Jess."

"I've never thought of Jessica as a tranquilizer," Molly muttered, studying her daughter and Luke even more closely.

Jessica glanced toward her mother with a scowl that warned Molly not to say any more.

"Thanks for dinner," Luke said, heading for the hall.

Jessica glanced toward her mother. "I'll be right back." Her tone let her mother know that she didn't want Molly accompanying her. Quickly following Luke into the hall, she reached him as he retrieved his old, worn sheepskin coat from the closet and pulled it on.

"You need to button up," she insisted, when he reached for the door handle with his coat still open. "It's cold out there, and it sounds like it's still raining."

"And you sound like a mother hen," he teased, releasing the handle and turning to face her.

Her back stiffened. "I'm only trying to see that you don't get sick."

The amusement left his face. "I didn't mean to make you angry." Reaching toward her, he stroked her cheek. "It means a lot to me to know you care." Then muttering a quick goodbye, he left.

Jessica stood in the doorway watching him drive away, her mood matching that of the cold, rainy blackness outside.

"You want to talk to me about you and Luke?" Molly coaxed, slipping a comforting arm around Jessica's waist as she joined her daughter in the doorway.

"No," Jessica replied, blinking back the tears of frustration that threatened to fill her eyes.

"He's a good man, one any woman could be proud to love," Molly said gently.

Jessica frowned out into the night. "He thinks of me as a sister, a lifelong friend, and that's what I'm going to be

or him. Right now he's under enough stress without my
adding to it.''

"Being a friend is as important to a successful marriage
as being a lover,'' Molly said philosophically.

Jessica turned toward her mother, her expression grim.
'Just don't say anything to Luke, and don't start planning
a wedding. I doubt very much he would ever consider me
or his wife.'' The frown on her face deepened. "Besides
this is probably just a phase I'm going through.'' One that's
asted for years, she added mentally.

Glumly she recalled the other men she'd dated in her at-
empts to get Luke out of her system. It hadn't worked.
She'd always ended up comparing them to him and they'd
ost. Idiot! she chided herself.

Molly rewarded her daughter with a look of indigna-
ion. "Of course I won't say anything to Luke. It's never
good to forewarn a man of impending capture.'' A mischievous twinkle sparkled in her eyes. "I do believe you
could fit into your grandmother's wedding gown.''

With a shake of her head and a final threatening glance
aimed at her mother, Jessica said good-night and went to
bed.

Chapter Six

The next morning Jessica awoke in the predawn hours and couldn't go back to sleep. She was too worried about Luke. Saying a silent prayer that the state lab would turn up new evidence in his favor, she wandered down into the kitchen and started a pot of coffee. But sitting at the table only made her more edgy. She remembered being there with Luke only hours earlier. He'd asked her if she'd ever learned how to cook. He probably thinks I can't even boil water, she mused. Without really thinking about what she was doing, she rose, found a mixing bowl and began throwing in the ingredients for a pie dough.

By the time her mother entered the kitchen a couple of hours later, Jessica was taking two cherry pies out of the oven.

"I must be dreaming," Molly muttered, eyeing her daughter speculatively.

"I couldn't sleep," Jessica explained with an edge of self-consciousness.

Molly's gaze traveled past the two freshly baked pies to the partly eaten and whole one she had made the day before. "I suppose we could freeze a couple."

"Actually I thought I would take one to Luke," Jessica said without even realizing until the words were out that this thought had been in the back of her mind all along. Stiffly she added as justification for her proposed action, "He fell asleep before he had any last night."

"Now that does sound like a good idea," Molly said, smiling brightly. "I've always been a strong believer that the way to a man's heart is through his stomach."

"Mother, please!" Jessica pleaded in exasperation. "This is only a show of friendship, to let him know we're on his side."

Ignoring her daughter's disclaimer, Molly poured herself a cup of coffee. Then, seating herself at the table, she studied Jessica with a worried frown. "Just how serious is this Strope business where Luke is concerned?"

"Very," Jessica replied, shifting her gaze to the dawn breaking outside the window.

"But there is no solid evidence against him, is there?" Molly persisted.

Jessica shook her head. "Not yet. But the circumstantial evidence is exceedingly strong."

"They can't try a man on circumstantial evidence," Molly said with conviction.

"Yes, they can. And they can convict him, too."

Molly's gaze leveled on her daughter. "Then you'll just have to find a way to clear him."

In spite of her depression, Jessica smiled. "Now I'm the one who must be dreaming."

A little later, as she drove toward Luke's place, her lightened mood was gone. She'd had second thoughts about taking him one of her pies. But her mother had refused to allow her to back out.

Molly had said that if Jessica did not deliver the pie, she would take it to Luke. This threat had sent shivers down Jessica's spine. She knew her mother well enough to know that Molly would have made it very clear to Luke that Jessica had baked the pie especially for him. Molly might even make a few other things clear to him that could embarrass Luke and place Jessica in a very difficult professional situation.

As she pulled into the drive leading up to Luke's house, Jessica noted that the place looked quiet. Only Luke's truck was parked out front. Carrying the pie, she mounted the porch steps and knocked on the front door. There was no answer. She considered leaving, but the thought of her mother bringing the pie out later changed her mind. The front door was locked, but if Luke was out in the barns working, the back door was bound to be open, she reasoned. She could leave the pie on the kitchen table with a note saying it was from her mother.

But as she rounded the house a movement caught her eye. Glancing toward the corrals, she noticed a saddled mount. It was a thoroughbred. Changing directions, she walked toward it. As she reached the animal, she saw the Strope brand tooled into the leather of the saddle. A hard knot formed in the pit of her stomach. Then she heard the sound of voices. Looking in the direction from which they were coming, she saw two figures standing in the entrance of one of the near stables. It was Luke and Melinda Strope. Luke's back was toward her and Melinda was concentrating her full attention on the rancher and hadn't noticed the deputy's arrival.

A part of Jessica wanted to turn and run and forget she had seen the two of them together at this early hour of the morning. But the policewoman inside of her would not allow her to turn away from reality, and she walked toward them.

"I'm so sorry you've been placed in this position," Melinda's soft, sympathetic tones floated toward Jessica. The woman's long, blond hair was hanging loose down her back and even with the March chill in the air, the silk blouse she wore with her elegant riding habit had been left partially unbuttoned, exposing what Jessica considered an indecent amount of cleavage for someone so newly widowed.

As Jessica drew closer, Melinda raised up on tiptoes and kissed Luke lightly on the lips with an air of familiarity. Jessica's progress came to an abrupt halt, her legs refusing to carry her either forward or backward. She'd trusted Luke and he'd betrayed her! He'd lied to her. He'd used her! She felt sick to her stomach, but pride kept her chin high and her stance rigid.

At that moment Melinda Strope turned to leave and, seeing the deputy, her eyes widened in panic and a scarlet flush highlighted her cheekbones. "I hope you won't misunderstand," she stammered. "I was simply out riding and stopped by for a neighborly visit to assure Luke...Mr. Brandson, that I don't hold him responsible for my husband's death."

"That is very generous of you," Jessica heard herself saying coolly, her attention never leaving Luke.

His gaze narrowed as he read the accusation clearly visible on her face.

"I think I should be going," Melinda murmured, moving swiftly toward her horse. "Margaret will miss me if I'm not back in time for breakfast."

Neither Luke nor Jessica spoke or moved while the woman mounted and rode off with guilty haste. But the moment she was out of sight, Jessica became suddenly mobile and, turning abruptly, started back toward her car. She was too angry, too hurt to confront Luke right now. She needed time to regain control.

Before she had gone five feet, Luke's hand closed around her arm. With a grip like steel, he pulled her around to face him. "That wasn't either the way it looked or sounded," he said in a terse growl.

"Her widow's weeds were very attractive," Jessica snapped, attempting to pull free.

"She was telling the truth." His other hand fastened around her other arm and he shook her slightly in a wordless demand to stop struggling and pay attention. "She stopped by to tell me she didn't feel I was responsible for her husband's death. She thinks I killed him in self defense."

"That's very benevolent of her," Jessica replied dryly. "Especially the part where she added the supportive kiss."

Luke's jaw tightened. "I was as shocked as you were."

Cynicism etched itself deeply into her features. "I didn't notice you struggling."

"You also didn't see me participating," he returned with equal venom. "The truth is, I was so stunned, I didn't have time to react."

Only a fool would believe him, Jessica told herself. She continued to regard him coldly, the betrayal she felt causing the knot in her stomach to tighten even more.

Issuing an exasperated snort, he released her. As his gaze traveled over her, he noticed for the first time the pie she had managed to hold on to. "Is that for me?" he asked gruffly.

The desire to shove the pie into his face was strong. But instead, she simply turned the pan upside down and then dropped it. "Oh, how clumsy of me," she said frostily as the pie hit the dirt and splattered.

"Jess, damn it!" Again his hands closed around her upper arms, only this time he pulled her against his muscular frame. "If I had been kissing that woman you would have known it." His face was only inches from hers. The feel of his warm breath against her skin played havoc with her senses, threatening to destroy the rigid control she was holding over herself.

"When I kiss a woman, she and everyone who sees it knows she has been kissed." His voice was low and tense as his face descended toward hers.

Her lips parted in the beginning of a protest, but before she could utter a sound, his mouth claimed hers, as if by this example he could convince her that she had not seen what she knew she had seen.

A battle raged within her. In spite of the scene she had just witnessed between him and Melinda Strope, in spite of the anger behind this kiss, her knees weakened. She hated Luke and she loved him. She wanted to be free of his touch and she wanted him never to let her go.

The palms of her hands spread flat on his chest, but they offered no real resistance. Tears of frustration began to trickle from her eyes.

The salty wetness reached her lips and mingled with the kiss. "Damn," he muttered under his breath, breaking the contact to brush light kisses over her tear-wet cheeks. Releasing his hold on her arms, he gently enfolded her in his embrace.

She closed her eyes tightly in an effort to cut off the flow of tears. She ordered herself to break free from him but her body refused to obey. The tenderness of his touch held her a thousand times more powerfully than the angry grasp he'd used a moment earlier.

He kissed the lids of her closed eyes. "Jess, I'm sorry," he apologized huskily. "I didn't mean to frighten you. I would never hurt you, never."

The embrace tightened until she could barely breathe. Then abruptly he freed her and stalked back toward the barn, leaving her feeling suddenly deserted.

Shaken and confused, she walked to her car and drove back to town. A dozen times during the drive she called herself a fool. He had kissed her in anger to prove a point and then in apology because he thought he'd frightened her. But there had been no passion in any of it. Yet her body continued to hold on to the memory of how it felt to be held by him. And she still wanted to trust him.

When she arrived at the jail, the sheriff sent her out on an early-morning patrol. Her mind was only half on her job as she cruised the quiet streets. A thousand times she reviewed the evidence against Luke. Adding in what she'd seen this morning, he looked unquestionably guilty. Her stomach knotted again as the image of him and Melinda Strope in the entrance of the barn continued to plague her.

"The sheriff is on the phone with the state lab," Harriet informed Jessica upon her return to the jail.

Surprised registered on Jessica's face. "So soon?"

"He had all the evidence hand-carried to them yesterday and asked for a rush job on the gun," Harriet explained. "His job is on the line if he doesn't take some action fast. Charles Strope was an influential man in this town." She paused briefly, then added incisively, "He was an influential man in the state."

Frowning worriedly, Jessica approached the sheriff's office and knocked on the door.

"Enter," Paul Pace's bark sounded from the other side.

He was hanging up the phone when she opened the door. "What did they say?" she asked stiffly, stepping into the office and closing the door behind her.

"There were no identifiable fingerprints other than Strope's on the weapon. The prints on the handle were badly smudged. The blood didn't help, either. It's their opinion that whoever else held the gun was wearing gloves."

Jessica was not surprised to hear this. If Luke had been framed, the murderer would surely have worn gloves. The problem was, they had Luke's blood-stained gloves in the evidence bag.

"And there was powder residue on Luke's gloves," the sheriff continued grimly.

"Could they determine how old it was?" she questioned sharply.

"Not precisely. There was blood mixed with some of it," Paul replied, adding even more grimly, "Charles Strope's blood."

In spite of what she'd seen that morning, Jessica couldn't stop herself from defending Luke. "He's a hunter and he likes target practice. He even has a range set up down in the gully."

"I know all that." Paul drew a terse breath. "And I understand how you feel, Jessica. I like Luke too. But the law's the law and it's up to us to see that it's enforced. We can't suppress evidence or overlook it just because we like someone. If a man kills another man, he has to pay."

Jessica's jaw tensed. She was suppressing evidence right now. She hadn't told the sheriff about seeing Luke and Melinda. She knew she should, but the words stuck in her throat.

The sheriff glanced at his watch. "I have an appointment with the district attorney in half an hour."

"Are you going to ask him for an arrest warrant for Luke?" she asked.

"It's up to him to decide, on the basis of the evidence, if we have a case," he replied noncommittally. The scowl on his face deepened as he rose from his desk. "There is one thing you should know. There were no powder burns on Strope's clothing and no powder residue on his hands. That means that when the gun fired, he wasn't holding it and the person who was was probably further than a couple of feet away. I'm not saying it still couldn't have been an accident. If he and Luke were struggling, they could have broken apart with Luke gaining control of the gun and as Luke fell back, the weapon could have accidentally discharged. But it's the kind of evidence that can be used either way." Setting his Stetson on his head, he added, "You're in charge until I get back."

Jessica watched him leave in silence. This last bit of evidence was truly damaging.

The rest of the morning dragged by painfully slowly. At noon Jessica made another patrol of the town. It seemed unusually quiet, as if even the buildings and trees were waiting for something to happen. By the time the sheriff finally returned at two, her nerves were as tight as a bow string.

"Come on, Deputy," he ordered, sticking his head in the door for only a moment.

"Do you think...?" Harriet began to ask in hushed tones only to have Jessica pass her desk and disappear through the door before she could finish her question.

Reaching the patrol car a minute later, she found the sheriff waiting behind the wheel. "I have an order for Luke's arrest," he informed her grimly as she climbed inside and he shifted the car into gear. "The district attorney wants to go for murder. He thinks Strope went gunning for Luke, they quarreled, fought over the gun, Luke took it away and shot Strope in cold blood."

Jessica stared out the front windshield. "I refuse to believe Luke would shoot anyone in cold blood," she said tightly.

"If the rumors about him and Mrs. Strope are true he could've. She's one hell of a good-looking woman, and men have killed for passion before," Paul pointed out.

"Luke might have seen the opportunity to get rid of the one obstacle that was in his way to have her all to himself."

The scene from that morning played through her mind for the millionth time. Was she being a complete fool where Luke was concerned? She had to admit that the kiss she'd seen didn't look like it held the sort passion people killed for. "I still don't believe he'd kill in cold blood," she heard herself saying with conviction. She could have believed self-defense or an accident but not cold blood.

The sheriff glanced toward her. "You've seen the evidence. If Luke wasn't a friend of yours, would you be so quick to defend him?"

She heaved an exasperated sigh and continued to stare out the front windshield. "No," she admitted reluctantly.

Luke was standing beside one of the corrals with Slim Morely when they arrived. He never once looked toward Jessica while the sheriff informed him of his rights. He behaved as if he had been expecting this to happen and broke his stoic silence only once to affirm that he understood what the sheriff had said.

Jessica's stomach became a hard knot as the handcuffs were fastened on Luke's wrists. She wanted to say something comforting but the black anger in his eyes kept her silent.

"I'll take care of things just like you told me, boss," Slim assured Luke as the sheriff started to lead him to the car.

He nodded to acknowledge the statement.

During the ride into town, Jessica sat beside Luke in the back seat but he ignored her presence entirely.

It wasn't until they reached the jail that he broke his silence. "I believe I'm allowed one call," he told the sheriff darkly.

Removing the handcuffs, Paul nodded toward the phone on Jessica's desk. "If I were you, I'd call a good lawyer," he said.

"Just what I plan to do," Luke replied, placing a call to Frank Lawson.

"We got some legal procedures to go through before Frank gets here," Paul said, guiding Luke toward a back room.

It was Jessica who did the fingerprinting for the official arrest record with the sheriff watching over her shoulder. Luke's hand felt cold, and his anger was like a physical force. Finally all the legal procedures were finished.

"We'll wait until Frank gets here to take your statement," Paul instructed. "Jessica, take him to his cell."

Luke continued to be silent until he and Jessica were alone in the back of the jail. "I suppose it was your version of what happened this morning that clinched my guilt," he said acerbically as he stepped into his cell and turned to face her.

Her jaw tensed. "I haven't said anything to anyone yet about this morning."

His expression lightened and he searched her face eagerly. "Then you did believe me?"

"Maybe I'm being a fool," she said, shutting the cell door between them. "Maybe I should have told the sheriff. I don't know."

His gaze narrowed. "I told you the truth, Jess."

"And I want to believe you," she replied tightly. Unable to face him any longer, she turned away and strode out into the main office.

Frank Lawson came in a few minutes later, and they all adjourned to the sheriff's office. Frank and Luke took the chairs in front of the sheriff's desk. Jessica chose to remain standing a little bit away so that she could see each man's face.

"I'll record what is being said and Harriet will transcribe it," Paul explained as he set up his tape recorder and switched it on. "Then I'll ask Luke to read over what she has typed and sign it."

"I'll want to read it too before he signs it," Frank stipulated.

"Fine." The sheriff nodded his consent. Then, turning to Luke, he asked him to describe his actions on the night of the murder.

Luke told the same story he had been telling all along. Every once in a while, Paul would interrupt to ask for certain details to be clarified. When Luke was finished, Paul continued to regard him narrowly. "Have you been seeing Melinda Strope?" he asked frankly.

"Only on a professional level," Luke replied firmly. "She was interested in purchasing a horse."

Remaining silent, Jessica watched him. The scene from the morning haunted her and again she wondered if she was allowing him to deceive her... to use her. She knew she wouldn't lie to protect Luke, but until she was sure of the meaning of what she'd seen, she wasn't going to say anything to condemn him, either.

"Your gloves had gunpowder residue on them." The sheriff continued to watch Luke closely. "You know how it got there?"

"A bobcat's been harassing my stock. Went looking for him the other day. Tried to scare him off with a few shots in the air. And I do a little target practice from time to time." Luke met the sheriff's gaze levelly. "But I didn't get powder on those gloves shooting Charles Strope. He was already dead when I found him."

"You can't be serious about charging my client with first-degree murder," Frank Lawson spoke up. "All you've got is rumor and circumstantial evidence."

"I suppose if Luke is willing to change his story. Say, maybe, to one where he met Strope on his porch, they went inside, argued, fought over the gun, Luke got shoved back and the gun accidentally fired, the DA might consider reducing the charge to manslaughter," the sheriff suggested. "Course I don't know if he'd go for that. It was one neat shot through the heart that killed Strope."

"I've told the truth," Luke growled. "And I'm not going to confess to a killing I didn't do."

Jessica tried to read what Frank Lawson was thinking, but his features were a mask of cool reserve. "What about bail for my client?" he asked, acknowledging neither the sheriff's suggestion nor Luke's protest.

"The judge set it at two hundred thousand when he signed the warrant for Luke's arrest," Paul replied.

Jessica paled, but Luke took the news without flinching. "Can you find a bonding company that will take my farm as collateral?" she heard him asking Frank as she escorted both him and his lawyer back to the cell area.

"If you can come up with twenty thousand in cash," Frank replied.

Luke nodded. "I've got it."

For a moment Jessica was surprised, then she realized that she shouldn't have been. Luke worked hard and his custom-built, four-wheel-drive truck was the only extravagance in which she had ever known him to indulge.

"Then I can probably have you out of here by tomorrow morning," Frank said.

"Make it as soon as possible," Luke ordered as he stepped inside the cell and Jessica again closed the iron-barred door.

"I will. But in the meantime, you talk to me before you talk to anyone else and keep your temper in check," Frank cautioned. "And," he added, "I'm going to look into finding you an attorney more experienced in criminal law. You're going to need someone who knows all the angles. Besides, with my handling Strope's affairs, there might be a legal conflict of interest."

"You do what you think is best," Luke replied.

Wanting a private conversation with the lawyer, Jessica followed him out of the jail. "Mr. Lawson," she called after him as he reached the sidewalk.

Coming to a halt, he turned toward her questioningly. "Yes, Deputy?"

"I understand that Mr. Strope was considering setting up a foundation for the youth in this state. Is that true?" she asked.

"You're asking for privileged information," he replied coldly.

"It's just a rumor I heard," she persisted, wondering how to rephrase the question.

"And why would a rumor like that interest you?" he asked.

"I was thinking that it would have involved a great deal of money to set up such a foundation," she replied, glad to keep the man talking.

"I suppose it would," he confirmed, studying her guardedly.

"And since I assume that Mr. Strope had not had time to act, his death was certainly convenient to whoever was to inherit the bulk of his estate," she said bluntly.

The lawyer's gaze hardened. "If you're suggesting that Luke killed Strope so that the widow would inherit the full estate, you're treading on slanderous ground, Deputy. Even if Luke was involved with Mrs. Strope, I'll never believe he would kill a man for money." Having said his piece, the lawyer turned abruptly and walked away.

Watching him, Jessica frowned introspectively. She had learned two things. One was that even Luke's lawyer thought he had shot Charles Strope. The second was that Melinda Strope was the major beneficiary to her husband's estate and the amount of that estate going to the widow would have been seriously lessened if the plans for the foundation had gone through.

Going back inside the jail, she found the sheriff. "If it's all right with you, I'd like to go out to Luke's place and unseal the study and clean it up."

"You still aren't ready to believe he's guilty, are you?" he asked.

"No," she replied. Her practical side told her she was being a fool but she still couldn't picture Luke as a murderer. There were too many elements that just didn't feel right to her.

The sheriff shook his head indulgently. "Then you go do your cleaning, and if you find anything we've overlooked let me know."

"You'll be the first to hear," she assured him.

Walking back to Luke's cell, she told him she was going out to clean his study. Seeing him behind bars was difficult. He was such a strongly independent person. He looked unnatural in the cell, like something wild that had been trapped.

"Is there anything I can pick up for you while I'm there?" she offered.

"There's a book on my bedside table." He sounded tired and for a moment looked as if he wanted to say something else. Then he thought better of it and instead walked over to the bunk along the wall and lay down.

Out at Luke's home, she used his keys to gain entrance. Going immediately to the study, she applied herself to cleaning up the mess her fingerprinting had left and in the process made another thorough examination of the room.

On the back of the large, leather upholstered wing chair near the fireplace, she found a single long blond hair. It looked as if it might belong to Melinda Strope. The woman had admitted to having been at Luke's place to talk about purchasing a horse. It would be reasonable that she would have come into his study. But evidence that she'd been here was not going to help Luke. "Not exactly the kind of thing I was looking for," she muttered, placing the hair in an evidence bag and stuffing the bag in her pocket. She knew it could be called withholding evidence, but she didn't plan to give the hair to the sheriff just yet. "You're getting real good at withholding evidence," she chided herself. "Let's just hope you're not playing a fool's game."

Her nerves on a razor's edge, she went upstairs to Luke's bedroom. The book he had requested was lying in front of a gold-framed picture of herself, Luke and Dan. It had been taken at the county fair the year she had graduated from high school. Her brother and Luke had taken her there as a graduation present. The photographer had dressed them in pioneer costumes that slipped on over their regular clothing, and they looked like settlers just beginning the long trek from Missouri to California.

Picking up the frame, a lump formed in her throat. She remembered the trip to the fair as if it had been yesterday. It had been fun but exhausting. On the way home she'd fallen asleep in the back seat and had woken as Luke was carrying her into the house. For a long time afterward she had remembered the feel of those strong arms holding her so easily. And something else that had never faded was the memory of how secure and safe she had felt and how gentle he had been. Her jaw hardened. Luke was neither a liar nor a killer. She was absolutely certain of that, no matter what the evidence implied!

Setting the picture down, she picked up the book and left the house.

Chapter Seven

Arriving back at the jail, she found Luke pacing his cell. As she handed him the book he caught her by the hand, drawing her close to the bars that separated them. "It has occurred to me that you might have gone out to my study, not to clean the place, but to conduct your own investigation," he said tersely. "I want the truth, Jess. Did you?"

"I was hoping to find something we had overlooked," she admitted.

His hold on her hand tightened. "I told you to leave the investigating to the sheriff."

She glared at him. "In case you haven't noticed, the sheriff feels he has completed his investigation."

"Then I'll do my own investigating when I get out of here. Maybe I'll hire a private firm." His gaze narrowed on her. "But I don't want you taking any risks."

Fury flashed in her eyes. "The risks are part of my job. I'm a grown woman and I'm a part of the law of this town. You seem to want to overlook those facts." Pulling her hand free, she stalked toward the door of the cell area.

"Jess," he called after her. "I know you're a grown woman. A man would have to be blind not to notice. And I know you're good at your job. I just don't want you getting hurt because of me."

Coming to a halt, she took a couple of calming breaths, then turned back to face him. So he had noticed she'd grown up, though not in the way she wanted him to notice. "Considering the fact that our prisoners normally get fed food from the café and Joe just lost his only good cook, at the moment your stomach is in more danger from this case than I am," she replied. Pivoting, she completed her exit.

It was already five. Telling the sheriff she was going to get Luke some dinner, she drove home. Being in jail was bad enough for him. The least she could do was to see that he got some decent food. She was filling a picnic basket with roast beef sandwiches, salad, a large helping of cherry pie and a thermos of coffee, when her mother entered the kitchen.

"You fixing that for Luke?" Molly asked.

"The café's food has been pretty bad since Barbara left," Jessica replied.

"You ought to take some for yourself and eat with him," Molly suggested coaxingly. "He could probably use some friendly company."

"I was planning to," she admitted, and flushed at her mother's knowing smile.

Arriving back at the jail, she started to enter the cell block but froze in her tracks when she saw Lydia Matherson standing outside Luke's cell. Inside, he was examining the contents of a picnic basket. "I fixed all of your favorites," the woman was saying in sugary tones. "Fried chicken, salad and some cherry pie."

Well, Luke had his friendly company, Jessica thought acidly as she turned to leave. But before she could make good her escape, Luke glanced past Lydia's shoulder and saw her.

The teacher, suddenly deprived of Luke's undivided attention, followed his line of sight and, turning toward Jessica, smiled sweetly. "Oh, Deputy Martin, I hope you don't mind but I couldn't bear the thought of Luke being forced to eat jail food. I'm sure you can find a dog who won't mind having whatever you have in there." She crinkled her nose in distaste as her gaze shifted momentarily to the basket Jessica was carrying.

A carefully schooled mask of indifference settled over Jessica's features. "I'm certain I can."

"Jess." Luke called after her, but she was already halfway across the main room. The sheriff's office door was open, so he could keep an eye on the jail. Without pausing to wait for him to invite her in, she entered.

"Looks like Luke is going to be eating better than a king," Paul said as she set the basket on the desk.

"Actually I thought you might want this. We wouldn't want to overfeed the prisoner," she replied coolly.

"Having Luke here is going to play havoc with my waistline," Paul said with a mischievous grin as he uncovered the basket and examined the contents. "However, I'm not complaining." He unwrapped a sandwich and a more serious expression came onto his face. "Harry called a few minutes ago. Strope's viewing is set for tonight and tomorrow. Can't stand those things. I'd like to pay my respects tonight and get it over with. Would you mind baby-sitting our prisoner for an hour or so?"

"When do you want me?" she asked, wondering if Lydia planned to spend the evening, also. Jealousy was not an emotion she found easy to handle.

"It starts at seven. Thought I would go around eight-thirty," he replied.

"I'll be here," she promised.

Leaving the sheriff's office, she could hear Lydia's honeyed tones drifting out of the cell area, and it took some control to keep from slamming the front door on her way out.

A few minutes later, as she sat at the kitchen table eating soup and a sandwich with her mother, she focused her concentration back onto the matter of helping Luke. Her instructors had always told her to start with the obvious. In this case that meant determining who would gain the most by the victim's demise. She was now fairly certain that Melinda Strope would gain the most financially, but it never hurt to get a second opinion. "Mom, if you had to hazard a guess, who would you say Charles Strope left his money to?" she asked, interrupting Molly's dissertation concerning a customer's husband problems.

Pausing in mid-word, Molly frowned thoughtfully. "I would say that unless he changed his will because of the rumors about his wife and Luke, he left nearly everything to Melinda. He was crazy about her when he first married her. That was one of the reasons Chuck hated her so much. And, of course, old Mrs. Chambers, Chuck's grandmother on his mother's side, helped the ill feelings along. She wanted Chuck to inherit everything, and when Charles rewrote his will to divide his wealth equally between his new wife and his son, she was up in arms."

"Do you know for certain that he rewrote the will in those terms?" Jessica questioned.

Molly nodded. "According to Mrs. Chambers. And she said that if either Chuck or Melinda died, the other would inherit the whole thing."

Jessica frowned. "Was she absolutely certain about the terms?"

"She honestly believed those were the terms," Molly assured her. "I think Charles threw the information at her during one of their fights. The two of them used to snipe at each other continually. Anyway, I remember the day she came in and told me. I was trying to cut her hair and she was so angry she could hardly sit still. I've never heard a woman speak about another woman in such vindictive terms as Norma Chambers was using about Melinda Strope and, believe me, I'm used to a bit of backbiting. If she hadn't become so arthritic and moved to Arizona to be with her other daughter, I'd feel certain she was the one who started those rumors about Luke and Melinda."

Taking a sip of her iced tea, Jessica studied her mother thoughtfully. Molly was a boundless source of information. "What do you know about Melinda Strope?"

Molly's mouth formed a thoughtful pucker. After a moment she said, "Not much. According to what I've heard, she was orphaned young, then raised by a maiden aunt who has since died. There was money from a trust her parents had left that allowed her to live comfortably. She's quiet, doesn't like to talk about herself. She's a good listener. That's probably one of the reasons people like her. It's been my experience that a great many people are looking for someone who will listen to them talk."

Jessica acknowledged this statement with a knowing smile. Her mother had learned to become a listener. It was good for business. What astonished Jessica was the amount of personal information Molly's customers divulged. Luckily for her patrons Molly was not an ardent gossip. She told Jessica most of what she heard, but anything that could be embarrassing or hurtful to a customer never went any further. The real problem was separating fact from fiction.

"And," Molly continued, getting back to Melinda Strope, "she's such a tireless worker. The Christmas Bazaar was a huge success this year and all because of her."

"Then she is still well liked in spite of the rumors about her and Luke?" Jessica questioned.

Molly frowned thoughtfully. "I have to admit that those rumors did some damage, but she has handled the situation with such dignity that I can't help but admire her, and many others feel the same. It can't be easy to have your reputation and your marriage threatened by vicious gossip. In fact I would have to say that she is what we used to term a 'real lady.'"

Melinda Strope was beginning to sound more and more like a paragon. Paragons had always grated on Jessica's nerves, especially ones who behaved like this one had earlier this morning. "Are you certain she has no relatives?"

"None that anyone knows of. I think that's why it bothered her so much that she couldn't have a child. She wanted family ties. And, speaking of family ties..." Molly again picked up the thread of gossip she'd been relating about her last customer's husband.

Shutting out what her mother was saying, Jessica considered Melinda Strope. If Luke was telling the truth about not being involved with the woman, and Jessica wanted to believe him, then Melinda's kiss this morning didn't make any sense. The woman had an affectionate nature, but to give a man she hardly knew, who was being accused of killing her husband, a supportive kiss was going a bit far.

Jessica knew she needed to know more about Melinda Strope, but the kind of information she wanted was not as easy to uncover as most people believed. And to make matters worse she didn't have much time. There was one possible shortcut and it was almost as if fate had delivered it into her hands. This was Thursday, and Max Johnson was not due back until tomorrow.

Realizing that the room was suddenly quiet, Jessica glanced toward her mother only to be met by an impatient stare.

"You haven't been listening to a word I've said," Molly accused.

"I'm sorry," Jessica apologized hurriedly. "But I was thinking about Charles Strope. The viewing is tonight."

"And tomorrow," Molly reminded her.

"I promised the sheriff I'd go back to the jail for a while tonight so he could go pay his respects," Jessica rushed on ignoring her mother's addendum. "We can't leave the place unattended when there's a prisoner. And I was thinking that since I have to go out anyway, why don't we go by the funeral parlor tonight and get that over with before I have to go to the jail."

"But I'm not dressed and the dishes have to be done," Molly balked.

"You could be dressed in no time, and I'll stack the dishes in water and wash them when I get back," Jessica insisted.

"But..."

"Please, Mom, humor me," Jessica pleaded. Interrupting a second protest, she added in determined tones, "I'll call Sheriff Pace and tell him that I might be a little late."

"Humoring you is probably where I went wrong in the first place," her mother muttered, shaking her head in self-reproach as she rose from the table and headed upstairs to change.

Dialing the jail, Jessica wished she could keep her mother out of this, but she needed an unsuspecting accomplice who would lie convincingly for her if it became necessary, and Molly was perfect for the role. Also, she was the only person available.

On the way to the funeral home, Molly continued to complain while Jessica listened patiently. It wasn't until they were approaching the door that she laid the foundation for her next move. "I've got an errand I need to run before I return to the jail, so we have to make this a very short condolence."

Molly rewarded her with a reproving glare. "First you rush me here and now you're going to rush me away. There are times, Jessica, when I really wonder about you."

Feeling guilty, Jessica followed her mother inside. She would have liked to have told Molly the truth, but given time to think, her mother would probably refuse to help, or, at the very least, waste a great deal of time arguing about possible mishaps and repercussions.

As she paused to sign the guest book, the heavy perfume from the baskets of flowers lining the walls and surrounding the casket assailed her. Vivid memories of her father's funeral washed over her, and she was glad they would not be remaining long.

Joining her mother beside the coffin, she looked down at Charles Strope. As usual, Harry had made the corpse appear as though he had entered death with total peace of mind.

Remaining only a few moments, she caught her mother's arm and guided her to where the widow sat. Melinda's long blond hair was pulled back severely and fastened into a tight bun at the nape of her neck. She wore only a touch of lipstick. The half-face veil attached to the small pillbox hat that matched her black sheath did very little to hide her tear-swollen eyes. She was, in every way, the perfect picture of the grieving widow. If it hadn't been for the scene she'd witnessed that morning, Jessica would have experienced strong twinges of guilt for what she was about to do. But her gut instinct told her that the widow was the key to solving the murder of Charles Strope and if she was going to help Luke, she had no choice.

As Jessica had assumed would be the case, Margaret Demis sat beside her mistress, her manner much like that of a mother hen protecting her young. Both women greeted Jessica with an underlying guardedness.

"If there is anything I can do to help you through this difficult time, just let me know," Molly said, giving Melinda's hand a comforting squeeze.

"Margaret is taking care of everything, but thank you, anyway," Melinda refused politely in brave tones.

"Are you certain there are no relatives we could contact to help you through this?" Jessica offered, once again trying to discover some link to Melinda's past that might lead her to more information about the widow.

"No." A tiny stream of tears trickled from under the veil. "There is no one left on my father's side of the family and, as I told the sheriff, my aunt was not on speaking terms with my mother's family. As a result I have completely lost contact with them."

"How awful for you to be so all alone," Molly said consolingly, throwing Jessica a reproving glance that said she saw through her daughter's ploy and found it distasteful that Jessica would attempt to interrogate the widow at the viewing.

Reaching over, Melinda patted Margaret's large, strong hand. "Actually I don't feel alone. I have Margaret."

"And you have many other friends in this town, too," Molly assured her.

Melinda smiled weakly. "Thank you."

"It's no wonder people get edgy when they see you coming," Molly reprimanded Jessica in hushed tones as they moved away from the widow to allow other mourners to offer her their condolences. "Not only is that uniform intimidating, with its gun, handcuffs and whatever else you carry, but you go prying into their lives at the worst times."

So her mother had also noticed the widow's guardedness. However, in all fairness, Jessica had to admit Molly had a point. Under the circumstances it would only be natural for Melinda to be anxious. Especially recalling the scene she'd witnessed that morning. That kiss didn't make any sense if Luke was telling the truth about not having had an affair with Melinda. But then the widow could still be in shock and not in total control of her actions. People had been known to do silly or unusual things during times of stress. "I was merely trying to be helpful," she replied with schooled innocence.

"I'd already told you she didn't have any family," Molly returned in the same lowered, disapproving tones. "And according to her, she'd already told the sheriff the same thing."

Jessica shrugged. "I just wanted to be certain she hadn't forgotten someone."

Molly rewarded her daughter with a disgruntled frown. "I expect you to behave the rest of the time we're here."

People were beginning to fill the room and again Jessica caught her mother's arm. "We really should be going," she murmured, guiding her mother back toward the widow.

Molly gave her daughter a startled look but followed Jessica's lead.

"We really must be going," Jessica addressed the widow in apologetic tones. "I hate to leave so quickly but the smell of the flowers reminds me of my father's funeral, and I'm afraid I don't feel very well."

"I understand." Melinda held out her hand in a gesture of sympathy and farewell. Jessica was also certain she caught an edge of relief in the woman's voice. "Thank you so much for coming."

"I feel awful about making such a quick exit," Molly fumed as she climbed into the car a couple of minutes later. "There has to be something sacrilegious about leaving a viewing after barely fifteen minutes."

"Believe me, I've spent enough time with that body for both of us," Jessica returned tersely.

Molly's manner became solicitous as she studied her daughter. "Do you really feel ill?"

"A little," Jessica admitted, rolling down her window to breath deeply of the crisp night air.

Reaching over, Molly patted her on the hand. "I don't mean to fuss so much."

"I know." Jessica glanced toward her with a crooked smile. "It's just that I'm not turning out exactly the way you had hoped."

"You've turned out just fine," Molly assured her. "I simply need a little more time to adjust to the metamorphosis."

A look of tenderness came over Jessica's face. "Thanks, Mom."

Molly touched her daughter's cheek gently. "You're welcome. Now let's get on with this errand. By the way, I don't think you mentioned what it was."

"I thought I would drive out by Luke's place to make certain everything is secure."

Molly nodded, accepting the explanation without question.

So far, so good, Jessica sighed mentally, struggling to appear relaxed. But as they neared the Strope home, she tensed her entire body. "Did you see that?"

"See what?" Molly demanded, peering into the night.

"That flash of light from the top floor." As she spoke, Jessica turned into the Strope's drive and brought the car to a halt in front of the house.

"I didn't see anything." Molly frowned and looked hard at the second-story window. "You must have seen a reflection from the headlights."

"I'd better check it out," Jessica insisted, reaching for the flashlight she had conveniently left on the backseat. "We wouldn't want the widow to return home and discover she's been robbed. You wait here and keep the doors locked."

Molly caught her daughter's arm as Jessica started to leave the car. "I think we should call the sheriff."

Molly reached for the police radio Jessica carried in her car for just such emergencies, but Jessica stopped her. "The sheriff can't leave the jail unattended. He'd have to call in Vince or Joe to come in as acting deputy before he could come out here to join us. I don't want to go causing an uproar unnecessarily. If you're right and it was only a reflection of my headlights, I'd never be able to live it down."

Panic flooded over Molly's features. "You can't go up there alone. If there is someone in the house, you could get hurt."

Jessica frowned. "Now you sound like Luke. I'm a police officer. See the uniform. See the badge. See the weapon. Now you sit here quietly and I'll be back as soon as I can." Without giving her mother another chance to protest, Jessica climbed out of the car.

Approaching the front door, she quickly extracted a small kit from the pocket of her jacket. It contained an assortment of picks used by burglars to gain entrance to homes. She had purchased the tools as part of a research project designed to find out how accessible such equipment was. Surprisingly she had found all sorts of things available to her. Most she had bypassed, but the set of tools had been too inviting. She'd played with them enough to get the knack, but she'd never actually planned to use them illegally.

Working swiftly, she managed to unlock the door in only moments. But as she opened the door and started to enter, she heard a footstep behind her and a hand suddenly closed over her arm. Startled, she jerked around to find her mother had joined her.

"You can't go in there alone," Molly said anxiously, her hold on Jessica tightening. "If that door was unlocked then there is obviously someone inside and they could be dangerous." The panic on her face intensified. "It's probably the real murderer."

"You scared me half to death," Jessica said tersely, beginning to breathe once again. "Now, please go back to the car and wait for me. And," she added, suddenly worried about her mother's nervousness, "don't go disturbing the sheriff."

Molly shook her head. "No. I draw the line at allowing you to place yourself in a position where someone is very likely to jump out from a dark corner and bash your head in."

Breathing an exasperated sigh, Jessica realized she was going to have to tell her mother the truth. "There is no one inside. I opened the door myself with these." Displaying the tools for a moment, she snapped the case shut and slipped it back into her pocket.

Molly looked appalled. "Jessica!"

"You said you wanted me to help Luke and this is the only way I've come up with so far," Jessica argued in her own defense.

Molly continued to look appalled. "Breaking and entering?"

"I need to know more about Melinda Strope," Jessica replied. "I can't get rid of the feeling that she's the key."

Molly shook her head in disbelief. "And I can't believe this is happening."

"I want you to go back and sit in the car." Taking her mother by the arm, Jessica led her toward the vehicle. "If anyone comes, honk twice."

"How many years will I get for being an accomplice if we get caught?" Molly questioned caustically, reluctantly climbing back inside.

"None if you stick to the story that we saw a light and found the door open," Jessica replied as she closed the car door.

But before Jessica could start back to the house, Molly was again out of the car. "I swear I can feel someone watching us," she said nervously.

"You're just edgy," Jessica assured her. "There's no one here."

Molly looked around one last time to convince herself. "I guess you're right," she conceded. "But you be careful."

"I will," Jessica promised impatiently. Hurrying into the house, her first objective was a small secretary desk in a corner of the living room. Going through it quickly, she found nothing pertaining to Melinda Strope's life before she came to Blue Mill Falls. An address book in the top drawer did not contain a single name or address of anyone from her previous existence in New York. It was as though her life had begun with her marriage to Charles Strope.

Going upstairs to the master bedroom, she rummaged shamelessly through the woman's drawers hoping to find an old packet of letters, anything that would lead her to Melinda Strope's past. In the far back of a bottom drawer, she found a medium-sized locked box. Practically holding her breath, she used her tools to open it.

A deep frown furrowed her brow. Inside was a large supply of birth control pills. A prescription tag gave the name of a doctor in St. Louis and was dated within the past year. "Now why would a woman who professes to want to have children have a secret supply of birth control pills?" she mused, her expression hardening as she closed the box and slipped it back into its hiding place.

The hairs on the back of her neck suddenly prickled as if she could feel someone watching her. "Mom?" she said in hushed tones, concluding that her mother had disobeyed her instructions and had come looking for her. But there was no answer. Jessica's body tensed for action. Jerking around, she played the light of her flashlight around the room and out into the hall. There was nothing. "My conscience probably," she muttered. "After all, I am supposed to be upholding the law, not breaking it."

Returning her attention to the drawer, she closed it. But as it slid into place, she was certain she heard a board creak. This time she stood and played the light more slowly over the shadows while she extracted her gun from its holster with her free hand. Determining that there was no one in the room with her, she moved toward the hall. Suddenly something large and furry ran into the room. Jumping onto the bed, it sat, its green eyes watching her. "A cat!" Her own green eyes focused on it accusingly. "You scared me half to death," she scolded the creature. "Now behave."

Moving to the closet, she glanced over the large assortment of designer clothes. A row of purses on the shelf caught her attention. All were obviously expensive and fashionable except for one very functional-looking, somewhat large, black handbag. It wasn't the kind of handbag Jessica would have expected to find in Melinda Strope's closet. It was, in fact, identical to one her mother, Kate Langely and several of the other women in town owned. The buyer at Carlson's Department Store had gotten a good deal on the purses and bought a large supply. They weren't the most fashionable bags, but they were real leather and well constructed. The store had held a sale on them and many of the frugal ladies of Blue Mill Falls hadn't been able to resist the bargain. But Jessica had never thought of Melinda Strope as a bargain hunter. Pulling the purse down from the shelf, she opened it. Inside were a couple of tissues and an old fingernail file. Frowning thoughtfully, Jessica replaced the purse carefully.

On the floor were several pairs of shoes neatly arranged on a shoe rack. Four pairs of boots formed a square to one side. In the far corner were a couple of shoe boxes sitting on what Jessica judged to be a boot box. Pulling out the shoe boxes, she discovered they were empty. The boot box, however, was heavy. Opening it, she found a locked metal fire box like those sold in office supply stores to prevent valuable papers from being destroyed in case a home should burn.

Noting that Melinda had gone to some trouble to hide it, Jessica opened it hopefully. Inside she found three marriage certificates and an insurance policy. After quickly jotting down the names, dates and places on the various documents, she returned them to their hiding place, being careful to replace everything just as she had found it. She'd have to find a way to come back later with a search warrant, if any of what she found turned out to be important.

Filled with nervous excitement she relocked the front door and returned to the car. Her mother was in a state of agitation bordering on hysteria.

"I was getting ready to come looking for you," Molly scolded. "I've been waiting here for hours."

"Only thirty minutes," Jessica corrected, starting the car.

"Well, it seemed like hours," Molly snapped.

Pulling out onto the main road, Jessica turned toward Luke's place. "Did you see anyone drive by?" she asked tentatively.

"No one drove by," Molly assured her.

"Are you certain?"

Molly scowled impatiently at her daughter. "Of course I am. I would have noticed. I don't know how criminals do it. I've never been so scared in my life."

"It's good for your system to have a shock once in a while. It starts the adrenaline flowing," Jessica said soothingly as she pulled into Luke's driveway, drove around to the back of the house and then out onto the main road once again.

Molly rewarded her with an indignant scowl. "And was it worth having my system shocked?"

"I hope so," Jessica replied. "I won't know until I've made a few phone calls, but I did find some very interesting documents."

Molly waited a moment, then frowned impatiently. "Well? Aren't you going to tell me about them?"

"Not yet," Jessica said, glancing at her watch. "I've just got time to take you home and get to the jail."

"Oh, no you're not," Molly stated emphatically. "I'm going to the jail with you. I want to be certain you don't do anything else dangerous tonight. Besides, I want to visit with Luke."

Jessica's facial muscles tightened. "He probably already has a visitor."

"Oh?" Molly raised a questioning eyebrow.

"Lydia Matherson." The name came out with a bitter edge.

Molly studied her daughter thoughtfully. "I understand she's an excellent cook and immaculate housekeeper. I've also heard that she'd be perfectly willing to give up her career and take care of a husband full-time."

Jessica kept her eyes on the road ahead. "If that's what Luke is looking for in a wife, then he's welcome to her."

"Of course he is," Molly muttered with an amused smile.

Refusing to be baited, Jessica remained silent until they were parked in front of the jail. "Mother," she cautioned, "please, remember not to mention a word of what happened tonight unless you want me in the cell next to Luke's. As long as no one saw us at the Strope place, it would be best to simply say we drove out to Luke's, looked around and came back."

Molly shrugged. "Fine. I'll tell everyone it was your driving that added the ten years worth of age lines to my face in the last forty-five minutes."

Seriously wondering if she had made a tactical error by including her mother on this little expedition into the shady side of life, Jessica led the way into the jail.

The sheriff greeted her with a welcoming grin. "Mighty fine dinner," he said as he handed her back the empty picnic basket.

Molly glanced toward her daughter questioningly. "I thought you brought that over for Luke."

"Lydia Matherson had already prepared all of his favorites," Jessica replied, unable to keep a catty edge out of her voice.

Being a prudent man, Paul Pace just set his hat on his head. "I'll be on my way so you two ladies can be getting home before long."

"And I'm going to visit Luke," Molly said to Jessica as the door closed behind the sheriff. "Are you coming?"

"No. I want to make a couple of phone calls," Jessica replied, telling herself that it was only her concern for solving the case, and not her fear that Luke would spot her jealousy in a minute, that kept her away from the prisoner.

Left alone she took out her notebook. The oldest marriage certificate, dated sixteen years previously, had been issued in Houston, Texas, to a Duncan Holston and Melinda Smith. The second was seven years old and had been issued in Los Angeles, California, to a Kenneth Lymon and Melinda Smith. The third was only a little over two years old and had been issued in New York to Charles Strope and Melinda Smith.

There had been no divorce papers, and the possibility that the new widow was a bigamist could not be overlooked. Following that line of thought, Jessica considered the possibility that one of Melinda's former husbands had caught up with her and killed Charles Strope in a jealous rage. However, that theory would have involved a great many coincidences when combined with the fact that Strope had been killed with his own gun in Luke's study.

On the other hand if one of Melinda's former husbands had caught up with her and decided that blackmail was more lucrative than jealousy, a few more alternatives presented themselves. Being a banker, Charles Strope probably kept a close eye on his money. After Melinda ran out of her own, she might have had some difficulty in satisfying the blackmailer's demands. By killing off Strope, the blackmailer would have again gained access to an easy money supply, and the widow wouldn't dare balk or she would lose the entire inheritance.

Then again there were other possibilities. But whatever the case, Jessica's next step had to be to trace down the men on the marriage certificates.

Calling Houston information, she asked if they had a listing for a Duncan Holston. The answer was negative.

She was disappointed but undeterred. After all, that had been sixteen years ago, and the couple might never have actually lived in Houston. Melinda had met and married Charles in New York City. Putting aside Duncan Holston for a moment, Jessica turned her attention to the second husband. Here she had been luckier. Sandwiched between the marriage certificates, there had been a life insurance policy which not only contained his address and telephone number but also had the business card of the insuring agent stapled to the top corner. Prudently she had copied the agent's business and home phone numbers too.

Breathing a silent prayer, she dialed Kenneth Lymon's home phone number. A woman answered. It took only a few moments for Jessica to realize her prayer hadn't been answered. The woman had never heard of Mr. Lymon. She and her family had moved to Los Angeles only a year ago and had been issued the phone number at that time. She knew nothing about whoever had had the number before them.

Next Jessica tried Los Angeles information. They had no Kenneth Lymon listed.

Fighting a bout of frustration, Jessica tried the insurance agent's home number. She got Mark Smythe's answering machine. Leaving her name and a message saying it was urgent that she talk to him, she hung up and frowned at the phone.

She still hadn't been able to entirely shake the chill she'd felt when she'd thought someone was watching her. "It's because you know you were breaking the law," she muttered to herself, determined to push it out of her mind. And the excursion had been worthwhile. At least she now knew that Melinda Strope had a much more involved past than she was willing to admit to.

Intent on her own thoughts, the ringing of the phone caused her to jump. Answering it, she heard the man on the other end identify himself as Mark Smythe in the politely friendly tones that are the hallmark of a good salesman.

Mentally she crossed her fingers hoping this call would lead to something that might help Luke. After identifying herself, Jessica asked the insurance man if he recalled writing a policy for a Kenneth Lymon.

"As a matter of fact, I do," he replied, interest sparking in his voice.

"I'm trying to locate him, but he seems to have moved," she explained, fighting to keep the excitement out of her voice. "I was wondering if you would have his current address or, perhaps, you could give me the number of your billing department and I could contact them."

There was a hesitation on the other end of the line, then in more guarded tones the insurance salesman said, "I don't believe you mentioned why you were looking for Mr. Lymon."

"I didn't." Jessica took on a more official tone. "It is a police matter and I would appreciate your cooperation."

Again there was a hesitation. "And who did you say you were?"

"My name is Jessica Martin and I'm a deputy sheriff in Blue Mill Falls, Missouri," she replied, allowing a hint of impatience to enter her voice. She didn't want to make the man angry enough to refuse to cooperate, but she did want to intimidate him enough to give her the information she needed.

"I've always tried to cooperate with the law, Deputy." Jessica was certain she heard a hint of amusement in his voice but it was gone when he continued, "But I'm afraid that if you are trying to locate the Kenneth Lymon for whom I wrote that policy you are not going to have much luck. That Mr. Lymon died a little over four years ago.''

Disappointment swept over Jessica. ''Died?'' she questioned tersely.

''He was shot to death during a burglary,'' Mark Smythe elaborated.

Kenneth Lymon had been shot to death? Taking a deep breath, Jessica forced herself to sound calm. ''I understand he was married. Was his wife also injured?''

''No, she was out playing cards with her bridge club at the time.''

Jessica's hand whitened on the phone. ''You wouldn't happen to recall the name of the policeman who handled the investigation of the robbery, would you?''

''It began with a *T*,'' the man answered thoughtfully. ''Let me check my files.'' After a moment he said, ''Thatcher. That's what it was, Detective Thatcher.''

Jessica jotted down the name. ''Do you remember what precinct he was with?'' she asked, wondering what time it was in Los Angeles at the moment and whether she could reach Detective Thatcher tonight.

It took Mr. Smythe a few more minutes but he finally came up with a number.

Jotting it down, she said, ''Thank you, Mr. Smythe, you've been very helpful,'' and prepared to hang up.

''Wait a minute,'' he demanded, refusing to release her so easily. ''You've piqued my curiosity. Can't you give me a hint as to why you were trying to contact Kenneth Lymon?''

''I'm sorry but, as I said before, this is a police matter,'' she replied firmly. Thanking him again, she hung up.

Immediately she began dialing Los Angeles information.

"Jessica Katherine Martin!" Luke's angry tones issued from the cell area. "I want to have a word with you!"

He had used her full name. That was a bad sign. It could mean only one thing—her mother had told him about their trip to the Strope house. Frowning darkly, she remained seated.

"Jessica, if you don't come in here this minute I will have a serious discussion with the sheriff when he returns," Luke threatened.

She knew it was a bluff, but it occurred to her that Paul Pace might enter during one of Luke's bellows, and then they would both be in hot water. Frowning, she cradled the phone. Marching into the cell area, she faced Luke sternly. "You wouldn't want to see my mother behind bars, now would you?" She countered his threat with a threat of her own.

"Molly, would you leave us alone," Luke requested, never once taking his angry gaze off Jessica.

"I suppose it's safe since you are separated by iron bars," Molly muttered. The look on her face said she was beginning to think she had made a mistake by telling Luke what Jessica had done.

Like two warriors sizing up one another before a battle, Jessica and Luke regarded each other in silence while Molly made her exit.

"I'm going to say this one more time and I want you to listen carefully," Luke growled as soon as they were alone. "I don't want you investigating this case on your own. I especially don't want you breaking the law to do it."

Jessica's stance remained rigid. "I realize I might have acted a little rashly, but this situation called for certain unorthodox procedures. And I will not be told what I can do and what I can't do by a chauvinistic cowboy who prefers his women completely domesticated like a well-trained house pet!''

His gaze narrowed. "I'm only thinking of your safety, Jess," he said gruffly.

Worried suddenly that her outburst had let him see how deeply she cared for him, she flushed with embarrassment and indignation. "My safety is my own business, and investigating this death is part of my job," she informed him with cool dignity. Then, before he could respond, she pivoted and stalked out of the cell block.

There was amusement in Molly's eyes as she watched Jessica seating herself once again at her desk. "A well-trained house pet?"

Jessica glared at her mother accusingly. "I thought I asked you not to tell anyone!"

Molly shrugged. "Since Luke is practically an accomplice, I didn't see any harm in talking to him. I've had quite a shock and it's not natural not to say anything to anyone about it."

Jessica's jaw hardened. "He's not an accomplice. He's a pain in the neck!"

Concern etched itself into Molly's face. "Sounds more like a pain in the heart," she said softly.

"Mother." There was a harsh warning in Jessica's voice.

Rewarding her daughter with an encouraging smile, Molly moved toward the door of the cell block. "I think I'll go back and visit with the pain in the . . . neck for a while longer."

"Try to be discreet," Jessica pleaded, hoping her words did not fall on deaf ears.

With a reassuring wink her mother disappeared into the back. Jessica watched her departure with an anxious frown. Worrying about what her mother might or might not say to Luke wasn't going to help him, she told herself. Picking up the phone, she dialed Los Angeles information. A couple of calls later she learned that Detective Thatcher was on vacation and wouldn't be in until Monday. After explaining her need to reach the man as soon as possible, she was given his home phone number. His wife answered and told her that the detective was out fishing with their son.

Fighting down an attack of impatience, she left a message saying that she was interested in the details of the Lymon robbery and murder. Then, giving the woman her home phone number and that of the jail, and explaining that the detective should ask to speak to her, she thanked the woman and hung up.

The sheriff returned a few minutes later. Going back to find her mother, Jessica fought a bout of nervousness. Even without Molly informing Luke about how she felt, she was worried he might be a little suspicious after her outburst.

Luke's expression became shuttered as she approached, and it occurred to her that if he had guessed how she felt, he was probably embarrassed by the situation. It must seem to him as if he's dealing with a schoolgirl crush, she thought tersely, furious with herself for letting her jealousy get the better of her.

Avoiding looking directly at him, she informed her mother that it was time for them to leave. But as she turned to exit, Luke suddenly reached through the bars and caught her by the arm. "I want your promise that you'll go home and stay there," he murmured. "No more nightly excursions alone."

She met the cold steel of his gaze with a haughtiness she hoped would make him believe her earlier outburst had had no personal foundation. "I thought I made it clear that I don't appreciate your interference in my life or my job."

Releasing her arm, he traced the line of her jaw. "I know catching criminals is your job and you're good at it. I read your record from your previous job and I've admired the way you've handled yourself since you became deputy here. But don't ask me to stop worrying about you. I've been doing that for too long."

His touch left a trail of fire. Frustration filled her. She'd had as much of this big-brother routine as she could stomach. Afraid he might guess the effect he was having on her, she stepped back, breaking the contact. "You're right, you have been worrying about me for too long. It's time for you to stop."

Withdrawing his hand through the bars, he ran it through his hair in an agitated manner. "Damn it, Jessica, a man has been murdered. It's hard enough for me to be caged and unable to clear my name, without the added worry that you'll do something foolish and get yourself hurt."

The green of her eyes sparked with anger. "I do not behave foolishly!" Then, because he did look exhausted and because she knew that a part of him was dying with each moment he was in this state of confinement, she relented. "But for your information, I am going home and do not plan to leave there for the rest of the night."

"Promise, Jess." It was a command and a plea both at the same time.

And because she loved him, she could not deny him. "I promise," she muttered gruffly, then turning quickly away, she left.

"I hope whatever you learned tonight is going to help Luke," Molly said as she and Jessica walked to Jessica's car.

"I hope so, too," Jessica replied, mentally going over the information she had gleaned and wondering how to piece it together. Walking into the street to go around her car and climb in behind the wheel, she heard the sound of an approaching vehicle. Glancing over her shoulder, she saw it weaving around the courthouse square. Its lights were off and obviously the driver was drunk.

Molly screamed as the car accelerated and headed directly for Jessica.

Acting purely on an instinct for survival, Jessica dove over the hood of her car. The other car whizzed past, missing her by a hair, and continued at its accelerated speed, weaving its way out of town.

"Jessica!" Molly called after her, as Jessica scrambled off the hood and into the driver's seat.

Ignoring her, Jessica popped the portable siren on top of her car and took off after the speeding drunk. But, by the time she got to the first intersection, he had disappeared.

Going back to the jail, she found her mother inside being comforted by Paul Pace.

"Guess you didn't catch him," Paul said, seeing her enter alone.

"Didn't even get close," she admitted grudgingly.

"That man nearly killed you!" Molly said shakily, rising to put her arms around her daughter.

"Drunks are very good at killing people other than themselves," Jessica replied, a disgusted look on her face as she recalled the last accident she'd witnessed in which a child had died because of a drunk driver.

Releasing her daughter, Molly again sank into the chair. "I don't think I've ever been so scared."

"Did you get a look at him? Did you recognize the car?" Paul questioned sharply.

"No and no," Jessica replied. "He was driving with his lights off. It all happened so fast, I didn't really see anything except something large coming at me. I can't even swear it was a man driving."

Paul regarded her worriedly. "You hurt?"

Following his line of vision, Jessica realized she was rubbing her arm. "Just a bruise," she replied.

"What's going on out there?" Luke demanded from the cell block.

"Jessica was almost killed by a drunk driver," Molly yelled back.

"Jess, I want to talk to you!" Luke demanded.

Knowing it would be futile to refuse, Jessica straightened her uniform and went back to see Luke. "What is it now?"

"Has it occurred to you that the driver of that car might not have been drunk?" he demanded, in lowered tones. "That bit of snooping you did tonight could have made the real murderer nervous."

"No one knows I was at Melinda Strope's house except for you and my mother," she insisted. Then she remembered the chilled feeling of being watched that had run down her spine. "And the Strope's cat," she added.

"I want your word that you'll let this alone," he demanded. "You turn the information you found over to the sheriff and let him handle this."

"He'll want to know where I got it," she replied coolly, adding, "It was just a drunk driver."

"His timing was extremely convenient for anyone who might not want you meddling in this investigation," Luke countered tersely.

"Coincidences happen," she replied. "Now I'm going home and getting a good night's sleep and you should do the same." Without giving him a chance to say anything else, she left the cell block.

But as she drove home, she had to admit that her quiet, peaceful little town did suddenly feel much less safe.

Chapter Eight

The next morning Jessica entered the kitchen to find her mother making blueberry muffins. "You can take some to Luke along with a thermos of coffee," Molly said. "It'll help wash out the taste of the café food."

Breathing a frustrated sigh, Jessica poured herself a glass of orange juice. "Lydia probably brought him a soufflé or, better still, maybe she brought a hot plate over to the jail and prepared fresh hot eggs."

"Well, it won't hurt you to fight fire with fire," Molly scolded. "You're a good cook when you put your mind to it."

Sitting down at the table, Jessica stared at the glass of juice. "Right now Luke needs someone to help him, not add more stress to his life by placing him in the position of having to deal with a woman he thinks of as a sister but who wants to be thought of as something quite different. So, could we please drop the subject?"

Molly studied her daughter with concern. "Only until Luke is free. Then you and I are going to have a serious talk about the art of pursuing the male of the species."

"When Luke is free," Jessica agreed, glancing toward the phone and praying silently that Detective Thatcher would call her soon. With any luck he would have some information that could lead her in the direction of Strope's real murderer. Almost as if her prayer had been heard, the phone rang and Detective Thatcher was on the other end.

"I hope I didn't wake you," he apologized. "Just got in. My son and I were doing a bit of night fishing. Thought I'd take a chance on getting through to you before I went to bed."

"I'm glad you called," she assured him. "What can you tell me about the Lymon case?"

"For starters, it's still unsolved." Sounding hopeful, he asked, "You wouldn't happen to have a solid lead for me, would you?"

"I don't know what I have," she admitted. "Could you fill me in on the details?"

"Lymon designed and made jewelry. He kept gold, silver and precious stones in a safe in the workshop at his home. Apparently he was working late one evening and someone came in, shot him to death and robbed him. We figured it had to be someone he knew, or someone posing as a customer he thought he could trust. The place had an extensive alarm system. Anyone attempting to break in would have set it off, and if he thought he was in danger he could set it off with a button built into the floor or one built into his desk."

"What about the wife?" Jessica questioned.

"I couldn't connect her. According to their friends, she adored him. Like a lot of artist types, he was a bit eccentric but she put up with his moods without complaint. The night of the robbery, she had been picked up by one of her female friends, a Sandra Craven. Mrs. Craven said she went inside to say hello to the husband. He was working on an exceptionally expensive piece of jewelry commissioned by one of our leading families. Mrs. Craven mentioned seeing a diamond that was approximately ten carats lying on the table, among an assortment of other precious stones. Anyway, after saying a few words to the husband, Mrs. Craven and Mrs. Lymon went to their bridge club. Mrs. Craven said Mr. Lymon seemed in good spirits when they left him and he and his wife were definitely on good terms. The two women returned a few hours later. Mrs. Lymon invited Mrs. Craven in for a cup of coffee and that's when they found the body. Good thing the Craven woman was there. The widow became totally hysterical. It was two days before she calmed down enough for me to get any coherent answers from her."

"But you still suspected her?" Jessica probed, pursuing his original statement that "he couldn't connect her."

"During my years in homicide, I've discovered that some people are very good at faking emotions, especially hysteria. With an insurance policy that had a double-indemnity clause and paid off to the tune of a half a million dollars, I couldn't totally overlook the possibility of her involvement. But there was never any evidence to suggest her guilt, and the robbery motive was solid. It was common knowledge on the street that Lymon had the stones I mentioned, in addition to his usual supply of goods. If it's of any interest to you, the insurance company hired their own investigator who also came to the conclusion that Lymon was killed by a thief."

But the thief still hadn't been caught. For the first time Jessica felt encouraged. At least she had something to work on. "During your investigation, did you ever run across the name Duncan Holston?" she asked, trying to fit all the pieces of her puzzle together.

"I don't remember the name," he replied after a moment of thought. "But it's been a long time since I worked that case. I'll check my files when I get in to work on Monday. Can you give me a hint as to who he might be?"

"I have reason to believe he's the widow's first husband," she replied, hoping to spark a memory in the policeman's mind.

"I don't recall anything about an ex-husband," Detective Thatcher said, the interest in his voice increasing. "Would you mind telling me what is going on and why you contacted me?"

"First, I was wondering if you could give a description of the widow. I want to be absolutely certain we're talking about the same woman."

"It was a long time ago, but in this case, yes. She was a real looker, slender, natural blond. Looked as if she would break in two in a strong wind."

"Definitely the same woman," Jessica muttered.

"And now I think it's time for a fair exchange." Detective Thatcher's voice hardened into more official tones. "What do you know about the Lymon case?"

"Nothing except that the widow is a widow once again," Jessica replied.

"Another large insurance policy and a perfect alibi?" he questioned sharply.

"Not exactly. I haven't heard about any huge insurance policy, but the husband was extremely wealthy and she inherits everything. However, it does look as if it's going to be difficult to tie her into the murder." This last statement was a lie. If the district attorney could prove Luke and Melinda were having an affair, he could build a case for conspiracy to murder against her. But now that it was becoming common knowledge that Charles had also accused her of having an affair with the minister, people were willing to discount any stories of her sexual misconduct and beginning to question Strope's ability to be rational about his wife.

Only the scene Jessica had witnessed early the other morning gave any credence to rumors of adulterous behavior. And, while a disclosure might bring the widow under suspicion, it would also make Luke's position even more precarious.

"Well, let me know how your case is resolved," Detective Thatcher was saying. "With my present work load, I can't devote much time to a four-year-old case, but I'll check on Duncan Holston for you." Pausing a moment, he found a pencil and had her spell it out for him. "I'll run this name through our computers, too, and see if anything turns up," he added. "Do you have a description?"

"Sorry, no," she replied.

"Too bad. He might have been using an alias. Anyway, I'll let you know if I find anything," he promised.

Thanking Detective Thatcher for the information, she hung up.

"Who is Duncan Holston and who was he married to?" Molly asked.

So intent on her own thoughts, Jessica had completely forgotten about her mother's presence. "Duncan Holston is a name I don't want you to mention to anyone and I mean *not anyone,*" she ordered firmly. "In fact I want you to forget everything you overheard this morning."

Molly studied her daughter levelly. "All right, I won't say a word to *anyone,*" she promised. "But tell me one thing, is what you've learned going to help Luke?"

"I hope so," Jessica replied. The problem was she wasn't certain how. She had a lot of loose ends. If she was going to help Luke she had to find a way to tie them into a neat little package. Right now she still wasn't certain how to string any two of them together.

A little later she entered the jail with a paper bag full of still-hot muffins and a thermos of coffee. The sheriff greeted her with a broad smile. "If those are your mother's muffins and they're for Luke, I have a feeling I'm going to get lucky again this morning."

"What do you mean?" she questioned evenly, setting the food on her desk and schooling herself to appear indifferent when he informed her that Lydia had already fed the prisoner.

But his information was quite different. "Frank Lawson sprang Luke about an hour ago."

"I hope whatever smells so good is for me," Luke's familiar tones sounded from behind them.

Jessica had heard the door open, but had assumed it was just Harriet arriving for work. Startled, she swung around. He had obviously gone home, showered, shaved, changed into fresh clothes and then returned immediately to the jail. "What are you doing here?"

He regarded her amiably. "At the moment, starving."

"Mom sent these over." She shoved the bag of muffins and thermos of coffee to one corner of her desk as she sat down and began shuffling papers. After her slip last night, she was determined to appear totally indifferent to his presence.

"You here to see me?" Paul Pace asked the rancher.

"Nope." Picking up the bag of muffins, Luke offered it to the sheriff.

"Thanks," Paul said, taking two muffins. "Since you don't want to see me," he said, "I've got work to do." Going into his office, he closed the door, leaving Luke and Jessica alone.

Pulling a chair up next to Jessica's desk, Luke set the bag down and poured himself a cup of coffee.

In spite of her resolve, Jessica was unable to ignore his presence. She glanced toward him irritably. "I can't believe you came back here just for some food."

"Is that a statement or a question?" he asked dryly.

"It's a question," she growled.

"In other words you want to know why I'm here," he elaborated in the same dry tone.

She eyed him levelly. "Yes."

He met her gaze evenly. "I'm here to make certain you behave yourself."

Indignation etched itself into her features. "You must be joking! You can't loiter around the jail. Go home!"

Remaining seated, he regarded her coolly. "Then let's say I'm here to observe how your investigation of my case is proceeding and to decide if I need to hire a private investigator."

"You can't stay—" she cut herself off in mid-sentence as Harriet came through the door.

"Sorry I'm late," the woman said with a bright smile that changed to a reproving frown when she saw Luke. "Are we letting the prisoners leave their cells for meals?"

"Luke's out on bail," Jessica explained stiffly.

The dispatcher-secretary continued to frown at the rancher. There was an anxiety in her eyes that suggested she wasn't totally certain he was safe to be around. "I would think you would have seen enough of our jail by now."

"Don't worry. I never harm lovely women." Luke flashed her a charming smile that brought a flush to her cheeks.

"I never meant..." she muttered embarrassedly, then letting the sentence fade, she went to her desk and began sorting the mail.

"You're not making yourself very popular," Jessica hissed. It was obvious that Harriet believed Luke had killed Charles Strope, and Jessica worried that the majority of the townspeople might be thinking the same now that the DA had charged him with the murder and some of the evidence had been made public. It didn't seem right that these people who had known Luke all his life could think he would kill anyone in cold blood. But the case against him did look strong, she reminded herself. "Try to behave," she ordered him.

"I thought I was." He winked playfully at her only to be rewarded with a deepening frown. Tilting his chair back against the wall, he picked up the bag of muffins.

Jessica glared at him. "Would you please go home. You have a farm to run and I have some police business to conduct."

"Go right ahead," he replied, remaining where he was. "Just consider me a piece of the furniture."

"That shouldn't be difficult," she returned. "You're acting as if your head is made of the right substance."

Rewarding her observation with an oversweet smile, he continued to eat.

Pursuing a long shot, she called the Houston police and asked if they had any records on a Duncan Holston. They had nothing. Next she phoned the FBI and asked if they would check their records for her. They said it would take a little time and they would have to call her back.

"Who is Duncan Holston?" Luke asked in low tones as she hung up the phone.

"Furniture neither hears nor asks questions," she replied, wishing he would leave. She was having a very hard time maintaining an indifferent attitude toward him.

Luke frowned impatiently. "Jess—"

The entrance of a tall, blond-haired stranger interrupted him. Jessica judged the newcomer to be in his early to mid-thirties. His soft brown eyes settled on her with more than casual interest and long, deep dimples added an extra touch of charm to the smile that came to his lips. His voice was rich and mellow when he spoke. "I'm looking for Deputy Martin."

"You've found her," Jessica replied.

A definitely masculine gleam sparkled in his eyes. "This is my lucky day."

"That remains to be seen," Luke muttered, his gaze traveling over the stranger in a critical appraisal.

"I'm sorry." The man's attention shifted to the rancher, then back to Jessica. "I see you're busy. I'll just take a seat and wait my turn."

As he started toward a chair a few feet away she stopped him. "I'm not busy."

"Oh?" A question etched itself into his features as he glanced toward Luke.

"He's practicing to be a part of the fixtures around here," she said with a practiced nonchalant shrug.

He smiled that charming smile again. "I see." Then, glancing toward Luke once again, he frowned uncertainly. "Well, actually I don't."

"Never mind." Rising, Jessica walked around her desk and held out her hand. "I don't believe you've told me who you are."

After accepting the offered handshake, the man continued to maintain the contact. "I'm Mark Smythe."

Her eyes widened in surprise. "Mr. Smythe?"

"Mark," he corrected.

Frowning, Jessica withdrew her hand. "I don't understand why you're here."

"I'm here because women don't control the market on curiosity," he replied, smiling once again. "You refused to tell me what had happened here that prompted you to call me, so I came to have a look for myself."

Jessica studied him, her frown deepening. "Would the former Mrs. Lymon recognize you if she saw you?"

"I don't know." His smile vanished as his expression matched hers in seriousness. "Maybe. I did see her a couple of times. Could her recognizing me spoil something for you?"

"I don't know," Jessica replied. "But I'd rather not lose the element of surprise just yet. If you don't mind, I'd like for you to keep out of her way for now at least."

"I'm a very cooperative kind of guy," he assured her. "Would you like for me to wear a disguise?"

There was a mischievous gleam in his eyes that was hard to resist. I'll bet he sells a lot of insurance policies, she mused. That kind of charm was attractive, but it could hide a multitude of sins. Jessica narrowed her gaze on him. "I still don't understand why you're here. From Los Angeles to Blue Mill Falls is quite a trek just to satisfy your curiosity."

"Actually I'm here because the Lymon case has always interested me," he replied openly. "In fact, I would rather be an insurance investigator than an insurance salesman, but the salesman's job is a more reliable income. However, with the sum of a half a million dollars at stake, I thought I might try my hand at a little detective work. And, of course, there are the stones that were never recovered. They were insured for another million."

Now she understood. "In other words, the thought of the ten percent recovery fee has helped to keep your spark of interest in the Lymon case alive," she elaborated.

"If you insist on being crass, yes." He smiled to show he was not offended. "I hope you won't hold my greed against me."

"Not if it helps me solve my case," she replied honestly.

"Good." Escorting her around her desk, he pulled out her chair and waited for her to seat herself. Then, finding himself a chair, he pulled it up next to her desk on the side opposite from Luke. "Now that we understand one another, why don't you tell me what has happened in your fair town that concerns Kenneth Lymon's widow?"

Briefly Jessica related the details of the case.

When she finished, his gaze shifted to Luke then back to her. "Isn't it unusual for the chief suspect to be involved in an overseer's capacity during the investigation?"

"He's not overseeing the investigation," she replied coolly, but did not elaborate further on Luke's presence.

"It certainly looks that way," Mark persisted, his tone making it clear he didn't approve of Luke being there.

Jessica had to admit that allowing Luke to hang around was unorthodox. But then she hadn't exactly "allowed" him to remain. She shot Luke a disgruntled glance. "Well, looks can be deceiv..."

"Jessica!" Paul Pace bellowed from his office door. "I'd like to see you in here on the double."

"Yes, sir." She was out of her chair in a flash. The sheriff was generally an even-tempered man. Frantically she wondered if somehow he'd found out about her excursion into the Strope home.

"Close the door," he ordered when she joined him inside his private sanctum.

Complying, she then stood in front of his desk, her hands clasped behind her so he could not witness her wringing them.

In calmer tones, he said evenly, "Would you care to explain to me why the FBI called just now to inform me that they have no records on a Duncan Holston?"

"Because I asked them to check on him for us," she replied, mentally kicking herself for not telling Harriet to route that call to her when it came in.

Paul Pace continued to study her closely. "And why are we interested in Duncan Holston? Even more to the point, who the hell is Duncan Holston?"

Knowing lying would only cause her more trouble, Jessica said stiffly, "I have reason to believe he was Melinda Strope's first husband."

The sheriff scowled. "You have what?"

"I have reason to believe..." she began to repeat.

He held up his hand. "I heard you the first time. Were you aware that, according to Mrs. Strope, she has never been married before?"

Jessica's jaw tensed. "I have reason to believe she is lying."

"And what is your reason?"

"An impeccable source?" she suggested tentatively.

Paul's frown deepened. "Why do I get the feeling that it would be futile for me to pursue this line of questioning?"

"You really don't want to know," she assured him.

Running a hand through his thinning white hair, he tilted his chair back and studied her intently for a long moment. "Who is the stranger sitting at your desk?"

"An insurance salesman," she replied.

"You thinking of taking out a little life insurance just in case I totally lose my temper with you?"

Knowing it was not smart to push Paul Pace too far, Jessica met his gaze levelly. "No, sir. He's the insurance salesman who sold Melinda Strope's second husband a large insurance policy."

Paul shifted his chair back onto all four legs. "Her second husband?"

"Yes, sir." Succinctly, Jessica proceeded to relate what facts she knew about Kenneth Lymon.

"Are there any more husbands you haven't mentioned?" he asked when she finished, an underlying edge n his voice hinting that he found all of this a bit hard to believe.

"None that I know of."

Rubbing one hand across his mouth, Paul continued drumming with the fingers of the other while he studied Jessica. "You honestly believe Luke is innocent, don't you?"

Jessica straightened her shoulders. "Yes, sir."

"And you're determined to continue to investigate this on your own to prove you're right."

Jessica shrugged. "You know how stubborn I am."

A tiny smile curled one corner of Paul's mouth. Easing himself out of his chair, he walked over to the door. Opening it a small amount, he looked out toward Jessica's desk. After a couple of moments he closed it again and returned to his desk. "All right, this sounds like a lead worth pursuing. I'd like to find we've been wrong about Luke. When I was about that insurance man's age, I was a sucker for a pair of green eyes. In fact, I still am. You go ahead with your investigation. I'm sure that salesman will tell you things he wouldn't tell me. But I want to know everything you turn up. In the meantime, I'll do some checking on my own and see if I can come up with anything on this Duncan Holston character."

Relief swept over Jessica's features. With or without the sheriff's approval she had planned to keep investigating. But it would be much easier to have him on her side. "Thanks."

With a wave of his hand Paul shooed her out of his office.

"Anything wrong?" Mark asked, rising to greet her when she returned to her desk.

"Just a little bit of paperwork I didn't do properly," she replied, slipping past him and seating herself.

Luke shot her a curious glance but remained silent.

"Speaking of paperwork." She pulled a notepad into position in front of her. "I would be interested in the name of the investigator your company hired to look into the Lymon killing."

"I can give it to you if you want it, but that's not really necessary. I have a copy of the file he turned over to us," Mark informed her.

Again surprise registered on her face. "Here?"

"In my briefcase." He tapped the sleek leather case sitting on the floor by his chair.

"I'd like to see it," she said, holding out her hand.

"How about over lunch?" he bargained, his voice taking on a softly coaxing quality that suggested he wasn't thinking only of business. "Just you and me. I don't mean to be rude, Brandson." He glanced toward the rancher. "But I find third parties inhibiting."

"I'll bet you do," Luke muttered.

"Lunch sounds perfect," Jessica agreed quickly before Luke's big-brother instincts could cause a scene. "Why don't you come back around twelve-thirty?"

"Fine." Smiling warmly as he rose, he added conspiratorially, "In the meantime, I'll keep a low profile." He was almost to the door when he came to a halt and turned to face Luke. "If you decide you want that policy, just let me know."

Luke merely nodded in acknowledgement.

"That's got to be the best-looking male to stumble into these parts in years," Harriet said sighing as the door closed behind the insurance salesman. "If I were you, Jessica, I'd change into a dress and skip talking about police business."

"I'll consider the suggestion," Jessica replied, continuing to stare thoughtfully toward the door. It was nice to have a man look at her as if she were a desirable female. Especially one as handsome and as charming as Mark Smythe. Suddenly feeling the hairs on the back of her neck prickling, she turned to face Luke. "You discussed buying an insurance policy from Mark? Won't Sam Jordan be angry if he discovers you're doing business with someone other than him? Besides, I could have sworn you weren't impressed by Mr. Smythe."

"I wasn't," Luke said coolly. "He's too smooth for my taste. But I wanted his business card to find out what company he claims to be working for." Handing her the receiver of her telephone, he shoved the card in front of her. "Don't you think you should contact them and make certain he is who he says he is?"

"Of course he is who he says he is," she scoffed.

Luke's jaw hardened in a determined line. "If my understanding of what I have overheard is clear, you have now involved yourself in the investigation of two murders. Don't you think it would be prudent to check on any strangers who suddenly appear out of the blue offering valuable information?"

"He didn't suddenly appear out of the blue. I called him," she pointed out tersely. "And the financial compensation for anyone who can prove that Lymon was killed for the insurance money and regain most of it would be enough justification for several abrupt appearances. Not to mention the jewels that were stolen."

"What could it hurt to call?" he insisted.

She couldn't argue with that. She grabbed the receiver. Punching the number for Information she asked for the number of the insurance company listed on the card. It was the same as that printed in the lower left hand corner. Rewarding Luke with a caustic smile, she dialed the number. A woman answered and informed her that Mr. Smythe was out of town and asked if she would like to speak to another of their representatives.

"No," she replied. Then, determined to play this out fully so that Luke couldn't fault her for not being totally cautious, she continued in a slightly flustered voice, "I've been talking to representatives of several firms. And, I'm a little embarrassed to admit it but I'm afraid I might have gotten a few of the names and faces confused. Just so I can be certain that Mr. Smythe is who I think he is, would you mind describing him to me?"

"He's hard to forget." There was a lusty admiration in the secretary's voice. "He's a little over six feet tall, thirty-two years old, has blond hair, a great body, the most wonderful soft brown eyes, and he's single."

"I do believe I remember exactly who he is now," Jessica said assuredly, giving Luke an "I told you so" look. "And when he smiles, he has very sexy dimples."

"That's him," the woman confirmed. "Who shall I say called?"

"Jessica Martin. He has my number," she replied, then after thanking the woman, she hung up. "Satisfied?" she asked Luke with an edge of aggravation.

"I suppose I have to be," he conceded with a scowl, slipping the card into his pocket. "Now tell me why you're interested in this Kenneth Lymon's death."

Studying his cool expression, it suddenly dawned on Jessica that down deep inside she'd been hoping that his objections to Mark Smythe had been tinted with jealousy. She'd even added the part about the dimples just to needle Luke. But he wasn't jealous. He was simply being protective. "That's police business and I can't discuss it with you," she replied stiffly.

His expression became even colder. "You obviously discussed it with Smythe."

"He had information I needed," she returned tersely.

He regarded her sternly. "You also lied to him."

Jessica frowned in confusion. "What?"

Luke's eyes narrowed as he leaned toward her. "Paul Pace would never lose his temper over a piece of paperwork. Did he find out about your little escapade last night?"

"No." She glanced anxiously toward Harriet, but Luke had lowered his voice and she didn't think the dispatcher had overheard. "And you are trying my patience."

"You're right," he agreed abruptly. "And I have been making as ass of myself by hanging around here bothering you when you'd probably rather I was in the next county." He drew an impatient breath. "I've got a farm to run and some arrangements that'll need to be made if I'm going to spend more time in jail."

Startled by this sudden change in his attitude, Luke was almost to the door before Jessica caught up with him. She was glad to be getting rid of him. But she hated for them to part in anger. Placing a hand on his arm, she halted his exit. "I'm doing everything I can to see that you don't have to spend time in jail," she assured him. Her tone and manner became more official. "What you have heard in here this morning was part of a police investigation. I want your word that you will not mention either Kenneth Lymon or Duncan Holston to anyone."

"You have my word," he promised gruffly, then turned and left.

"I don't know how you put up with that man," Harriet said as the door swung closed and Jessica returned to her desk. "He absolutely unnerves me, especially when he's angry." She shivered slightly to give emphasis to her words, then added, "With him being so strong, you'd think he could have gotten that gun away from Charles Strope without shooting him with it.''

"Try to keep in mind that he's innocent until proven guilty," Jessica suggested scorchingly.

Harriet's back stiffened with self-righteous indignation. "Of course he is. But the district attorney wouldn't have charged him if he didn't think he had enough proof to win a conviction."

A grimness came over Jessica's features. "I admit that it does look bad for Luke at the moment. But as people involved with the law, we should keep an open mind."

Harriet rose from her desk. "My mind is as open as anyone else's in this town," she stated. With her head held high, she stalked into the ladies' room.

"That's what I'm afraid of," Jessica muttered beneath her breath.

And, although no one really believed the rumors Mrs. Wakley was spreading, they weren't helping improve the town's mood toward Luke. But rumors weren't the real problem. In bold letters, she wrote the word *proof* on the scratch pad in front of her. That was the one part of this mess that nagged at her continuously. Even if she knew for certain in her own mind who the real guilty party was, how was she going to prove it? Luke had been very carefully and very securely framed. All of the evidence pointed directly to him. He had even helped by producing a pair of bloody, powder-stained gloves.

The atmosphere in the jail for the rest of the morning bordered on hostile, and it was a relief when Mark Smythe returned.

"Where's your shadow?" he questioned, glancing around the room expectantly.

Jessica glanced toward him in confusion. "What?"

"Brandson. The way he was hovering over you, I half expected him to insist on accompanying us." A mischievous gleam sparkled in his eyes. "I don't think he trusts me."

"He doesn't," she admitted. "But don't take it personally. He's always had a big-brother complex where I'm concerned."

"He's not going to jump out of the woodwork if I make a pass, is he?" Mark demanded with mock anxiety.

Jessica scowled. "Luke Brandson is a good man."

Pausing with his hand on the latch of the passenger door of the rental car he was driving, Mark's manner became serious. "I'm a little confused. You tell me that Brandson has a big-brother complex where you're concerned. That implies the two of you have had a reasonably close relationship through the years. And just now you defended him. I've been keeping my ears open since I left you this morning and from the talk I've heard, the evidence against him is strong, but with a good attorney and a change in his story he could probably get off with manslaughter. It's my guess the killing was an accident. Brandson got scared and invented that ridiculous story which only made him look more guilty. But your DA's going for murder one, and it looks like you're going to help him by trying to connect the widow to this. That would give credence to the rumors about the affair and make Brandson less sympathetic in the eyes of any jury."

Jessica's jaw tensed. "I'm trying to prove that Luke's story is the truth. I believe he was framed."

A look of disbelief registered on Mark's face. "You believe him?"

"Yes," she replied without reservation.

Mark gave a low whistle. "You've got your work cut out for you."

"I know," she admitted, as he opened the door and stepped aside to allow her to climb in. She waited until he had seated himself behind the steering wheel, then said, "I thought I would fix us something at my place. That way we can have a private discussion without worrying about being overheard. Besides, I have an ulterior motive. My mother mentioned that Melinda Strope and Margaret Demis are coming to her shop today to have their hair done. I want you to get a good look at both of them. I want a definite identification of the widow, and I also want to know if you recognize Margaret."

"Too bad." The mischievous gleam again sparkled in his eyes. "I was hoping you had something else in mind."

It had been a long time since anyone as good-looking as Mark had flirted with her, and his manner was appealing. She couldn't resist giving him a look of mock reproach and returning the prescribed banter. "You men are all alike."

"But you women aren't and that's what makes life so interesting and challenging," he countered with a laugh.

There was an underlying confidence about him and she guessed he rarely lost a match with a women he seriously set his mind to win.

Arriving at the house, she barely had time to get him into the kitchen before Melinda and Margaret arrived. As they walked across the drive to the salon, he studied them intently from the window of the back door. "The blond is Melinda Lymon all right. She's barely changed. I'm not certain if I've ever seen the other woman before. But I don't think so."

"Could she be the friend who found Lymon's body with the wife?" Jessica suggested. "She could have altered her hair color and her weight."

He shook his head. "No. That woman was nearly sixty. Besides, she had a large family and was a lifetime member of the community. She wouldn't have been involved in any 'murder for profit' scheme.''

"It was a long shot," Jessica admitted as they left the window. Motioning for him to sit down at the table, she went to the refrigerator and began taking out sandwich fixings and setting them on the table.

"You honestly believe the widow is involved, don't you?" he said, adding thoughtfully, "Has it ever occurred to you that she just might be one of those unlucky people who seem destined to be followed by tragedy through their lives?"

"It has," she admitted, setting plates and flatware on the table. "To be perfectly honest, I'm not sure what I believe except that Luke is telling the truth."

"I hope Brandson knows how lucky he is to have someone with so much faith in him." Mark smiled wistfully. "Wish I could find someone with that much faith in me. I'd marry her in a minute."

Ignoring the knot that formed in her stomach at the thought of Luke and marriage, Jessica glanced toward Mark. "You don't really strike me as the settling down type," she said trying to keep up her end of their banter.

"Maybe I just never met the right woman," he replied, his tone of voice hinting that she might be the one to change him.

"Maybe," she conceded but made no effort to continue this light flirtation. She had much more important matters to pursue if she was going to save Luke from jail or worse. "You want iced tea, coffee or soda?"

"Iced tea sounds good," he answered. He watched in silence as she got out glasses and filled them. As she carried them to the table, he suddenly asked bluntly, "Are you in love with Brandson?"

Jessica's jaw tightened. It was bad enough that she'd admitted her feelings to her mother. She wasn't going to let a stranger know the truth. She schooled her face into a look of haggard impatience. "He's a long-time family friend. Actually he's been a real pain in the neck to me most of my life. But he's always been around when I needed help." She added, "And even when I didn't." Her mouth formed a determined line. "I can't turn my back on him."

There was relief in Mark's eyes as he smiled up at her warmly. "Just want to know how strong the competition is."

Jessica was flattered but she was more concerned about Luke. So far every path she'd taken had proved to be a dead end. "I could use a lead on a man by the name of Duncan Holston," she said, seating herself across the table from him. "Did you come across that name in your investigator's report?"

He shook his head regretfully. "I've read the report a dozen times. I could swear that name isn't in it anywhere." Opening his briefcase, he pulled out a manila envelope. "But you're welcome to check for yourself."

"Thanks," she said, reaching for the folder.

Mark continued to hold it captive for a moment. "You get the folder when you tell me who Duncan Holston is," he bargained.

Jessica was in no mood to be evasive. She just wanted information. "I believe he's Melinda Strope's first husband," she replied. "Now may I see the folder?"

Mark regarded her in stunned silence for a moment. "She had a first husband?" he questioned, releasing the folder to her. "How did you uncover him? Did she reveal all while under your mother's hair dryer during a particularly boring afternoon?"

"No." Jessica avoided his eyes. While on the surface, Mark Smythe seemed to be merely a smooth-talking charmer, out looking for a little excitement and monetary reward, he was a sharp observer. "How I found out is of no importance. The question is, where is Duncan Holston now? And, in your case, where was he when Kenneth Lymon was killed?"

Confusion again registered on Mark's face. "I still don't understand why he's so important."

Setting the folder aside for the moment, Jessica met his gaze levelly. "What if there was never a divorce? What if he was blackmailing his wife each time she remarried? And then, what if he got tired of the small payments and wanted a large lump sum? By killing off the husbands, he provided himself with a new bankroll."

"I hope you won't be offended but that is a pretty far-fetched theory. Divorces are easy to come by, and Melinda Strope never struck me as a bigamist." He smiled a crooked smile. "Besides, if that theory is correct, I don't get my reward."

"Sorry about that," she said matching his light manner. Then her expression became serious again as she persisted in outlining her theory. "Maybe she thought she had a divorce. Maybe Duncan Holston told her he had gotten one. Then, after she was married to Lymon, Holston showed up and blackmailed her. When Lymon died, he could have told her that for a price he would go somewhere and get a real divorce. He could even have had some phony papers drawn up. Then he pulled the same trick when she married Strope—he showed up here to blackmail her again."

Mark studied her dubiously. "What does your sheriff think of your scenario?"

"I haven't told him," she admitted. "I know it sounds as if I've been exposed to one too many television detectives. And maybe I am grasping at straws. But I've known Luke Brandson all my life and I believe he's innocent.''

''But you don't have any proof to corroborate your theories?'' he asked skeptically.

''Only the names and the fact that Melinda Strope has lied about her past marital status.'' Determination glistened in Jessica's eyes. ''But I'm determined to turn up something that will give Luke a fighting chance.''

Mark smiled encouragingly. ''Let it never be said that Mark Smythe deserted a lady in distress. As long as I've come all this way, I might as well try to help.''

She could tell he didn't think they had much of a chance. But she was willing to accept any aid made available to her. ''I appreciate the offer, and I hope this works out to your advantage, too.''

Reaching across the table, he took her hand in his. ''It very well could.''

The warmth in his eyes brought a flush to her cheeks. She found herself wishing that just once, Luke would look at her like that. Working her hand loose, she began to make her sandwich.

As Mark too began making a sandwich, he said in businesslike tones, ''Now that I'm committed, tell me what you know about this Duncan Holston other than the fact that he was married to the former Mrs. Lymon.''

Jessica frowned in frustration. ''So far all I know is that they were married in Houston.''

''No doubt if he is following her around doing evil deeds, he has changed his name and developed a whole new identity,'' he pointed out.

''No doubt,'' she agreed, refusing to let the bleakness of the situation undermine her determination.

Again Mark reached across the table to take her hand in his. ''Before we go any further there is one thing I have to say. I will help you all I can, but you should keep in mind that your trust in Brandson might be ill placed. The evidence against him is pretty solid. And being confined in a jail cell can be terrifying to a man whose whole existence has been directed toward having no boundaries. It still seems most likely to me that he killed Strope by accident but is afraid to own up to it.''

Jessica shook her head. "If Luke killed Strope, he would have said so.''

"I hope you're right.'' Releasing her hand, Mark's eyes glistened with mischief. "Because if Brandson did do it, I definitely lose out on my finder's fee.''

While they ate, Jessica went over the contents of the folder. She found nothing helpful. "Do you mind if I keep this file and copy it?'' she asked as they drove back to the jail. "Maybe there's something I missed.''

"Anything to be of assistance,'' Mark replied gallantly. "Do you think that if I went to see the widow on the pretext of offering her my condolences it might shake her up enough so that she would come forward and tell the truth?'' he suggested.

"It might merely warn her and put her on her guard,'' Jessica cautioned. "Let's wait for a while. In the meantime, you could contact the investigator who made this report on the Lymon case and ask if he has Duncan Holston's name in his private files or anywhere in his notes.''

"I doubt that he does. I'm certain he gave us a complete report, but I'll check and get back to you.'' They were parked in front of the jail and, catching her under the chin with the tips of his fingers, he tilted her face upward and kissed her quickly and lightly on the lips. "Any excuse to remain in touch with you is welcome. I never realized until now what a weakness I have for green-eyed police officers with curves in all the right places.''

With a forced smile Jessica slipped out of the car. Mark Smythe was good for her morale but he wasn't Luke.

Chapter Nine

Jessica spent the next couple of hours making peace with Harriet. It was not going to help her investigation, or anyone's nerves, if the staff at the jail was fighting amongst themselves. Luckily Harriet was basically a good-natured soul and accepted the overtures toward renewed harmony with relief, allowing things to settle back to normal.

Mark called in the middle of the afternoon to say that he had finally managed to speak to the investigator who had handled the Lymon case. The man had searched through his files and drawn a blank on the name Duncan Holston. "He did, however, give me several tips as to how I might locate Holston, and I've arranged to fly out to Texas early in the morning and begin."

"I'd like to hear what he had to suggest," Jessica said, toying with the idea of flying out to Houston herself. She was beginning to feel desperate. All she had were theories, and those were pretty weak. She had to find Holston. "Would you be interested in coming to dinner this evening? My mother's a wonderful cook."

"I'd come even if she burned everything," he assured her.

A small frown played at the corners of Jessica's mouth. She wasn't in the mood for flirting. She chided herself. For

Mark this was a game. He didn't understand how personally she was involved. But, even more important, she didn't want him guessing how she really felt about Luke. She forced a lightness into her voice she didn't feel. "Come around six. That will give us time to talk in private while Mom is watching over things in the kitchen."

"Now that does sound inviting," he said in suggestive tones. "I'll be there."

"Was that Mr. Smythe?" Harriet asked as Jessica hung up.

"Yes," Jessica said, forcing a smile. She knew what was coming next. Harriet was an ardent matchmaker.

"I wouldn't let that one get away if I were you," the dispatcher advised.

"He is charming." Jessica had worked too hard to reduce the tension in the room to do anything to inflame the situation again by informing Harriet that just because a man was good-looking and had nice manners didn't mean he was a good catch. Then, because it was necessary and it also cut off further conversation about Mark Smythe for the moment, she phoned her mother. One of the customers answered and informed her that Molly was in the middle of a streaking and couldn't come to the phone. Knowing that if she mentioned Mark's name it would be spread all around town by evening, she simply left a message that there would be an extra person for dinner.

As soon as she hung up, Harriet began making suggestions as to how she should dress and hinted that she thought Jessica could use a little more makeup. Jessica fought the temptation to snidely ask the woman if she would like to come over and supervise her preparations for the evening, but prudently she refrained.

On an impulse Jessica placed a call to Sandra Craven, the friend who had been with Melinda when Lymon's body was found. She told her that she was reopening the Lymon case and asked Mrs. Craven if she would mind telling her again what had happened the night of the murder. To her relief the elderly woman's memory was very good. But to Jessica's disappointment, she discovered nothing new. The woman had never heard of a Duncan Holston. She was a neighbor of the Lymons and assured Jessica that she'd never seen any unaccounted-for strangers hanging around the place. Several times she mentioned how wonderful a person Melinda was and how sweet.

"I was so worried about her," she said with motherly concern. "Her having no family and being left on her own. Guess she just couldn't stand being in the house where the murder took place. Moved out barely a month later. I was hoping she'd keep in touch but she didn't. Guess the memories were too awful for her. I've never seen anyone go to pieces like she did when we found the body."

Thanking her for her help, Jessica hung up. Glancing at the clock, she noticed that it was nearly two. Time for her to go out on patrol. Grateful for the excuse to get away from Harriet and have some private time to think, she left.

Blue Mill Falls looked the same as it always had, but it didn't feel the same. She couldn't shake the sensation that there was danger lurking on these quiet, shady, tree-lined streets. The bruise on her arm hurt a little as she accidentally pressed it against the door. "It's only natural to be a bit nervous when you've nearly been killed by a drunk," she reasoned aloud, trying to lessen the tenseness she was feeling by listening to her own voice. It didn't work.

A prickling sensation on the back of her neck caused her to glance over her shoulder. No one was there. A crooked smile played across her face. Grandma Martin would have said it was her sixth sense warning her to be careful. But she didn't need any sudden chill to warn her there was danger.

She was convinced that whoever had murdered Strope was a cold-blooded, calculating killer. And a person like that wasn't going to sit back smugly and assume the job was done. He or she would be keeping track of the investigation. "And if I get close enough, they might act against me," she muttered. Her jaw tensed. "But risking that could be the only way to clear Luke."

Arriving back at the jail a couple of hours later, she was checking her messages when Melinda Strope came through the door with Margaret Demis hovering protectively behind.

The blonde looked white as a sheet and her hands were trembling. Approaching Jessica's desk, she came to a halt, her posture rigid. "I must speak to you and the sheriff."

"I really think you should go home and rest," Margaret encouraged. Then, shifting her attention to Jessica, she said, "I don't know what has gotten into her. She went up to her room to rest and a few minutes later came back and told me that she had to see the sheriff and you. At first I refused to drive her. But she said she would drive herself if I didn't and she's in no condi—"

"Margaret, please," Melinda interrupted the dissertation on her state of mind. "This is important. It has been bothering me and I cannot rest until I've spoken to Deputy Martin and the sheriff."

"If you'll follow me," Jessica instructed, keeping both her voice and manner calm, while frantically hoping the widow was going to provide the information that was needed to vindicate Luke. Knocking on the sheriff's door, she waited for his response. Then, after opening the door, she stepped aside to allow Melinda Strope to enter ahead of her.

Pausing in the doorway, Melinda blocked Margaret's way. "You've been a good friend to me through all of this," she said gratefully. "But what I have to say is difficult, and right now I only have enough courage to say it in front of the sheriff and the deputy."

Concern etched itself deeply into Margaret's features. "Are you certain you'll be all right?"

"I'll look after her," Jessica promised.

This assurance was rewarded by a hostile glance from the housekeeper.

"Please," Melinda said, indicating a chair near Harriet's desk with a frail gesture of her hand.

Casting a second threatening look in Jessica's direction, Margaret stalked over to the chair and sat down.

Nervously Melinda entered the sheriff's office. Jessica followed, pulling the door closed behind her.

Rising, but remaining behind his desk, Paul Pace gestured toward one of the chairs facing him. "Won't you be seated, Mrs. Strope?"

Melinda seemed to sink onto the wooden structure as if her legs had suddenly become too weak to support her.

"What can we do for you?" the sheriff asked in sympathetic tones as Jessica seated herself in the companion chair.

"I don't know exactly how to say this." Melinda's voice shook and her eyes flooded with tears.

"Take your time," he said soothingly, glancing toward Jessica and raising a questioning eyebrow. She answered with an "I have no idea what's going on" shrug.

"I don't know what you'll think of me, but I beg of you not to judge me too harshly." A slow trickle of tears escaped and rolled down the widow's cheeks. "I lied to you."

Jessica had to fight to keep a calm outer countenance. Maybe Melinda was going to clear Luke, and this nightmare would be over.

"Go on," the sheriff encouraged, his manner fatherly. "And don't feel too bad. We're used to people not being completely honest. I appreciate you coming forward."

"Thank you." She forced a weak smile as she dabbed at her tears with a hankie. "But you may not feel so kindly toward me when I'm finished. This wasn't a small lie. It was a monster." She glanced beseechingly toward Jessica who was remaining silent.

"We all have our secrets we would prefer not to disclose," Jessica said, matching the sheriff's friendly, comforting manner. A sudden knot formed in her stomach. What if Melinda had come to confess to having had an affair with Luke? Jessica's jaw tensed. Despite the scene by the barn, Jessica still believed Luke was telling the truth when he said he'd never had an intimate relationship with this woman. She waited anxiously to hear what Melinda had come to say.

Still continuing to hesitate, Melinda looked down at her lap, where her hands now rested. She studied them for a long moment. Then, with a resolute air, she lifted her head and met the sheriff's gaze. "I have been married before. Twice."

"That is not a crime in this day and age," he assured her.

"Yes, but my second husband also died violently. He was a jeweler." Loving admiration was strong in her voice. "He created marvelous pieces, truly works of art." The muscles in her face suddenly tightened as if she was fighting another flood of tears, and a look of horror entered her eyes. "But to do his work properly, he kept gold and precious stones in his workshop safe. He was shot to death during a robbery. You see, he was working on this very special piece. It was to be set with a huge diamond and several other gems. He had everything he needed for it in his workroom." The tears she had been trying to control began to pour freely down her cheeks. "I feel like a jinx, as if by marrying a man I put the mark of death on him."

"What about your first husband?" Jessica asked, finding it difficult to keep her voice gentle and coaxing. If he was dead, too, she had no suspect.

Fear entered the widow's eyes as she fought to regain control of her emotions. "I married him when I was very young. It took several years, but eventually I got up enough courage to leave him and demand a divorce." She shivered as if this memory caused her fear. "He was not the kind of man I thought he was. He was . . . cruel."

"Do you happen to know where he is at the moment?" Jessica probed hopefully.

"No." The answer came out sharply, edged with fear. "If I never see or hear from him again it will be a blessing."

"Have you had any contact with him since your divorce?" Jessica persisted.

Melinda shook her head. "No, none."

"Do you happen to know where he was from or do you have any idea where we might contact him?" Paul Pace asked.

Melinda looked up at the sheriff with a perplexed frown. "Why would you want to contact him?"

"I don't like loose ends," he replied with an encouraging smile. "Do you have any idea where we might be able to locate him?"

"We met and married in Houston and lived there after our marriage, but I don't think he was from there originally," she replied, closing her eyes in an effort to concentrate. "The truth is, I never knew much about him. I discovered very quickly he had lied to me about himself. When I confronted him, he was very secretive about his past, and after we separated, I never saw him again."

Jessica studied her closely. "How did you obtain your divorce?"

"He obtained it in Mexico and called me when it was finalized. That was the last I heard from him." The woman rose rigidly. "Now that I have told you everything, I will be going. I apologize for not being totally honest with you in the first place but it is difficult for me to face the fact that I am a blight to the men I love."

"Just for the record," Paul Pace interrupted her retreat. "What were your husbands' names?"

Standing with her hand on the handle of the door as if she needed the support, Melinda turned to face him. "The first was Duncan Holston and the second was Kenneth Lymon."

"You said you met and married Holston in Houston and you lived with him there. Do you happen to remember the address?" he asked, his tone official.

She thought for a moment. "It's been a long time," she replied hesitantly. "And it's not something I really want to remember." Then, after another moment, she gave him a street and house number.

"And where did you meet Kenneth Lymon?" he questioned after jotting down the information she had just given him.

"We met in Los Angeles, and that was where we lived for two wonderful years." With another crying binge threatening, she added the address of that house and Detective Thatcher's name to the information she had already given him. "Now, if that is all, I . . ." Slowly she began to sink toward the floor.

Jessica was there in an instant to place a supportive arm around the widow's waist.

Taking several deep breaths, Melinda straightened. "I'm so sorry." Embarrassment caused her to flush, producing red splotches on her cheeks that contrasted harshly with her paleness. "I really must be going."

The sheriff had joined the two women by the door. "Are you certain you'll be all right?" he asked solicitously.

"I'm fine. I just felt a little light-headed for a moment," she assured him.

Dubiously he opened the door and stepped aside. "Thank you for coming in and talking to us."

Immediately Margaret was at Melinda's side. "Now I absolutely insist you come home and rest," she said. Tossing both the sheriff and Jessica accusatory glances, she added, "You look like death."

"Yes, I would like to go home now," Melinda agreed tiredly. Holding her head proudly, she preceded Margaret out of the jail.

Jessica followed Paul Pace back into his office and closed the door. "Well, what do you think?"

"I think I would like to find this Duncan Holston and ask him a few questions," he said, reseating himself at his desk. Meeting her expectant gaze, he added, "But this still doesn't change the evidence. The fact that Lymon and Strope were both shot to death could be pure coincidence. Lymon had placed himself in a high-risk position by keeping both precious stones and metals in his home, and Strope had gone gunning for Luke."

Jessica knew the sheriff was being the voice of reason, and she did not attempt to argue with him. It would serve no purpose. He was dealing with facts, and she was playing hunches.

Driving home a while later, she went over what had happened in her mind. The result was not encouraging. Even though Melinda Strope had come forward, they still knew as little as they had known before and Luke was still the prime suspect.

She noticed two customers' cars parked in the wide drive as she pulled in and parked near the house. She was glad Molly would be busy for a while. She wanted a little time to herself. Passing through the kitchen, she paused to check the oven and discovered that her mother already had a pot roast cooking. At least she would not have to change in a rush so that she could start dinner.

Upstairs in her room she stripped off her uniform and climbed into a warm shower. The muscles in her neck were as taut as bow strings. Infuriated with herself, she admitted grudgingly that she had missed Luke's presence during the afternoon and wondered how he had spent the rest of the day. The image of Lydia Matherson comforting him did nothing to help her nerves, and she made the water hotter and washed her hair.

Later, after having blow-dried it into soft waves, she looked through her closet. Her gaze came to rest on a kelly-green shirtwaist dress with white piping. It was not too dressy, while at the same time it flattered her figure and set off her eyes. She pulled it out and slipped it on.

Going back downstairs, she was setting the table in the dining room when her mother came in.

"My, don't you look pretty," Molly smiled approvingly. "Luke should be real impressed."

"Luke?" Jessica questioned sharply, then, realizing her mother had simply made a false assumption, she said, "No, not Luke. My guest is Mark Smythe. He's an insurance salesman I ran across during this investigation. We're going to discuss some revelations that have come to light about Melinda Strope. I don't want you repeating anything you might overhear."

A sparkle came into Molly's eyes. "Well, Luke is going to be here, too. He called a few minutes ago and, naturally assuming he was the guest you had called to warn me about, I mentioned dinner. He said he'd be here. So I guess you'd better set a fourth place."

Jessica groaned aloud. It wasn't that she didn't want to see Luke. She wanted to see him too much. What she didn't want was to spend the evening acting as buffer between Mark's unwanted flirtation and Luke's unwanted big-brother protectiveness. She wasn't certain she could keep up her pretense of indifference toward Luke and she didn't want either him or Mark to suspect how she really felt.

"It won't hurt Luke to see you with another man," Molly was saying with a womanly smile.

"He's already met Mark and they mix like oil and water," Jessica replied.

"Then we won't seat them next to one another at the table," Molly said over her shoulder as she returned to the kitchen, a mischievous gleam in her eyes.

"I would prefer not to seat them in the same room," Jessica muttered under her breath as she took out another place setting.

Mark arrived at precisely six, and after introducing him to her mother, Jessica led him into the living room. As he seated himself on the couch, she prudently chose a nearby chair. He was regarding her with a steadily warming gaze, and before the conversation could turn to a personal vein, she directed it toward their investigation. "Melinda Strope came to the jail today."

His smile said that he saw through her ploy, but was willing to acquiesce. "Why does that sound so ominous?"

"She confessed to her previous marriages," Jessica elaborated.

His posture straightened and a seriousness came over his features. "No kidding?"

"No kidding," she replied.

Mark studied her with interest. "What about Duncan Holston? Did she tell you where to find him?"

Jessica shook her head. "She swears she has no idea. She says she met him in Houston, married him there and lived with him there for a few years. It seems that he was not the nicest person in the world. It's obvious she's afraid of him."

"Gus Aimes, the investigator I talked to, gave me the names of some of his contacts in Houston. He said they'd cooperate in any way they could. With any luck I might be able to get a lead on this very elusive character," Mark said encouragingly.

"It would be terrific if you could get a description or, better still, a photograph," Jessica suggested hopefully. "If he's the one we're looking for, if he did frame Luke, then he would have to be someone we've seen around. He would have to have been in a position to have kept an eye on Strope and to have bided his time until the perfect opportunity presented itself."

A gleam of understanding sparked in Mark's eyes. "I see what you're getting at. He would have to be one of your community, or he would have been spotted as a stranger and his presence would attract attention."

"Exactly," she confirmed.

Mark's voice became conspiratorial. "Do you have any idea as to who it might be?"

Jessica's mouth formed a thoughtful pout. "There are several possibilities. I'll keep an eye on them and have the sheriff run a couple of checks. Hopefully I'll have a more definitive answer by the time you return."

"And if we do turn up a positive identification on this Holston character, then what? How do we link him with Strope's death? All the evidence still points to Brandson."

Determination hardened Jessica's features. "We convince the widow to cooperate. If Holston is the one who killed Strope, Melinda Strope should be able to supply us with a motive, and we could work from there."

Mark looked worried. "Do you think you can convince her to help?"

"She's pretty shaken up and feeling very guilty. If we can convince her that she will be safe and free to lead a normal life after Holston is behind bars, she might be willing to testify against him in a court of law." Jessica drew an eager breath. "At least I hope so."

"And what if we're wrong about Holston? What if he hasn't been harassing his former wife? What if he's never been within five hundred miles of Blue Mill Falls?" Mark's gaze become sharply penetrating. "What will you do then?"

"I'll look for someone else with a motive to want Strope dead," she replied without hesitation.

"You're determined not to give up on Luke? You won't even admit that he might have shot Strope accidentally?" he prodded, a hint of exasperation in his voice.

Jessica shook her head. "I know he's innocent."

A wistful smile played at the corners of Mark's mouth. "I wish I had someone who had that much faith in me."

Jessica smiled encouragingly. "I'm sure you'll find—"

"I hope I'm not interrupting anything," Luke's gruff tones announced his entrance, his manner contradicting his polite words. "I came in through the kitchen and your mother sent me out here."

"No, of course not." Jessica smiled uncomfortably as the atmosphere in the room suddenly tensed.

Luke continued to focus his attention on her as he lowered his large frame into a chair near hers. "You look very pretty tonight." There was a hint of accusation in his voice as if he resented the fact she had tried to make herself more attractive for Mark.

For a moment she found herself wishing this was jealousy on Luke's part, but she was not the kind of person to delude herself. He simply didn't like Mark. He'd made that clear. And because he didn't like Mark, he didn't want her having anything to do with the insurance man. "Thank you," she muttered, her back stiffening defensively.

"It's my opinion that Jessica would look good in a flour sack," Mark said, smiling softly as he accepted Luke's unspoken challenge, his eyes seeming almost to caress her.

Jessica's hands tightened on the arms of the chair. She didn't want Luke arguing with Mark about her. She wanted Mark's help to clear Luke and he'd be a great deal more cooperative if the two men weren't feuding. "Mark and I were discussing your case," she said coolly, determinedly changing the subject. "Tomorrow he's flying to Houston to try to uncover a piece of evidence that might help."

"Be happy to drive you to the airport," Luke offered, continuing to regard the other man dourly.

Mark smiled good-naturedly. "No, thanks." His gaze shifted to Jessica. "I'm hoping Jessica will volunteer. It's always nice to have someone to kiss goodbye."

"I'll bet you're an expert at that," Luke muttered.

The smile vanished from Mark's face. "I admit I haven't always been a saint where women are concerned. But in Jessica's case I don't think I could ever get bored." His voice took on a coaxing quality as he turned toward her. "In fact, I've been thinking. If this case works out well for us, maybe we should consider starting our own private investigative agency. I've got a lot of contacts in the insurance business, and I could continue as a salesman on the side until we made a reputation for ourselves."

"That's an interesting proposition," Jessica admitted. In the back of her mind she had begun to think that once she had cleared Luke, it might be a good idea to leave Blue Mill Falls again. There was obviously no future for her here, and becoming a private detective could be the right course for her.

"If you'll excuse me," Luke said, his manner cutting. "I seem to have lost my appetite."

"Too bad," Mark said with a smile, as Jessica hesitated, searching for something to say to defuse the situation. She hadn't meant to upset Luke. He had enough on his mind as it was. But, before she could speak, he left the room. The front door slammed and a moment later they heard his truck start and drive away.

Jessica's stomach churned.

Coming out of the kitchen to see what all the door slamming had been about, Molly frowned at her daughter. "What happened to Luke?"

"He decided not to stay for dinner," Jessica answered, her tone warning her mother not to ask any more questions at the moment.

"Well, I know it wasn't my cooking he was objecting to," Molly threw over her shoulder as she returned to the kitchen.

"Brandson sure has a temper," Mark commented as soon as he and Jessica were alone. The underlying edge in his voice suggested that he thought she was behaving ill-advisedly to overlook this aspect of the other man's personality.

"Not usually," she replied in Luke's defense. "I admit he can be a bit on the gruff side, but generally he's not this difficult to get along with. Being charged with murder has him on edge. And then there's his big-brother complex." She frowned at the doorway through which Luke had left.

"No wonder you're not married," Mark said, placing a hand over his heart in a gesture of mock horror. "Having to face Luke Brandson's wrath would scare off all but the bravest of souls." A smile suddenly spread across his face. "But have no fear. I am one of the bravest."

"Or the most foolhardy," she amended banteringly as she returned his smile. Mark's attempts to build himself up in her eyes at every possible opportunity were flattering, though she didn't believe he would ever be able to make her forget Luke.

"Or foolhardy," he agreed with a good-natured laugh.

Too worried about Luke to indulge in any further light banter, Jessica turned the conversation back to the more immediate concern of clearing Luke. "What specific suggestions did Mr. Aimes give you for finding Holston?" she asked.

"He had several, but the one I'm going to start with is to visit the neighborhood Holston and Melinda lived in. Someone there might remember them."

Jessica nodded approvingly. "Sounds like a good idea."

"Dinner's ready," Molly announced from the doorway.

"That sounds like an even better one," Mark said, rising and waiting for Jessica to precede him.

During the meal, as if by mutual consent, no further mention was made of the Strope murder. Molly insisted on asking questions about Mark's personal life. When Jessica attempted to stop her prying, Mark intervened, saying that he enjoyed talking about himself. Thus, the rest of the evening was filled with listening to anecdotes from his youth.

Unable to get Luke's angry departure out of her mind, Jessica only half listened and was grateful she did not have to contribute more than a word or two at appropriate intervals.

Being careful not to overstay his welcome, Mark rose to leave around ten. "I hope I haven't bored you," he said, addressing Molly with a charming smile.

"Not in the least," she assured him, the sparkle in her eyes saying that she not only did not find him boring but also considered him a suitable companion for her daughter.

"This is my weekend off. I'll be happy to drive you to the airport," Jessica offered as she walked him to the door.

Mark's gaze warmed noticeably. "I'd like that very much." He paused and tilted her face upward. "I've enjoyed this evening immensely." He lowered his head toward her slowly as he spoke and as his last word faded, his lips found hers for a gentle kiss.

Mark seemed perfect for her. He was interested in the same things she was. They could even share a career. She willed herself to feel something . . . anything. The faintest little spark would do for a start. But there was nothing. "You'd better be going," she said, easing away from him before he could kiss her again. "If I'm going to pick you up at five-thirty tomorrow morning, we both need to get some sleep."

The blue of his eyes deepened. "You don't exactly inspire me to sleep." Again he captured her chin. This time he placed a light, quick kiss on the tip of her nose. "But I know better than to argue with the law," he quipped, and in the next instant he was out the door and on his way toward his car.

Watching him leave, Jessica frowned in frustration. Why couldn't Luke see her the way Mark did? Because Luke thinks of me as family, she answered her own question. Trying not to think about the enigmatic rancher, Jessica went into the kitchen to help her mother with the dishes.

Molly grinned widely when Jessica joined her. "It looks as if some good may come out of this murder after all."

Jessica frowned as if questioning her mother's sanity. "What good?"

A Cheshire-cat grin spread over Molly's face. "I should get a son-in-law out of this one way or another."

"Don't count on it," Jessica warned with a scowl, again recalling the bland feeling Mark's kiss had caused.

"You're certainly in a bad temper for someone who has just spent an evening with a very charming man," Molly observed, pausing to look hard at her daughter for a long moment. "And speaking of bad tempers, why did Luke slam out of here without any dinner? It's not natural for him to pass on one of my meals."

Avoiding meeting her mother's gaze, Jessica picked up a glass and concentrated on drying it. "I told you that he and Mark didn't get along, and this murder business has him operating on a pretty short fuse these days."

"But what sparked him off?" Molly persisted, still watching Jessica closely.

Bowing to the inevitable, Jessica set the glass in the cabinet and faced her mother. "Mark mentioned something about him and me starting a detective agency of our own if this case worked out well. I didn't say I would do it. I only said it sounded like an interesting idea, and it does. But Luke probably went right home and called Dan, and tomorrow I'll get a call from my dear brother warning me not to do anything rash."

"Are you really considering the possibility of opening a detective agency?" Apprehension showed on Molly's face. "That would mean moving back to a big city, wouldn't it?" A plea entered her eyes. "I thought you liked living here."

"I do," Jessica replied. Her jaw tightened in frustration. "But if I can't make Luke notice me as a woman, I don't think I can stand to remain in this town and watch him marry someone else," she admitted honestly.

"You do have it bad," Molly said. She put an arm around her daughter's waist and gave her a hug. "Well, don't look so bleak. I'm certain we can come up with something that will make the man straighten up and take notice."

Jessica had strong doubts about this but she was in no mood to continue this conversation. "Maybe," she hedged. "But right now my only concern is making certain he doesn't go to jail. After that is settled, then I'll consider the future."

Chapter Ten

The next morning when Jessica picked Mark up, she found herself studying him closely. He was handsome and charming and he obviously found her a desirable woman. He also seemed to respect her professional skills.

"I'm sorry we don't have time for breakfast," he said as she drove him toward the small, private airfield a few miles outside of Blue Mill Falls. They were a good three- to four-hour drive from the major airports at St. Louis and Kansas City. But they were close to the Oklahoma border. So Mark had opted for hiring a private plane to fly him to Houston. "Barnes has flying lessons to give this afternoon and he wants to be back in time for them. Besides, I don't fly well on a full stomach."

"I understand," she assured him.

His warm gaze traveled along her profile. "Ever since I left you last night I've been thinking about what I said about us forming a detective agency. I honestly think it's a great idea. I hope you're willing to at least give it some thought."

Again Jessica found herself wishing he could stir her the way Luke did. But all she felt was anxiety. "I am giving it some serious thought," she admitted.

His smile broadened. Very gently he combed a curl of her hair behind her ear with the tip of his finger. "Come with me to Houston."

If Luke had asked her to go someplace with him in a voice like that, she'd have followed him to the edge of the earth. But Mark wasn't Luke. In that moment, she made a firm decision. If she did become a private investigator, it wouldn't be in partnership with Mark. Although she had, at first, been flattered by his flirting, she was already becoming bored with it and with him. Also, flying to Houston, at this moment, wouldn't help Luke. Mark could do the basic ground work there by himself. Her time would be more profitably spent in Blue Mill Falls, working on other parts of the puzzle. Getting Luke out from under this murder charge was her only priority right now. Afterward, she'd decide whether to leave town and start her own investigating firm. Putting distance between her and Luke hadn't worked the first time but maybe it would if she gave it another try. "I appreciate the invitation, but I've got some things I need to do here," she replied.

Mark frowned disappointedly, then concern overshadowed his disappointment. "I want you to be careful," he cautioned. "If Luke isn't the murderer, I'm sure the real murderer isn't happy about you continuing the investigation."

"I will," she promised.

Standing there in the dim predawn light she watched the plane take off. A crisp breeze stirred her hair as an unexpectedly strong sense of being totally alone suddenly swept over her. Her gaze traveled over the two large hangars and the line of parked planes. She'd always loved these quiet early morning hours. But right now, standing alone at the deserted airfield, she felt a chill move along her spine and she shivered.

Luke wasn't the murderer. Every fiber of her being told her that. And Mark was right—the real murderer would not be happy about her continued prying. She recalled the feeling of being watched she'd experienced at the Strope place, and the bruises she had taken to avoid being struck by the car that had disappeared so quickly.

"At the Strope place it was just the cat, and the driver of the car that almost hit me was a drunk," she told herself curtly. Still she couldn't shake off the feeling of foreboding. Climbing back into her car, she drove toward town.

Charles Strope's funeral was this morning, and she wanted to get to the church early and watch the mourners arrive. She wasn't certain what good that would do but she was hoping to spot something out of the ordinary in one of the participant's behavior.

Automatically her foot pressed down on the accelerator as she climbed the snaking incline that wound around Miller's Ridge. She had chosen this route because it was the fastest way back to Blue Mill Falls. It was also the prettiest. The rocky face of a forty-foot-high cliff bordered one side of the road. Signs warned motorists to watch out for falling rocks. The other side of the road was bordered by a deep gorge. A metal guard rail had been constructed to keep drivers who took the road too fast from plunging into the ravine. Usually the wild beauty of this undeveloped countryside relaxed Jessica, but this morning was different. The anxiousness she had felt at the airport stayed with her.

A slight scattering sound suddenly caught her attention. Glancing toward the cliff face she saw a small stream of gravel sized rocks sliding down toward the road. Suddenly a loud rumbling filled the morning air. Looking up she saw the shadowy form of a huge boulder rolling downward, dislodging smaller rocks and boulders on its way. If she got caught below the slide there was a chance the rocks would roll toward her. Caught underneath she wouldn't have a chance. Her car would either be crushed or pushed into the ravine. Pressing harder on the gas, she prayed no one was coming in the other direction. Flooring the accelerator, she swung into the oncoming traffic lane, speeding across the path of the falling rock. Ignoring the sound of the smaller, faster pebbles striking the side of her car, she concentrated on the road. A hairpin curve was just ahead. Slamming on her brakes, she left a trail of rubber as she managed to stay on the road. Her heart was pounding wildly as she came to a stop on the other side of the curve. She parked and climbed out of her car. Behind her she heard the huge boulder as it hit the roadway then continued down into the ravine. Walking on shaky legs, she made her way back around the curve. Smaller rocks and pebbles were still slowly sliding down the side of the cliff like a gravelly waterfall, scattering across the road. The metal guard rail was bent downward where the huge boulder had rolled over it.

Standing there, Jessica stared up at the ridge of the cliff. It looked peaceful now. "Well at least that solves the problem of Oley's Boulder," she muttered. The huge boulder that had fallen was the last of the large boulders on top of Miller's Ridge. It had been given the name Oley's Boulder several years back when one of the townsmen had suggested it was the same shape as the nose of the town's major, Oley Smith. Both, everyone had agreed, were decidedly prominent but not unattractive. At the last few town council meetings several people had suggested dislodging the boulder and getting rid of the threat it posed once and for all. Everyone in attendance had agreed that getting rid of it was a good idea. The problem was it was under the jurisdiction of the county road department, and getting them to act was like getting molasses to run on a winter day. Walking back to her car, Jessica kept glancing upward but no more rocks came down.

Using her police radio she called in the report of the slide to the sheriff.

"You all right?" he asked.

"Fine," she replied.

"You seem to be attracting a lot of accidents lately."

Jessica heard the concern in his voice. "Yeah," she conceded, adding tersely, "I'll set out some flares. Then I'm going to take a little climb while I wait for John and Claude to show up to clean up the road."

"I'll be there as soon as I can. You be careful," he cautioned.

"I will," she promised.

Twenty minutes later she stood on the crest of the cliff looking down. There was nothing to indicate that the boulder had been purposefully dislodged. On the other hand there was no proof that it hadn't.

"From those skid marks you left, I'd say you were right lucky," Paul Pace said when he joined her a little while later. "I should have come out here and gotten rid of that boulder myself right after that last rain. Damn lucky you weren't killed."

"I know," Jessica replied, frowning down at the road below where John and Claude were already clearing away the rock.

"You haven't made old Beatrice Clay angry lately and had her put one of her curses on you, have you?" the sheriff questioned, trying to sound light but missing the mark.

Beatrice Clay was an old woman who lived in a cabin down by the river. She told fortunes and periodically threatened to put the evil eye on those who crossed her. "No, I haven't made Beatrice angry," she replied stiffly.

"And maybe this wasn't an accident. Maybe the real murderer is worried about me getting too close to the truth."

"There's enough rocky surface, a person could have reached the ledge without leaving any footprints," Paul admitted. "But I don't see any sign of force. It's my guess you were just in the wrong place at the wrong time. That rock was bound to come down sooner or later. And that last big rain probably loosened it quite a bit."

Jessica couldn't argue with him. Coincidences happened. She just didn't like the way they were happening to her, all of a sudden.

"But maybe I should just take over this investigation," Paul was saying. "Wouldn't want you to take any chances."

The last thing Jessica wanted was to be removed from the case. "I'm sure you're right about it being an accident," she said quickly. Then, glancing at her watch, she frowned. "I've got to get going. The funeral's at ten and I've got lots to do before then."

"You take it easy," Paul called after her as she made a hasty retreat.

She knew the sheriff honestly thought the close calls she'd had the past couple of days were just accidents. And she had to admit that on the surface they did look that way. But the instinct that had kept her alive and well on the streets of Kansas City was now warning her, loud and clear, to keep an eye on her back.

"I'm beginning to think you should spend the weekend locked in your room," Molly said as she and Jessica drove toward the church a couple of hours later. "You do seem to have a knack for being in the wrong place at the wrong time these days." She shook her head. "Oley's Boulder should have been gotten rid of a year ago."

"Well, it's gone now," Jessica replied drily as she pulled into the church parking lot.

"And I don't understand why we had to get here so early," Molly complained a few minutes later as she and Jessica entered the church to discover they were the first to arrive.

"Because I want to get a seat where I can watch the principal mourners," Jessica replied in low tones, motioning her mother into a pew near the front. "You want to help Luke don't you?"

"Yes, but I don't see how watching people at a funeral will do any good," Molly retorted in matching tones.

Jessica breathed a tired sigh. "I don't know, either," she admitted. "But I've got to try everything."

Molly read the frustration on her daughter's face. Putting her arm around Jessica's shoulders, she gave her a hug. "I don't mean to be difficult," she said apologetically. Then, settling back in the pew, she too watched the door as people began to file in.

Melinda entered looking drained and pale as she made her way to her seat. She trembled occasionally during the service and once in a while dabbed at a fresh trail of tears. Margaret sat beside her, obviously attempting to offer aid and comfort to her mistress. Her concern was clearly for Melinda Strope and not for the man in the casket.

Max Johnson sat behind the women. Dressed in a suit, with his hair combed and his face freshly shaved, he was not bad looking in a roguish sort of way. It was not inconceivable, Jessica mused, that an impressionable young woman might find him attractive enough to overlook his rough points long enough to marry him and discover how really rough he could be. He did, in fact, fit her mental image of Duncan Holston very closely.

He also fit the other qualifications she had imposed if the man was to be the murderer. He had come to Blue Mill Falls only after Charles Strope had married Melinda Lymon and he led a loner's existence both before and since. There was no one to check on his comings and goings while, at the same time, he was in the perfect position to know all of Charles Strope's movements.

The trip to Kentucky had taken much longer than was actually necessary. He could have flown back, watched Strope, hoping for a chance to kill the man, found the opportunity during Tuesday night, returned to Kentucky, picked up the colts and driven back slowly enough to prevent any injury.

There was still the question of how he had gotten into Luke's home, but, if he was the criminal type, he probably had access to several methods. If she applied herself to it she was certain she could come up with the answers to the logistics problems.

Immediately following the church service, she informed her mother that she had a headache and didn't feel that she could go on to the grave site. Molly regarded her skeptically but made no protest as they drove home. As soon as they were at the house, Jessica dashed upstairs and changed into her uniform.

"I thought you had gone to your room to rest," Molly said with a frown when Jessica came back downstairs. Her gaze narrowed further when she saw how her daughter was dressed. "And why in the world do you have your uniform on? You're not supposed to be on duty today."

"I just remembered something very important I need to attend to," Jessica replied. "It simply can't wait." Giving her mother a quick kiss on the cheek, she dashed out of the house before any further questions could be asked.

Assuming it would take the mourners at least another forty-five minutes to complete the long process of loading the casket into the hearse, driving to the grave site and then having a small graveside ceremony, she figured she would have time to check out Max Johnson's apartment before he returned.

"Maybe a private agency is where I belong," she muttered as she turned into the drive of the Strope place. "At least then I wouldn't have to feel so guilty about breaking the law."

Her fit of conscience grew as she drove around the house and parked near the stables. Then, recalling Luke pacing in his cell like a caged animal, she was out of the car in the next instant and pulling her small tool kit out of her pocket. It took a couple of minutes to unlock the place. Apparently Max Johnson thought he had something very valuable, because he had added an extra heavy lock in addition to the regular one. Luckily she had a tool that would flip that one, too.

"You mind telling me what you think you're doing?"

Jessica nearly dropped her tools as she jerked around to find herself face to face with Luke. "What are you doing here?"

"Your mother called me. She said you'd made an excuse so you wouldn't have to go to the cemetery, then you'd taken off almost as soon as the two of you got home. She put two and two together and concluded that you might have decided to make another excursion out here while everyone was away. So I drove over to the service road on the edge of my property and kept an eye out. Saw you turn in here. I would have been here sooner but I thought it wouldn't look good for anyone to spot my truck here, so I left it on the service road and came on foot." His gaze narrowed on her. "Now I want you to climb back into your car and go home."

"No," she refused flatly, then glanced at her watch anxiously. "And I don't have time to argue." Opening the door, she started to go inside the apartment.

Luke laid a hand on her shoulder, stopping her. "What you're doing is against the law you're supposed to be upholding."

Jessica turned back toward him. "I know, but it's necessary." Letting her anxiety show, she added, "The case against you is strong and to be perfectly honest I'm getting a little desperate. Now I'm going to go inside and take a quick look around and I want you to go home."

"I have to admit that I'm feeling a little panicky myself about the outcome of this investigation," Luke said gruffly. Then his jaw hardened with determination. "But if one of us is going to break the law, it should be me. You go home and I'll take a look around."

"No," Jessica said, blocking his way. "You can't afford to be caught."

"You can't either," he countered. "You're an officer of the law."

"I've talked my way out of stickier situations than this," she informed him. Again glancing at her watch, her frown deepened. "We haven't got time for this." A pleading note entered her voice. "Please, go home before anyone sees you." Then, before he could continue the debate, she slipped inside the apartment. To her relief, Luke didn't follow.

The apartment was surprisingly tidy. Going through Johnson's desk she found a few old photographs of horses, some with Max standing beside the horse and some with the horse standing alone. There was a switchblade and a couple of small, sharp pointed, metal discs like the ones used with such deadly accuracy in Ninja movies. They were nasty-looking weapons, but there was nothing in the desk that would identify Max Johnson as Duncan Holston.

Breathing a frustrated sigh, she headed for the bedroom. Suddenly the door of the apartment was flung open. Whirling around, expecting to see Luke, she saw instead Johnson's large bulk blocking the entrance. The sun glistened on the barrel of the forty-five he held aimed at her.

"Well, well, if it ain't the deputy," he said with a cynical sneer. "I ain't never liked the law, and I particularly don't like female lawmen. And I especially don't like them snooping around my place." As he pulled back the hammer on the gun, his expression became even more threatening. "You got a search warrant?"

"No," she replied calmly, her eyes shifting from the gun to his face. The hatred in his eyes was easy to read. He was just looking for an excuse to pull the trigger. "I came by to ask you a few questions. Your door was slightly ajar so I stepped inside. Considering the fact that we've had one murder, I wanted to make certain you were all right."

His gaze traveled around the interior, the anger on his face increasing. "I don't like my privacy disturbed."

Jessica's shoulders stiffened as she schooled her face into a look of self-righteous indignation. "I was only making certain you weren't hurt."

Johnson's jaw twitched. He smiled a nasty smile. "I've got half a mind to shoot you. After all, you are on my property uninvited."

Jessica's ears perked up. "I'm on Melinda Strope's property," she corrected him, watching him narrowly.

He shrugged as if her distinction was unimportant. "You're in *my* apartment."

His hand on the gun tightened and Jessica fought to remain calm. If he was the killer surely he wouldn't shoot her here. Whoever had framed Luke was smarter than that. Of course if he wasn't the killer, he might just be stupid enough to pull the trigger. Recalling her boast to Luke that she could talk herself out of difficult situations, the urge to laugh bubbled in her throat. Realizing this was due to panic and not humor she swallowed it back. "I'm here because I'd like answers to a few questions," she said in her best official tone, attempting to turn the tables and put him on the defensive.

"Don't see any reason why I should answer any questions you ask," he sneered. "I just caught you breaking and entering."

"I told you the door was open," she retorted, adding, "and, like I said, I only came inside to make certain you weren't hurt and in need of help."

"Well, I wasn't." The sneer on his face broadened. "And you knew it. I seen you and your mother at the funeral. You thought I was at the cemetery so you could just come over here and have a look around. Too bad for you, I don't like cemeteries. Soon as I could get away, I took off."

"If I were you, I'd put that gun away before someone gets hurt and you end up in jail," a threatening male voice said from behind Johnson.

Twisting around, the trainer found himself facing Luke. Still sneering, he carefully lowered the hammer. "Just having a little fun. Caught the deputy snooping around my place without a warrant."

"I was not snooping. I was waiting to ask him a few questions," Jessica interjected curtly. A part of her was extremely grateful Luke hadn't left, while another part was humiliated that she had needed him to rescue her.

Luke's attention shifted to Johnson. "I can guarantee you won't like it in jail."

"Guess you should know," Johnson replied, casually letting the hand holding the gun drop to his side. A cynical smile played across his face. "Women are nothing but trouble. But I don't need to tell you that. You sure got yourself into one hell of a mess over one."

Ignoring Johnson's reference to the rumors about him and Melinda Strope, Luke's gaze shifted back to Jessica. "*Trouble* is this one's middle name," he muttered, adding, "Come on, Jess."

She wanted to run to him, but didn't dare do anything to give Johnson the impression that Luke had come with her. A charge of accessory to breaking and entering was the last thing he needed right now. "I came to ask Mr. Johnson a few questions."

"You can ask all you like but I ain't answering," Max replied. "If the sheriff has any questions, he knows where he can find me." Suddenly his attention turned to Luke and his gaze narrowed speculatively. "You sure turned up convenient like."

Luke shrugged as if the insinuation that he was with the deputy was preposterous. "This case hasn't been going so well for me. Went out for a walk and got to thinking that you might know something useful. Before I knew it, I was here. You mind answering a few questions for me?"

Jessica held her breath, hoping Johnson would buy this explanation.

He gave a snort. "I ain't answering no questions for anyone."

Jessica began to breathe again. He had bought it. Meeting Johnson's hostile gaze with a calmness she didn't feel, she said, "You'll be hearing from me." Then, brushing past him and Luke, she walked toward her car.

As she reached it, Luke caught up with her. "You're going to give me a ride to my truck then we're going to my place. We need to talk."

She started to tell him that she would take him to his truck but she had no intention of having a talk with him. However, Johnson was watching them and she didn't want to make a scene. Besides, Melinda Strope and Margaret would be returning soon, along with some of the other mourners, and Jessica wanted to be gone before they arrived. "Fine," she muttered, still intending to leave him as soon as she took him to this truck. Climbing in behind the wheel, she waited for him to say "I told you so" or chide her about her boast that she could talk herself out of difficult situations.

Instead a tense silence filled the car as she drove him to the service road where he'd parked. His berating her would have been easier to take, she decided as she pulled up and set the brake.

Climbing out of her car, he finally broke his silence. "You'd better follow me home or I'll follow you," he said, as if he'd read her mind and knew of her intent to flee.

She gave a shrug in an attempt to appear nonchalant. "We can have a little talk another time. Mom is expecting me for lunch."

"Your mother is pacing the floor, worried to death about what you might be getting yourself into," he snarled. Anxiety and self-recrimination mingled in his eyes. "And she should be. I can't believe I let you go into that apartment."

Jessica's shoulders squared. "It wasn't your decision to make."

He drew an impatient breath. "Jess, follow me," he ordered. Then, after slamming her car door shut, he stalked over to his truck.

She knew if she disobeyed, he'd follow her home and they'd have their confrontation in front of Molly.

That she didn't want. Grudgingly, she shifted into gear, backed out onto the main road and drove to his place.

As soon as they were inside, she made a run for the phone and called her mother. She didn't want Luke telling Molly he'd found her with Johnson pointing a gun at her.

"If you behaved more prudently, you wouldn't have to worry about what people might tell your mother," he said pointedly as she hung up, letting her know he'd seen through her ploy.

"My behavior is really none of your concern."

He raked a hand through his hair in an agitated manner. "Has it ever occurred to you that you're aging the people who care about you at a rapid rate with these comic-book antics?"

Comic-book antics! Hot tears of anger and frustration burned at the back of her eyes. "I'll have you know that before I made my foray into the Strope home you didn't have a chance in the world of getting out of this mess with less than a charge of manslaughter."

"You might be right," he admitted with a growl. "But you could have gotten yourself hurt today. Max Johnson is a rough character."

He had a point. But the crack about comic-book antics still stung. She faced him with cool dignity. "Like I said before, I'm glad you showed up, but I could have handled it myself. I've been in tighter situations before."

He paced across the room, then turned to face her again. "I went up to check out Miller's Ridge. I couldn't find any sign that it was anything other than an accident. But if you hadn't been taking Smythe to the airfield you wouldn't have been anywhere near there when the rock came down. If you'd been hurt or killed I would have felt responsible."

Jessica read the concern on his face. She wished it was something more, but she wasn't foolish enough to try to make herself believe it could be. "You can't blame yourself if I get hurt in an accident."

His gaze narrowed as he studied her darkly. "Jess, seeing you with a gun pointed at you scared the hell out of me. I want you to stop taking risks for me."

He made her feel like a teenager with a crush trying to get attention. "It's not for you. I just want to see justice done."

He raked his hand through his hair again. "Damn it, Jess. You're supposed to be enforcing the law, not breaking it. I've hired a good detective agency. Let them do whatever needs to be done. I don't want you risking your job for me."

A knock on the door interrupted. "I could hear your raised voices all the way out onto the porch," Lydia Matherson said, entering as if it was natural for her to come into Luke's house without waiting for him to answer her knock. Glancing toward Luke, she shook her head sympathetically. "I can't believe I've caught you two in another of your 'cat and dog' fights." Turning to Jessica, her look of sympathy turned to one of disapproval. "Don't you think Luke is going through enough without having to put up with one of your tantrums?"

It was hard enough to see the way Lydia made herself at home in Luke's house. But to have the woman speak to her as if she was one of her high school students was the final straw. Jessica turned and stalked out of Luke's home.

Her chin was quivering by the time she pulled into her own driveway. Relieved to see that her mother had a customer in the salon, she managed to get to her bedroom before the tears overflowed. She felt so frustrated.

"Jessica, are you all right?" Molly's concerned voice sounded from the other side of the door.

"No, I'm not," she answered grimly. Brushing at the streams of tears with her fists, she opened the door. "Why did you have to send Luke searching for me?"

"I was worried," Molly replied apologetically. Smoothing Jessica's hair back with a motherly caress, she studied her daughter anxiously. "What happened?"

"We had another fight." Jessica's chin trembled. "Then Lydia Matherson showed up." Her voice caught. Stiffening, she backed away from her mother. "I really don't want to talk about this anymore." Closing the door, she leaned against the wooden structure as a new flood of tears threatened. The situation between herself and Luke seemed hopeless.

Molly knocked again. "It can't be that bad," she comforted through the closed door.

Bad, Jessica thought acidly, was a mild description. Attempting to keep her voice level, she again brushed away the tears and opened the door. "I need to be alone for a while, Mom."

"All right," Molly agreed reluctantly. "I do have a customer with a permanent that I have to get back to before she begins to look like the Jacksons' French poodle. But as soon as I've finished, I'm coming back and we are going to have a very serious mother-daughter talk."

Not in the mood for a mother-daughter talk or a talk of any kind, Jessica splashed cold water on her face, changed into a pair of jeans and a sweater and left the house.

As she walked toward her car, her mother came running out of the beauty shop. "Where are you going?" Molly demanded anxiously.

"For a drive to clear my mind," she answered evenly, then added in stronger tones, "and I don't want you calling Luke."

Molly frowned uncertainly. "All right, I won't."

Jessica frowned. "I want your promise."

"I promise," Molly relented. "But you drive carefully."

"I always do." Breathing a tired sigh, Jessica gave her mother a hug. "Don't worry about me. Honestly, I'm only going for a drive. I need some time to think." Releasing Molly, she climbed into her car and drove out of town to the bluffs along the river.

Turning off onto a side road, she parked on the back side of a particularly high overhang. Leaving the car, she climbed the wooded, rocky slope. It was too early in the year for the wildflowers to be in bloom. Later the bases of the rocks as well as any tiny crevices in the rocks large enough to hold enough soil to support growth would be brightened by the colorful and unusual blooms of the columbines.

A breeze with the lingering taste of winter stirred her hair, and she wished she had thought to bring a jacket. Her destination was a small clearing on top of the bluff where her father used to come to think things out. He'd brought her here on several occasions. After his death she'd come on her own whenever she needed a place to work out her problems.

Reaching the clearing, she stood for a long moment looking down at the river running clear and clean fifty feet below. Then, choosing a spot a short distance from the edge, she sat down, crossed her legs Indian fashion and rested her elbows on her knees while cupping her chin in her hands.

A burst of yellow caught her eye and, glancing to her right, she smiled wistfully. It was a clump of daffodils. She'd planted the bulbs here years ago so that her father would have something colorful to look at before the wildflowers bloomed.

A part of her wanted to cry once again, but a stronger part refused her this luxury. Crying wouldn't change things. What she needed to do was to make plans for her future...a future that wouldn't include Luke. Again the thought of starting up the detective agency played through her mind.

The crunching of dry underbrush suddenly warned her that she was not alone. Her muscles tensed in preparation for the unexpected. Mentally she cursed herself for not bringing her gun along. If the boulder and the drunk hadn't been accidents, she'd been foolish to come up here. Rising to her feet, she moved further from the cliff edge while scanning the woods in the direction from which the sound had come. Catching sight of a blue shirt and a head of thick dark hair, she began to breathe once again.

A moment later Luke entered the clearing, waving a white handkerchief above his head. "I've come under a flag of truce," he said gruffly.

Embarrassment mingled with anger. Turning away from him, Jessica returned to her seat on the flat rock overlooking the river. "I can't believe my mother actually called you again."

"She didn't," he said, pocketing the handkerchief. "I went to your place looking for you, and when she told me you had gone for a drive to be alone, I figured you had come up here."

She glanced toward him. "You remembered this place after all these years?" she questioned incredulously, recalling how he and Dan had found her here after her father's funeral. She hadn't meant to cause anyone any trouble, but she hadn't been ready to say goodbye to her father just yet. While the others were in the living room, she had sneaked out of the house and walked all the way here from town. She had been so certain she would feel her father's presence in this clearing, and she had.

"I've been here myself a few times over the years," he said, sitting down beside her. "I hope you don't mind."

"It's a free country." Too embarrassed to face him, she picked up a twig and began to peel off the bark.

"I want to apologize for giving you such a hard time."

Chewing on her lip, she glanced toward him dubiously. "I'm either hearing things or hallucinating."

He regarded her grimly. "Being charged with murder hasn't been easy for me. That, coupled with worrying about you placing yourself in danger or, at the very least, in a compromising situation because of me, has set my nerves on edge. But I shouldn't have taken it out on you."

"I don't want to fight with you anymore, Luke."

"And I don't want to fight with you." There was a sadness mingled with the tiredness etched deep into his features that drew her to him. "I need your friendship, Jess."

A lump caught in her throat and tears welled in her eyes. "You have that," she assured him.

A tight, relieved smile played at the corners of his mouth. "Glad to hear that." Then the smile was gone. "Jess," he began in hesitant tones.

She'd rarely heard indecisiveness in his voice before. Her gaze narrowed on him worriedly.

As if unable to face her, he turned away and stared into the woods ahead of him. "I've never been a man to hide from reality. I know I'm in a pretty tight spot." He paused for a long moment, then continued grimly. "Everything that's important to me is here but I don't know if I can stand being locked up." His hand closed around hers. "I just want you to know that whatever I do, it will only be to buy time to find the real killer."

Jessica stared at his taut profile. He hadn't said it, but she knew he was talking about running and the way he was holding her hand was like a silent plea for her understanding. It was her duty to warn him not to leave. The words formed in her throat but the consequences of him staying terrified her. Innocent men had been convicted before and the way this case was shaping up, he could easily be found guilty and sentenced to life imprisonment or even death row. She couldn't make that decision for him.

But, as many times as she told herself that she wanted him out of her life, she couldn't bear the thought of him vanishing completely. "I want your word that no matter what happens, you'll keep in touch," she demanded. Then, not wanting him to guess how deeply she felt, she quickly added, "You're like a son to Mom and it would hurt her real bad if you just disappeared and we never heard from you."

"I'll keep in touch," he promised gruffly, drawing her into a friendly embrace. A chill breeze wafted around them but Jessica felt only Luke's warmth. Wrapping her arms around him she added her own strength to the embrace as an affirmation that she was there to support him.

Tenderly he held her head pressed against his shoulder and she tried very hard to think only of the friendship he had requested. But she wanted to share so much more with him. Fighting the urge to turn her head toward his neck and bury her face against his warm, sweet-smelling skin, she shivered. Suddenly afraid she was going to make a complete fool of herself once again, she released her hold and eased herself away from him. "The breeze is cold."

"It's always cold up here this time of year," he said gruffly, adding in paternal tones, "You should have worn a jacket."

She shook her head in exasperation. "You're worse than Dan or my mother."

He smiled a crooked smile. "I care about you, Jess. I don't have too many people in my life to care about and I suppose that causes me to be a little overbearing at times."

"A *little* overbearing?"

He shrugged. "So, I'm a country bred chauvinist."

"True," she returned in a matching bantering tone. Then, finding her imposed sisterly position a difficult one to cope with in her present state of mind, she added, "And you're right about the jacket. It is cold. I should have brought one and since I didn't, I think I should be going home."

Chapter Eleven

Jessica stopped at the house only long enough to assure her mother that she was fine but still did not want to talk. Then, after taking a moment to put on a touch of lipstick, she went in search of Paul Pace.

He was in his office and looked up in surprise when she entered. "You should learn to take your days off more seriously."

"I can't stop thinking about the murder," she said with a heavy sigh, seating herself across the desk from him.

"And what have you been thinking?" he asked with an indulgent smile.

"I've been wondering if you've done any checking on Max Johnson."

Paul frowned. "Why Max Johnson? He wasn't even in town at the time of the death."

"He's been living at the Strope place for nearly two years. He might know if Charles Strope had any enemies who hated him enough to want to kill him. You never know what a man might tell his horse trainer."

The sheriff studied her dubiously. "Why do I have the feeling that I'm being manipulated?"

Jessica smiled innocently. "I just don't want to leave any stone unturned."

He shook his head indulgently. "Well, I guess it wouldn't hurt to have him come in for questioning."

Jessica breathed a sigh of relief. "Thanks."

"There's something you should know," Paul said as she began to rise.

The tone of his voice caused the relief on Jessica's face to vanish. "What?"

"The preliminary report came in on the fingerprints. There were a few smudged sets that couldn't be identified firmly. But those that could be, matched Luke's, Kate's, the doc's and mine—seems I wasn't as careful about not touching things as I should have been."

"We already knew the murderer wore gloves," Jessica pointed out.

"That's right, he did," the sheriff confirmed pointedly.

Jessica knew he was thinking of Luke's blood-stained gloves. The blond hair in the plastic bag she had carefully tucked away played through her mind. She was certain it would match Melinda Strope's hair. The problem was, producing it wouldn't help Luke. The DA would use it as proof Luke was having an affair with the woman. He would probably claim that Luke had carried it into the room on a shirt he had worn during a rendezvous with Melinda . . . a little souvenir of their tryst. The memory of the kiss she had witnessed early Thursday morning again played through her mind. If anyone else had seen that little display they would have been convinced once and for all that Luke was guilty. But Jessica remained convinced of his innocence. She just wished she had a way to prove it.

Grudgingly she admitted that the hair might not even be a clue to the solution of the crime. Charles Strope could have carried it into the room on a piece of his clothing. Frustration filled her. Every path she found seemed to lead to a dead end. "I'll go call Max Johnson," she said stiffly.

Max Johnson wasn't happy to hear from her.

"Guess you went and told the sheriff about me pulling a gun on you," he snarled into the phone. "Well, just be ready for me to press charges against you for breaking and entering."

"I told you the door was open and I only went in to make certain you weren't hurt," she replied, determined to stick to this story. She did not, however, want the sheriff to even suspect she might have broken the law. "Besides, I didn't tell the sheriff anything about our little meeting. I thought we'd just keep that between the two of us."

There was a silence on the other end of the phone, then Johnson said grudgingly, "Yeah. Maybe you're right. No use stirring up trouble for myself. You've probably got the old man wrapped around your little finger."

"I'd suggest you get over here as soon as possible," Jessica ordered, letting him think he had the situation sized up perfectly.

"I'll be there when I'm good and ready," he snarled back, slamming the receiver down.

But he showed up within the hour.

Paul Pace greeted him cordially. As soon as the three of them were seated in the sheriff's office, Paul took out a small tape recorder and placed it on his desk. "I hope you don't mind. I don't want to be accused of getting anyone's words muddled," he explained before the protest in Max Johnson's eyes became verbal.

"You can record all you like," the trainer replied, casting a pointed glance in Jessica's direction. "I got nothing to hide. I wasn't even in town when Strope got himself killed."

"I'm not accusing you of having anything to hide or of being involved with the murder," the sheriff assured him.

"I merely want to know if you have any idea who might want to see Charles Strope dead."

The man shifted uneasily. "Don't know of anyone in particular."

"We thought that you being the only other man around his place, Mr. Strope might have confided in you about anyone he was worried or concerned about," Jessica said coaxingly.

Max gave her a dry look. "The only person he mentioned to me was Luke Brandson. Lately he'd been wanting to know if the man had been hanging around the place."

"And had he?" Paul Pace demanded sharply.

"No, not that I seen." Max shrugged. "Course that ain't saying there couldn't have been some hanky-panky between Brandson and Mrs. Strope. I'm no spy. My motto is Live and Let Live."

This wasn't helping Luke. Jessica decided to take a more blunt approach. "You were on your way to Kentucky when the death occurred. Is that correct?"

"Yeah." His posture stiffened with self-righteous indignation. "And I've got all the receipts to prove where I was and when...motels, meals, everything. Strope wouldn't pay for any expenses I couldn't show him a receipt for."

But Jessica wasn't ready to give up so easily. Her gaze narrowed on the trainer. "Have you ever lived in Houston, Texas, Mr. Johnson?"

The sheriff glanced toward his deputy but remained silent.

Genuine surprise registered on Johnson's face. "No."

"Never?" Jessica persisted, hoping he was just a very good actor. More dead ends were not going to help clear Luke.

"I ain't never been in the state of Texas, and I don't see that where I've lived or haven't lived should be any of your business," he replied belligerently. Turning his attention to the sheriff, he added, "I came down here to answer *your* questions, not hers."

Paul Pace studied the man calmly. "As long as you've got nothing to hide, I see no reason why my deputy's questions should upset you."

Johnson glared at Jessica, then turned his attention back to the sheriff. "I'm a man who regards his privacy as a sacred right. I've done nothing against the law and I don't like being dragged down here and given the third degree!"

"And we're investigating a murder," Paul Pace reminded him grimly.

"A murder that was committed while I was out of town," Johnson threw back. In the next instant he was on his feet. "So if you don't have any more questions about Strope, I'll be on my way. I don't intend to sit here and relate my life story simply to satisfy a female's curiosity." Glancing down at Jessica, a challenge glittered in his eyes. "If you're that interested in me, we can finish this in private."

Jessica merely stared back at him with cool dignity.

"Thanks for coming in." The sheriff's sharp tones carried an air of finality.

"It was no pleasure," the trainer replied with a snarl.

Alone again with his deputy, Paul Pace studied her thoughtfully. "So you think Max Johnson might be the elusive Duncan Holston."

"The thought has occurred to me," she admitted. "He fits my mental image of the man, and he was in a perfect position to watch over Strope and bide his time until he could arrange the moment for the perfect frame."

"You think he sneaked back to town, somehow lured Strope to Luke's place, got himself and Strope inside and killed him?" the sheriff asked, frowning dubiously. "Don't you think that's a little farfetched? I'm not saying I don't think Johnson is capable of killing a man, but he'd be more likely to do it in a bar fight. If Luke was framed, it was done by someone with brains and patience."

"Maybe he's a lot smarter and slyer than he wants people to think," she replied, refusing to give up too easily. "He might have figured on constructing the perfect alibi with a handful of receipts from places where people in charge don't like to answer questions and aren't too careful about their record keeping. Then he could have come back here and given himself a couple of days to see if Strope would place himself in a perfect situation to be murdered. He might even have been the one to plant the seed about Luke and Strope's wife in Strope's mind. Then, before he left, he could have fueled the fire with a few well-chosen remarks."

"Your theory contains a lot of *ifs* and a lot of loose ends," the sheriff pointed out skeptically. "And you still haven't explained how they got into Luke's study."

"I know," she admitted, then added hopefully, "but maybe if I keep stirring the pot something will rise to the surface."

Again Paul's manner became fatherly. "I just hope you're not disappointed. If Luke and the widow do have something going, it's very likely he saw Strope's gunning for him as the perfect opportunity to do away with him. It's my guess he panicked after he shot Strope and concocted the story he's telling, hoping to avoid a trial. But any day now I expect him to come in here and change his story so he can plead self-defense. If he can convince a jury he was only acting to save his own life, he could end up not only with the widow but all that money as well."

Jessica's expression hardened. "Luke would never kill a man for love or money."

Paul sighed at her innocence. "Jessica, the longer you're in this business, the more you're going to discover just how far humans will go for both or either of those commodities."

"Some humans," she corrected. "But not Luke."

Rising from his desk, Paul Pace placed a fatherly arm around her shoulders and led her to the door of the jail. "You go home and enjoy what's left of your weekend. And, if Luke doesn't turn out to be the innocent party in this mess, I may thrash him myself for disappointing so loyal a friend as you. In the meantime, I'll run a check on Max Johnson."

Unable to resist, she went up on tiptoes and planted a kiss on the older lawman's cheek.

"Now that is a first." He grinned. "I can't recall ever being kissed by a deputy before."

Jessica returned his smile with a wink, then she drove home. Entering the kitchen, she discovered her mother preparing a chicken for roasting. "I thought Saturdays were sandwiches in front of the television days."

"Not this Saturday. You go upstairs and change into something soft and feminine," Molly ordered, opening the oven and shoving the bird inside. "Luke is coming to dinner and I want the two of you to make up."

"We've already made up."

"Good." Molly straightened and smiled at her daughter conspiratorially. "Then after dinner he can take you to a movie or dancing. You could both use a little relaxation to take your minds off of this murder business."

"No," Jessica said swallowing back the lump that formed in her throat as she recalled Luke's plea for her friendship. "Luke has made it perfectly clear he cares about me in a brotherly way and that is the limit of his feelings. Any matchmaking plans you have will only be an embarassment to all of us, so I want you to put them out of your mind."

"You've got to fight—" The ringing of the phone interrupted her mother's protest.

It was Mark. "I've been to Holston's old neighborhood. The guy didn't seem to have made any friends. Fact is, those who remember him were glad to see him go and didn't care where he went. But I've contacted one of the people Aimes mentioned and I'm meeting him for dinner. Maybe he'll be able to give me some idea of where to go from here."

This wasn't good news but it also wasn't a total dead end. "Don't be surprised if you have company on your search by Monday," she informed him. "Luke has hired a private investigative firm to begin checking into the case."

"That doesn't say much for his confidence in me," Mark quipped with an edge of peevishness.

Jessica frowned at the phone. "He needs all the help he can get. This isn't a game for him."

"You're right." Mark sounded sincerely self-reproachful. "It's just that I find all of this so exhilarating. I want you to seriously consider my idea of us starting up our own firm. I don't think I'm ever going to be able to go back to simply selling insurance again."

"I have been thinking about going into the private sector," she admitted noncommittally. Her frown deepened at the sound of her mother setting the table in the dining room. "In fact, maybe I'll take you up on your suggestion that I join you in Houston. I'll talk to the sheriff and see if he can get Vince to come in as acting deputy for a few days and I'll fly out. Might as well see how well I can work without a badge." She told herself she wasn't running away. She would merely be leaving for a few days, and she would be working on the case while she was gone. She just needed to put some distance between her and Luke for a while.

"That sounds great," Mark was saying enthusiastically. "As soon as I've checked into a hotel, I'll call and give you my number. You call me when you've got your plans set, and I'll pick you up at the airport."

"Great," Jessica replied. "See you soon," she added as she hung up.

"What's this about you going to Houston?" Molly demanded from behind her.

"I'm not doing Luke much good here," Jessica replied with a shrug. "I'm going to talk to the sheriff about taking some time off and going to Houston to work with Mark."

"You're honestly thinking about starting a detective agency with him, aren't you?" Molly studied her daughter reprovingly. "I can't believe you're going to give up on Luke without a fight."

"There is nothing to fight for," Jessica said tersely. "Luke needs my help to clear him and he needs our support. That's all."

"You can't just hand him over to Lydia Matherson," Molly protested.

Jessica drew a tired breath. "He's not mine to hand over. I've accepted that and I want you to, too."

Molly shook her head disparagingly. "I can't believe that's what you really want."

It wasn't what Jessica wanted. What she wanted was to marry Luke, have his children and live out her life here among the people she loved. And, maybe, she added wistfully, become sheriff when Paul Pace retired. A wave of rustration swept over her. "It's the way things are," she said stiffly, more than ever determined to fly to Houston.

"Well, I think you're going about this all wrong," Molly persisted. "But then I'm only a mother. What do I know?" she added sarcastically. "One of these days you're going to actually follow my advice and I'm going to faint."

"No, you won't." Jessica gave her mother a hug. "You'll spend the rest of both of our lives making certain I don't forget it."

Molly hugged her daughter back. "I only want you to be happy."

"I know." Releasing her mother, Jessica said firmly, "But I want your promise that you'll give up on this matchmaking."

"It's against my better judgment," Molly replied with a lopsided grimace, "but I promise."

While Molly went back into the kitchen to check on dinner, Jessica phoned Paul Pace and got his permission to take a couple of extra days off. Then she called the airfield and arranged for Neil Barnes to fly her to Houston early the next morning. Momentarily she considered flying out immediately, but that would be cowardly. Luke would expect her to be here for dinner and she would be here.

When the phone rang again around six, she assumed it was Mark. But instead it was Luke.

"Apologize to your mother for me," he said in clipped tones. "I've got a touch of the flu and won't be able to make it to dinner."

"Do you have a temperature?" Jessica questioned, unable to hide her concern.

"Only a very slight one," he replied. "But I'm feeling pretty tired."

He didn't sound like himself, and it occurred to her that he might be sicker than he wanted her to believe. She thought about him being all alone and her hand tightened on the receiver. A friend would help a sick friend, she rationalized. "Take a couple of aspirins and go to bed. I'll bring some of Mom's chicken soup over in a few minutes. That's a definite cure-all."

"No." The word came out sharply. In more subdued tones, he added, "I don't want you getting sick, too. I don't feel that bad, and by morning I'm certain I'll be fine. It's probably more a case of exhaustion than the flu."

She didn't need him to paint her a picture. It was obvious he'd found a better way to spend his evening. "Take care of yourself and keep warm," she said stiffly.

Her hand was shaking as she hung up, and she wished fervently she'd gone ahead and made plans to leave for Houston tonight.

"What was that all about?" Molly questioned.

"It was Luke," Jessica replied levelly. "He's had a better offer for the evening."

Molly frowned. "What are you talking about?"

"He said he had the flu, then he changed it to exhaustion. The truth probably is that Lydia Matherson made him an offer he didn't want to refuse."

Molly's frown deepened. "I don't believe that for a minute. Luke would never turn down one of my meals for a woman."

"I admit your food is outstanding, but not that outstanding." Jessica tried to force a smile but it wouldn't come. Going into the hall, she grabbed a jacket from the closet.

"Dinner will be ready in half an hour," Molly said as Jessica passed back through the kitchen.

"I'm not hungry. I'll be back after a while," she replied tiredly and, without pausing, left the house by the back door.

Climbing into her car, she drove out of town. She hadn't had any particular direction in mind and ended up on the back road where she had parted from Luke earlier in the day. Turning off the motor, she sat in her car for a long time watching the bright pinks and oranges of the sunset fade into blackness.

She hurt too much to cry. It would have been easier if Luke didn't want her as a friend. Pride would have helped her let go of any feelings she had toward him. But as it was, she felt hopelessly trapped. She couldn't turn away from him, and yet, playing the role of the sisterly friend he wanted was tearing her apart.

Thinking didn't help. Restarting the car, she drove home.

"Mark called a few minutes ago," her mother informed her when she entered the house. "I told him you were out and I didn't know when you would be back. But he said he'd call back in half an hour. From the tone of his voice it sounded urgent."

Picking up the receiver, Jessica started to return the call immediately then realized she didn't have Mark's phone number or the name of his hotel. Refusing to call every hotel and motel in Houston, she paced the living room floor for the next twenty minutes hoping that he had uncovered information that would lead to a resolution of this case. The sooner she could put distance between herself and Luke, the better.

The phone rang a little before eight. "Have you uncovered something?" she questioned as soon as she heard Mark's voice.

"Not exactly," he replied hesitantly.

She frowned in confusion. "What do you mean by 'not exactly'?"

"It's about Luke." Again he hesitated.

"What about Luke?" she questioned sharply, Mark's tentativeness setting her nerves on edge.

"I'm not certain," he continued as if not really wanting to tell her what he knew but feeling he had to. "After I ate, I got to thinking about what you said about his hiring a firm of detectives. I figured there was no sense in them going over ground I've already covered, or at least we could pool our information. Anyway, I called him to give him the name of my hotel and to suggest that whoever he hired could contact me and I could tell them what I've learned so far. But he sounded strange."

Jessica scowled into the receiver, distracted for a moment by the sound of a musical clock signaling the hour. "You probably interrupted his evening."

"I don't think so," Mark said with conviction. "He was very cryptic. Said something to the effect that I should give up my wild-goose chase. That he was going to put an end to all of this before some innocent person got hurt."

Jessica's eyes narrowed and she frowned in concentration. "Maybe I had better go out to his place and have a talk with him."

"I don't know if I like that idea," Mark protested.

"I'll call you if I learn anything important," she assured him, then jotting down the name of his hotel and his phone number, she hung up.

"Is something wrong?" Molly questioned, watching Jessica anxiously.

"Something has been wrong with this case ever since it first began," she muttered, continuing to frown at the phone. Suddenly her manner became briskly businesslike. Grabbing up the jacket she had discarded earlier, she began to pull it on. "I'm going out to Luke's place to check on him."

Molly was on her feet in an instant. "I've got some chicken soup in the freezer. Wait a minute while I get it."

Knowing she would only lose the battle if she tried to refuse, Jessica waited impatiently.

"And I want your promise that you won't fight with him," Molly stipulated as she handed the container to her daughter.

"I promise." Pausing for a moment, Jessica gave her mother a quick hug, then left.

The phone call from Mark played through her mind as she climbed into her car. Her jaw tensed. She didn't know what was up with Luke, but she meant to find out.

Chapter Twelve

Parking in front of Luke's place, Jessica noted that only his truck was in the drive. The living room windows were dark but she thought she detected a slight movement near one of the curtains as she climbed out of her car. With the container of frozen homemade soup tucked under her arm, she mounted the porch and knocked on the door. It swung open slightly as if it had been improperly latched.

Cautiously, she pushed it open wider. "Luke?" she called out anxiously. She received no answer but the light in the study was on. Stepping into the entrance hall, she called out his name again. Again there was no response. She took another step forward. Even before she heard it snap shut, a slight breeze on her back told her that the door was swinging closed behind her. Pivoting, she found herself face to face with Mark Smythe.

"So glad you could make it," he said, switching on the light. He was holding a gun aimed at her chest.

"I thought—"

"You thought I was in Houston." His smile broadened. "Actually, I was. But after you told me Brandson had hired his own firm of detectives and that you had decided to come to Houston, we decided that this business has dragged on long enough. There were people there with in credibly good memories. Too much was becoming public knowledge and a trial was unthinkable.'' With a wave of the gun, he indicated that he wanted Jessica to precede him. ''The others are waiting for us in the study.''

Turning stiffly, she obeyed his unspoken command. Entering the room, she found Melinda Strope dressed in her fashionable riding outfit complete with a pair of leather gloves, holding a nasty-looking revolver. ''I see you've overcome your fear of guns,'' Jessica noted sarcastically.

A smile played at the corners of Melinda's mouth as she responded with a gentle shrug of her shoulder. Setting the gun aside, she moved over to where Luke was sitting behind the desk. He was bound securely to the chair and a gag had been stuffed in his mouth. ''He would have warned you, even if it had meant his own immediate demise,'' she said as she removed the handkerchief. Her tone indicated that she found such an act totally incomprehensible.

''You said you wouldn't harm her,'' Luke growled, his gaze promising revenge if he should ever get free.

''We had to say something that would persuade you to write a confession,'' Melinda replied matter-of-factly.

Continuing to stand in the middle of the room, Jessica looked at Luke questioningly. ''A confession?''

Perching herself on the corner of the desk, Melinda picked up a sheet of paper and read aloud.

I, Luke Brandson, did accidentally kill Charles Strope in self-defense. He was waiting for me when I returned home from playing cards. He forced himself into my home at gunpoint. We struggled and the gun went off. The fear of going to jail caused me to lie. However, I do not want to see innocent people put through an ordeal because of me.

Again I want to say that the death was accidental. But I fear that will not be the verdict if I remain for the trial. Therefore, I am leaving town to begin a new life somewhere else.

Sincerely,
Luke Brandson

"What happens now?" Jessica asked, knowing the answer already.

"A tragic accident, I'm afraid," Mark replied. "We had always planned on Luke dying before there could be a trial but I'm afraid there is going to have to be another corpse as well." He sighed regretfully. "And I shall be absolutely brokenhearted when I hear about it. Because of my phone call, you will have come out here and caught Luke in the act of leaving. You jumped into his truck and tried to persuade him to remain. But he wouldn't listen. He continued to drive. You argued. On the road above the cliffs outside of town he lost control of the vehicle. It plunged over the side of the cliff, crashed into the ravine below and burned."

"Why involve Jess?" Luke demanded, straining against his bonds.

Melinda regarded him with a mildly piqued expression. "It's a matter of survival. The deputy has displayed a strong bent toward both tenacity and loyalty. While these are admirable qualities, under the present circumstances they are quite detrimental to us. We discussed the situation and concluded that she has too much faith in you. There was the strong possibility she might not have believed the confession and might have continued searching for the truth, in order to clear your name."

Jessica faced the other woman with studied calm. "And the truth is that you murdered your husband."

"He brought it on himself."

The woman's self-righteous manner caused a chill to run along Jessica's spine. "Because he was going to use a sizable portion of his wealth to subsidize a foundation for the youth of this state?"

Melinda sighed in exasperation. "He was determined to immortalize his son."

Mark was studying the deputy during the exchange. "You've been fairly certain all along that Melinda was guilty, haven't you?"

"I wasn't certain who had pulled the trigger," she confessed. "But no matter how I worked out the husband's death, Melinda had to have played a key role, unless, of course, the whole thing was a string of coincidences, and that was too hard to believe. And then there was the black purse."

"I noticed your interest in it," Mark mused.

Jessica swung around to face him. "So you were there." Frowning thoughtfully, she added, "I suppose you have one of those answering machines on your phone that lets you call home and have your messages replayed to you. That's how you knew to call me later that night."

"Modern devices are so very convenient," he replied.

Jessica's jaw tightened. "I thought I sensed someone watching me. Then the cat came in, and I told myself it was just him and nerves that had me thinking someone else was there."

"I had gotten into town a little bit earlier and sneaked into Melinda's house to wait for her to get back from the viewing. Luckily for me, I was holding the cat when you came in. He proved to be an excellent diversion."

"Next time, I'll trust my instincts more," she muttered.

Melinda shrugged. "I suppose I should have thrown that purse away, but Margaret would have been certain to notice. She knew I had purchased it just before Christmas."

"What's a black purse got to do with this?" Luke demanded.

"It's a duplicate of the one Kate has been using this winter," Jessica explained. "And it's how Mrs. Strope got a set of keys to your house."

Luke's frown deepened. "I still don't understand."

"I suppose the feat was accomplished during the Christmas bazaar." Jessica looked toward Melinda for confirmation.

"Actually it was at the bake sale," the blonde corrected with an indulgent smile.

"That would have been more convenient," Jessica mused thoughtfully. "I should have guessed. You held that event in the front of Carlson's Department store, which is right next to the hardware store. All of the purses were shoved under the table. You excused yourself to run an errand, picked up Kate's purse and left. Entering the hardware store, you opened the purse and removed the keys to Luke's home which Kate keeps on a separate key ring from her other keys. Then you had duplicates made letting the folks in the store assume they were the keys to your home. Then you brought back Kate's purse and keys with no one the wiser."

"You are cleverer than you look," Melinda muttered cynically.

Jessica watched the woman coldly. "And I suppose you're the one who actually started the rumors about yourself and Luke."

"I simply made a comment to Mary Jordan about how jealous Charles was and that he was accusing me of having an affair with Luke. That woman is the most incorrigible gossip. Within hours she had it all over town, and by the next day half the town was ready to believe Luke and I were sneaking around." Melinda laughed. "It's just amazing how fast a story can spread."

"What I'd like to know," Luke growled, "is why you chose me as your scapegoat?"

The blonde's mouth formed a thoughtful pout. "The truth is you were only one of several possibilities. Margaret and Max were both under consideration, also. However, you were so very convenient...an unmarried male, with reasonably good looks, living so close. Charles already disliked and distrusted you."

"The scene I witnessed the other morning...you kissing Luke," Jessica said. "What was that all about? If I had thought Luke was guilty, that would have made you look like an accomplice."

"I had ridden over to make certain I hadn't left any telltale clues behind," Melinda replied with a bored sigh. "I hadn't planned on Luke being out so early, but he was and I was forced to make some excuse. So I told him that I had come over to say how sorry I was that he had been caught up in this mess because of my husband's irrational jealousy. I made it clear that I thought he had shot Charles, but that I felt certain it had been an act of self-defense. Then you showed up. Margaret had told me about your interview with her, and you were already beginning to worry me. When I saw the pie in your hands and caught the look in your eye when you saw Luke and me together, I realized I had misjudged your feelings toward him." She glanced toward Luke with a knowing smile. Jessica concentrated on the widow, not daring to look at him.

"Anyway," Melinda continued. "Impulsively I decided to shake your faith a little. It was chancy, but I wanted to see if you would tell anyone what you saw. If you did, I had a wonderful lie all ready. In a way I regretted not being able to use it. It would have sealed Luke's fate. I was prepared to tearfully tell how he had been the one to kiss me. I was even going to swear he had told me that he had been lusting after me and now he intended to have me for himself.''

Jessica realized it would have been her word against the widow's as to who kissed whom, and Melinda was a very convincing liar. The DA would have used Jessica's longstanding friendship with Luke to discount her testimony. Glad she hadn't fallen into that trap, Jessica shifted her attention to Mark. "I suppose you're the one who murdered Lymon."

He smiled rakishly. "Who would suspect the man's insurance agent?"

"Only someone who watched old Fred MacMurray movies, I suppose," she replied. "But what I don't understand is why you weren't the one to kill Strope so that your...'' she paused to glance toward Melinda questioningly.

"Sister," he filled the gap. "Twin sister."

Jessica kicked herself for not having seen the resemblance. Mark was much larger, but their coloring was the same, along with the shape of their mouths and noses. "So that your sister could provide herself with a really good alibi?" she finished.

"I was supposed to, but unfortunately I was tied up in another scheme, and Strope was planning to sign his new will on Wednesday." He smiled mischievously. "His death couldn't be put off, so Melinda chose to execute the plan herself."

The blonde shook her head in an indulgent fashion. "I will never get used to your punning."

Jessica saw the movement of Luke's shoulder and knew he was working on the ropes binding his wrists. Fervently she hoped he wouldn't succeed too quickly. There were answers she still needed. Quickly returning her attention to

Melinda, she said, "Just to satisfy my curiosity, what exactly did happen the night Charles died?"

"You're the clever one, you tell me," Melinda challenged.

"All right," Jessica agreed tightly. "First you drugged Margaret's hot chocolate, probably when you went in to tell her that you were going out. Since she's already a heavy sleeper, I assume you used a fairly light dose. You didn't want her waking up during your final confrontation with Charles, or while you were at Luke's place with him. But you didn't want her so drugged you couldn't rouse her enough to provide yourself with an alibi."

"Very good," the blonde said, smiling with acid approval. "Go on."

"Then you went over to the Jordan house on the pretense of doing church work, but your real motive was to set the stage for later. Since the rumors about Charles accusing you of having had an affair with the reverend were all over town the next day, I can only assume that while you were with Mary you mentioned how unreasonable your husband had become over the past few months. As proof, you told her that he had even accused you of having an affair with the reverend. You had probably already planted this information with Margaret a few weeks earlier but had sworn her to secrecy. You didn't want Charles to hear it because I doubt he ever made such a preposterous accusation, and you didn't want him denying it publicly." Jessica paused, her gaze narrowing on Melinda. "You'd always planned to kill him, hadn't you? Even before he decided to start the foundation."

Melinda shrugged nonchalantly. "I find I get bored with my husbands after a while." She smiled at Luke. "I will confess there were moments when I considered actually having an affair with you. But I couldn't afford to take the chance." She sighed wistfully. "Too bad. It might have been fun."

Luke responded with a look of distaste.

"On the other hand," Melinda muttered sarcastically, "you would probably have been even more boring than Charles."

"But before you got rid of the husband, you needed to get rid of the son so you would be the sole beneficiary," Jessica interjected sharply as the full truth dawned on her. "You were the one who gave Chuck the drugs."

Melinda sneered. "He was such a stupid child." She sighed as if she found the subject of Chuck Strope incredibly boring. "You were telling me how I managed the rumors about the reverend."

"Yes, the reverend," Jessica replied. She'd confronted killers before, but never one so cold-blooded. "After Charles's death, when, through Mary, it became common knowledge in town that he had accused you of having an affair with the reverend, and you, yourself, confirmed it to the sheriff, Margaret was there to swear to it as an absolute truth. Thus giving credence to the story."

"The majority of people will believe anything if it's fed to them properly," Melinda offered philosophically. "I learned that from my first husband."

"The illusive Duncan Holston?" Jessica questioned.

Melinda smiled wistfully. "I met and married him when I was sixteen. Mark and I had been living with a maiden aunt. But she was a bore. Duncan agreed to let Mark come live with us. We three made a great team. Duncan was an excellent con artist and he taught Mark and me everything he knew."

"That's why I couldn't let you come to Houston or let Luke's detectives start sniffing around. Several people from our old neighborhood recognized me," Mark interjected.

"It would never do for my connection to Melinda to be discovered."

Jessica's attention shifted back to Melinda. "Just for my own curiosity. Where is Holston?"

Melinda shook her head in mock sadness. "I'm afraid he's dead too. Like I said, he was a good con artist. He never got caught. But he was strictly small-time and refused to try to rise to greater heights. We had to get rid of him." She smiled as if recalling a pleasant memory. "It was the first con job Mark and I ever worked alone. I bruised myself and told our neighbors I'd gotten hurt by accident, while Mark, on the sly, told everyone Duncan was beating me. When Mark and I fled, it came as no surprise. Duncan, of course, followed. He had no idea what was going on. We met up in a small town in Mexico." She smiled toward her brother. "Mark took care of making certain no one would ever know what happened to the body. No one in Houston missed Duncan. The neighbors all thought he was scum. We'd been renting a furnished apartment so there was no property to dispose of. The three of us simply disappeared."

"And you resurfaced as Melinda Smith, and soon became Melinda Lymon," Jessica said. Turning her attention to Mark, she added, "And you as an insurance salesman."

"We all have to find our little niches in life," he replied. "The insurance business has been very good to me."

"Mark has developed quite an extensive wealthy clientele," Melinda said with admiration. "In fact, he found Lymon for me."

"But one has to be careful about having too many clients collecting large claims," Mark interjected in practical tones.

Melinda smiled broadly. "That's why he concentrates on the ladies. They do adore him."

Mark returned the smile. "Unlike my sister who prefers to marry for money, I prefer affairs with bored, wealthy women who are willing to pay handsomely to keep their husbands from ever finding out about their little indiscretions."

"Nice family," Luke said dryly.

Melinda cocked a cynical eyebrow in his direction, then turned her attention back to Jessica. "You were going to tell me how I managed Charles's death. But so far you've only got me as far as Mary's house."

Jessica frowned thoughtfully. "Actually I'm not totally certain about your next move. I considered the possibility that you stopped by Luke's place on your way home and unlocked the door. But that would have been chancy. Luke could have come home early and caught you, or your husband could have driven by and seen you here and you weren't ready for him yet."

"I did consider unlocking the door at that point," Melinda admitted. "But you're right. I decided it was too chancy. Go on."

"Okay. You didn't unlock the door then. You went directly home. Margaret was asleep, Max Johnson was somewhere between here and Kentucky, and Charles was pacing the bedroom floor. You stopped in the study and put his gun in your purse. You couldn't have done this earlier because someone might have noticed it was missing."

"He almost caught me," Melinda admitted, a slight flush reddening her cheeks as if the memory brought a rush of excitement. "He came storming down the stairs when I didn't come up immediately. I barely had time to get out of the study."

"I imagine he wanted to know where you had been," Jessica picked up the thread of the story. "Whatever you said instantly promoted another argument. You had the gun and the keys to Luke's house. You'd probably made certain, by some discrete question to Mary, that Luke was at his usual poker game that night with her husband."

Melinda nodded a confirmation.

"The stage was set," Jessica continued. "You demanded that an end be put to Charlie's ridiculous fits of jealousy once and for all. You insisted that he confront Luke that very minute." Jessica paused to study the widow narrowly. "Or did you let him think there really was something between you and Luke?"

"I prefer to play the part of the mistreated innocent," Melinda replied with a playful smile. "I'm very good at self-righteous indignation. Besides, Charles was half-crazed with jealousy. It would have been too dangerous to even hint that he might be right. But he was in just the right mood to get him to confront Luke."

"So the two of you rode over here in his car." Jessica paused. Frowning, she admitted grudgingly, "But I haven't worked out how you managed to maneuver him into Luke's study when Luke wasn't at home."

"That was a little tricky but much easier than you might imagine," Melinda said with a prideful smile. "When we drove up and he saw that Luke's truck wasn't in the drive, he wanted to go home and confront Luke in the morning. But I pointed out that Luke might have parked in the back and insisted that we go up to the front door and knock. Of course there was no answer. Then I suggested that Luke might already be asleep and insisted that Charles take a look around the back of the house to see if the truck was actually there. If so, I told him that I intended to pound on the door until Luke woke up. As soon as he rounded the corner of the house, I unlocked the door. When he returned to tell me that the truck wasn't there, I said I intended to stay until Luke returned but I wasn't going to wait in a cold car. I tried the knob, the door opened and I walked in. Charles protested violently, but he followed and when I sat down in the study, he remained too, now absolutely convinced I was much too much at home in Luke's house."

"And because you were in a room that faced the back of the house, you said it was stuffy and opened the window a bit so you would be certain to hear Luke's truck when he did pull in," Jessica added, putting all of the pieces carefully together.

"Very perceptive," Melinda complimented. "I had wondered whether anyone noticed the window. Admittedly being in the living room would have been more convenient for spotting Luke's arrival but I couldn't take the chance on him seeing me or becoming suspicious at seeing lights on in his house. And Charles wasn't going to sit around in the dark."

"So you and Charles waited together in the study, except for the few minutes when you left on some minor pretext and relocked the front door and opened the one in the kitchen so that nothing would slow down your flight."

Melinda nodded in confirmation.

"Now the scene was set," Jessica continued. "At a little past two you finally heard Luke's truck drive up. Charles rose to go confront him. At that point you pulled out the gun. He stared at you in confusion. You heard Luke slam his truck door and you fired. Charles fell forward. You shoved the gun under him and ran out the back door. By the time Luke unlocked the front door and discovered the body, you had fled out the back door and were on your way through the woods back to your own home. You went in, stuffed your gloves into a hiding place to be disposed of later, rinsed off the smell of gunpowder, and changed into a nightgown. Then you went downstairs to Margaret's room and, after resetting her clock to read a few minutes past two, you shook her awake. I suspect that was the only time all evening you actually might have panicked. She had to have been close to impossible to arouse, considering how much trouble I had a couple of hours later."

Melinda laughed. "I thought I was going to have to set dynamite off under her bed to get her to open her eyes," she admitted.

"But you were insistent and finally she woke up... very groggy but awake enough for your purposes," Jessica continued. "Not wanting to take any chances, you told her that it was nineteen minutes after two in the morning and showed her her clock to emphasize the time. Then you said that Charles wasn't home yet and you were worried. You asked her what you should do, knowing full well she would tell you to go to bed and not worry. You let her fall back to sleep, then reset the clock to the right time and began your wait for the sheriff to bring you the tragic news that you were a widow."

"It would appear that my sister's only mistake was you." Mark frowned reprovingly. "But considering the way you and Brandson fought, who would have thought you would have had so much faith in his innocence?"

"Still, she did have you as her safeguard," Jessica pointed out. "The frame was perfect as long as no one discovered a dent in her moral armor. If that happened, a new game had to be devised, and to survive she had to be one step ahead of the police at all times. That's where you came in. You were her backup in case anyone expressed interest in the Lymon case. It was natural you'd be contacted because you were the one who had sold him the policy. And I made it even easier for you. I contacted you directly."

"Next time I'll keep my papers in a safer spot," Melinda assured her, adding petulantly, "It's a shame Mark missed you with his car that night. This all would have been so much easier.''

"So you were the drunk?" Jessica mused, her gaze narrowing on Mark.

"I try to nip trouble in the bud, but you move fast," he replied. Turning to Melinda, he added chidingly, "But you're the one who missed her with the boulder."

"It's not easy to time a rock slide just right," Melinda returned in her defense.

"You're not going to get away with this," Luke growled.

"Of course we are," Melinda replied with a patronizing smile. "With your confession here, and the two of you found dead, the case will be closed. Sheriff Pace might keep looking for Duncan Holston for a while, but he'll never find him. Besides, he thinks you're guilty. He's only humoring Deputy Martin's wild flights of fancy because he has fatherly feelings toward her." She glanced at her watch and frowned. "Brother, dear. I really must be returning home. Margaret is safely tucked away but Max is out with his friends, and I need to get back before he does. We don't need any further complications."

"You're right. And I have to be getting back to Houston to ensure my alibi." Going around behind the desk, Mark cut the bonds holding Luke in his chair, but left the hands themselves tied. "Get up slowly and don't make any sudden moves. I've already thrown your hastily packed suitcases into the back of your truck, and now it's time for you and Jessica to take a ride."

Slipping off her perch on the corner of the desk, Melinda kept her gun aimed at Jessica.

Standing, Luke moved his shoulders as if they were cramped from having his hands tied behind him. Then he began to walk slowly around the desk, choosing the side that would bring him closest to Melinda. Jessica watched tensely, again hoping he wouldn't do anything rash and get himself hurt. But in case he did manage to play hero, she readied herself to help. The moment he had positioned himself between Melinda and Mark, he yelled, "Jess, run!" and, in the same instant, butted Mark in the chest with his head sending the man off balance.

Momentarily disconcerted, Melinda wavered, giving Jessica the opening she needed. She swung at the woman's gun hand with the container of frozen soup. Melinda let out a scream of anger and pain as her weapon sailed across the room.

In the same instant the sheriff, the doctor and two deputized townsmen rushed into the fray. It was over in moments.

Looking around for Luke, Jessica's heart caught in her throat. He was lying dazed on practically the same spot Charles Strope had occupied only days before. Blood was running from a gash on his head. Dropping to her knees, she began to untie the ropes binding his hands. They were stained with blood from his wrists where he'd torn the flesh in his struggle to free himself. "Luke," she breathed his name anxiously as the rope came loose.

Groaning, his hand went to his head as his eyes opened and he levered himself into a sitting position. "Jess, are you all right?"

"I'm fine," she managed to say without letting her voice shake, fighting the urge to wrap her arms around him. Taking a handkerchief from her pocket, she held it to the wound on his head.

"What hit me?" he growled.

"The desk," the doctor answered, kneeling opposite the deputy. "Smythe knocked you into it when you tried to play the hero."

Luke continued to frown in confusion as the sheriff and his two helpers slipped handcuffs on Melinda and Mark. "Where did the crowd come from?"

"Jessica invited us to the party," the doctor replied. "Now hold still while I take a look at that gash on your head."

Paul Pace finished reading the prisoners their rights. Ordering one of his temporary deputies to guard them, he sent the other one down the road to pick up the squad car and drive it up to the house. Then he joined Jessica and the doctor. "Is Luke going to be all right?"

The doctor paused in his examination. "He needs a couple of stitches and I'd like to check him into the hospital overnight for observation."

"I'm not going to any hospital," Luke said with finality.

"Joe and Vince can help me get those two—" Paul Pace nodded toward Mark and Melinda "—back to town. Jessica can stay here and help you with Luke. But I'll keep this little tool box of Jessica's for a while." He tapped the breast pocket of his shirt, indicating Jessica's collection of lock picks. "I'm not too certain I feel comfortable having my deputy running around with this type of equipment."

"They came in handy tonight," she pointed out.

"Actually Smythe left the front door unlocked after you came in."

"You were listening in the hall all of the time?" Luke asked, grimacing as the doctor began to clean the wound on his head.

"I was. The others were waiting on the porch, with the door open, ready to act on my signal." The sheriff glanced down at his stockinged feet. "Now, I've got to go put my boots back on and get back to town. Jessica, you want to give me that tape recorder?"

Slipping the small black box from her jacket pocket, she handed it to the sheriff.

Accepting it, he added, "I believe there is something on here about a search of the Strope house I think I'm going to have to ask you about later."

She rewarded him with a look of pure innocence. With a shake of his head he began ushering his prisoners out of the house and into the waiting police car.

"I think we'd better get Luke upstairs to his bed," the doctor suggested. "I want him lying down when I stitch him up." Rising to his feet, he extended a hand toward the rancher. "I've had too many of these tough guys pass out on me at the sight of a needle."

Getting to his feet, Luke was a little unsteady. Jessica slipped her arm around his waist, and he put his arm over her shoulders. Using her for support, he made it up the stairs without any difficulty.

Once he was lying down, she pulled his boots off while the doctor opened his black bag and began sorting out the equipment he would be needing.

"How did you know to bring the sheriff?" Luke asked, as she set his second boot aside.

"It was your musical clock." She had to fight the urge to touch his face with a gentle caress. "Mark must have used the phone in the hall, because the sound of the clock was faint. But I was certain I heard it in the background announcing eight o'clock in its less than tranquil fashion. I realize there are probably others like it in the world, but I figured the odds were close to a zillion to one that Mark would have one in his hotel room in Houston."

"Like I said before, I'll sleep better at night knowing Jessica is protecting us," the doctor commented with a smile. Then his expression became serious as he turned his attention to Luke. "I'm going to give you a shot for the pain. I hate being distracted by my patients' screaming while I stitch them up.''

Jessica stood by the window looking out on the dark night while the doctor worked.

Finishing with the stitches, he cleaned and bandaged Luke's rope-burned wrists, then shone his light again into Luke's eyes. ''The pupil dilation looks good and you weren't actually unconscious. Any feelings of dizziness or nausea?''

''None,'' Luke replied.

''Then Jessica can fix you an ice pack to hold on those stitches for a while to keep the swelling down, and I'll be on my way.'' As Jessica accompanied the doctor to the door, he added, ''It would probably be a good idea if someone were to keep an eye on Luke for tonight. He looks fine but I hate to leave a patient with a head injury completely alone.''

''I'll stay,'' she assured him. Then, remembering that he'd had to park his car a little ways down the road, she added, ''Would you like me to drive you to your car?''

''No. It's not far. The sky's clear. It's a lovely night for a walk.'' He smiled down at her. ''You stay and take care of Luke. I just hope he realizes how lucky he is to have you on his side.''

''Thanks,'' she managed to say around the hard lump that was forming in her throat. Standing on the porch in the midst of the still night, she watched the doctor walking away. That was what she was going to do as soon as possible. She was going to walk away from Blue Mill Falls and her feelings for Luke. He was safe now, so it was time for her to find a new place and begin a new life. She wouldn't stay here and live her life in a fantasy world, hoping that one day Luke would learn to care for her the way she cared for him.

Going into the kitchen, she fixed the ice pack and carried it upstairs. Luke was lying on his back, exactly as she had left him. Placing the ice pack on his stitches, she frowned down at the bloodstains on his shirt. "I'd better soak that in some cold water right now or those stains will never come out."

But, as she began to unbutton the garment, she knew she had made a mistake. In spite of the control she was holding over herself, her hands shook.

"I've been thinking," he said, watching her. "If I was married, I wouldn't have gotten into this mess in the first place."

"Probably not," she muttered, steadying her hands and finishing with the buttons before easing him into a sitting position.

"Besides, as you pointed out the other day, this place is too big for one man," he continued gruffly. "It should be filled with a family. Truth is, I've always wanted a wife and kids."

She turned away from him. How could he be so thickheaded? She was giving him the kind of support he wanted, but surely he must have guessed how she really felt. Melinda had practically spelled it out for him downstairs. How could he possibly think she would want to hear about his plans to marry someone else? That was more than she could handle at the moment. Pulling the shirt free, she stalked out of the room.

Without pausing, she went downstairs, through the kitchen and out the back door. She was still holding on to the shirt, and a part of her wanted to rip it apart while another part wanted to cling to it.

"Jess." Luke caught up with her and, capturing her by the arm, brought her to a halt.

"Leave me alone, Luke," she pleaded, fighting back the tears. It wasn't his fault he didn't love her. But she couldn't stand looking like a lovesick fool in front of him.

"This has been our problem all along," he said, turning her toward him and taking her hand in his.

Her jaw hardened as she fought for control. "What has been our problem?"

"We don't communicate enough."

Her control began to slip. She was in no mood to hear him tell her how much her friendship meant to him and he didn't want anything to destroy it. She couldn't look him in the face. Her eyes focused on the dark curly hairs of his chest. They blurred in front of her and a tear trickled down her cheek. Damn, she cursed mentally. "Luke, please," she pleaded, trying to pull free.

His hands tightened their hold. "Jess, I love you," he said gruffly.

"I know," she choked. "Like a sister."

"No," he growled. "Like the woman I want to marry."

She lifted her head to stare up at him in disbelief. The warmth she saw in his eyes caused her knees to weaken. "What did you say?" she asked, her heart pounding so hard she was certain he could hear it.

"I love you, Jess. I want to marry you." He leaned toward her and kissed her with a hunger that left no doubt as to his intentions toward her.

The blood raced hot through her veins. Releasing his shirt, she ran her hands caressingly over the warm solid flesh of his chest, then upward over his shoulders. She felt dizzy with excitement. Her mind whirled. He'd said he loved her. He wanted to marry her. Was she dreaming? When their lips parted, she buried her face in his neck for a long moment to regain her equilibrium.

He lifted her chin and kissed her forehead, then the tip of her nose. "I've been in love with you for a long time." There was pain in his eyes and his voice was husky with emotion. "At first I tried to convince myself that what I was feeling was strictly brotherly...that you were the sister I never had. But it was more, much more than that. When you went away to college, I missed you like hell.

"Then when you took that job in Kansas City, I couldn't sleep nights. I was so worried about you. But every time you came home we only seemed to fight."

"You were always so critical," she said in her defense.

"And *you* always took everything I said the wrong way," Luke replied. His arms closed around her even more tightly as if he was afraid she might try to get away from him again. "I thought I had convinced myself that it was ridiculous for me to hope we could ever have a future together. Then the job of deputy opened up and you applied. I pulled every string I could to make certain you were hired. In spite of my doubts about us, I wanted you here so badly it hurt. But after you came, we were at each other's throats even worse than before.

"Then this murder happened and I saw how much you wanted to believe in me. In spite of all the evidence against me, and after seeing me with Melinda the other morning, you still stood by me. And then there was that kiss. Afterward, when I found out you hadn't told anyone about seeing Melinda at my place, I thought about that kiss a lot. It occurred to me that fear might not have been the emotion you were experiencing. When I saw the look of jealousy in your eyes the night Lydia brought me dinner in jail, I knew I was right."

"All these years I thought you were seeing me with pigtails and freckles." She kissed the line of his jaw. Suddenly her mouth formed a pout. Looking at him, she demanded tersely, "Why didn't you say something to let me know how you felt? Do you have any idea how frustrated I've been?"

A self-conscious look came over his features. "Maybe was a little afraid you would reject me.... Maybe I was a lot afraid," he corrected.

She saw the hint of fear in his eyes, and for the first tim in her life she knew the real power of her womanhood. I was an exhilarating sensation. She arched more tightl against him, kissing the smooth hard flesh of his shoulder "But after you guessed how I felt, why didn't you sa something?"

A dark shadow seemed to pass through his eyes. "Be cause by then my situation looked pretty bleak, and I loved you too much to tie you to a man who was accused of a murder he couldn't prove he didn't commit." His hand moved with a firm caress over her back, then lower to fee the curve of her hips. "I was so jealous of Mark Smythe wanted to run the man out of town. When you started talking about starting up an agency with him, I nearly wen crazy with frustration."

Her body ignited beneath his touch. "I know that feel ing," she admitted huskily, trailing her hands along hi shoulders to the back of his neck. "I love you so much." Rising on tiptoes, she met his mouth for a lingering explo ration.

His breathing became ragged and she sensed his stron, male need. An aching hunger swept through her. Instinc tively her body moved against his, inviting an even mor intimate contact.

She felt him shiver. Suddenly conscious of the cold nigh breeze stirring around them, she frowned self reproachfully. "You must be freezing. Dr. Clark is neve going to leave me in charge of one of his patients again."

Taking his hand, she began leading him back into the house.

But as they reached the door, he came to an abrupt halt. "Before we go inside, I want an answer, Jess."

She frowned up at him questioningly. "An answer?"

His voice was low and husky, "Will you marry me?"

Her eyes sparkled. "Yes," she said, smiling. Then she kissed him lightly to seal the bargain. "Now, will you, please, let me take you inside."

A playful look came over his features as he pulled her into his arms. "This has got to be a first."

She frowned up at him in confusion. "A first?"

"This has got to be the first time you have agreed to something I have requested without a question or a protest," he elaborated.

"Now who's being incorrigible?" she demanded with a playful scowl. Then, her expression becoming serious, she said, "Will you, please, go inside. I don't want a bridegroom with pneumonia."

"Yes, ma'am," he replied, opening the door and allowing her to enter ahead of him. Without pausing, he slipped an arm around her shoulders and led her through the house to the front door. "And now it's time for you to go home."

"I can't." She reached up and locked and bolted the front door. "I promised the doctor I would stay and take care of you."

"Jess, you can't." He frowned self-consciously. "I want you too much. Now that I know how you feel, it's hell not to make love to you."

"I'm not leaving," she informed him firmly. Picking up the hall phone, she dialed her home number. When her mother answered she told her very quickly what had happened regarding Melinda Strope and Mark Smythe. She finished by explaining that Luke had been injured and, at the doctor's request, she was staying to keep an eye on him.

"I certainly hope you plan to spend this time with him wisely," Molly said cryptically.

"I do," Jessica assured her.

Hanging up, she turned to find Luke frowning down at her. "My condition isn't anywhere near as serious as you made it sound. I've been hurt worse—"

"Falling from a horse," she finished for him. "Yes, I know."

The frown remained on his face. "And you didn't mention our impending marriage. Are you afraid Molly will disapprove?"

"No," she assured him without hesitation. "But she's very, very old-fashioned. I am, too, except where you're concerned."

She smiled softly as she again ran her hands caressingly over his chest and along his shoulders. "If I had told her about us, she would have insisted on coming out here as a chaperon."

"Jess." His voice carried a strong note of caution.

Ignoring it, she tasted the hollow of his neck with the tip of her tongue. "She'll insist on at least two months to plan the wedding."

"Two months?" he asked huskily, his hands moving beneath her sweater to explore the soft curves beneath.

"At least." A smile curved her lips as she trailed kisses along the side of his neck, up to his earlobe and then nipped it.

Catching a glimpse of his stitches, she flushed self-consciously and drew away from him. "I'm sorry. I shouldn't be doing this. I should be giving you a couple of aspirins and tucking you into bed."

"I only have two stitches, and I've already taken the aspirin," he replied gruffly. "But tucking me into bed sounds like a very good idea." Slipping an arm around her shoulders, he guided her toward the stairs.

Much later, as she lay snuggled against him, her body felt a new kind of aliveness. A lingering excitement mingled with a sense of satisfied relaxation. She moved her head against his shoulder and looked up into his face. He was lying quietly, staring at the ceiling. "Penny for your thoughts," she said softly.

He smiled down at her. "I was thinking about how lucky I am and how this place finally feels like a home after all these years."

Raising herself up on one arm, she kissed him lightly on the mouth. "I feel pretty lucky myself."

Turning her back onto the pillow, he feathered kisses over her face while the curly hairs on his chest brushed sensually against her breasts, rekindling the flame of desire. Suddenly pausing abruptly, he lifted his head and looked anxiously into her face. "I didn't hurt you, did I?"

"Only for a moment," she murmured, her eyes darkening to an emerald green as his hand moved over her stomach and then downward, exploring with erotic provocation.

He smiled a quirky, relieved smile and kissed the tip of a hardening nipple. "It gets better."

Her fingernails gently raked his back. "Prove it."

"I intend to," he replied in a voice filled with purpose.

Harlequin Intrigue®

QUID PRO QUO

Racketeer King Crawley is a man who lives by one rule: An Eye For An Eye. Put behind bars for his sins against humanity, Crawley is driven by an insatiable need to get even with the judge who betrayed him. And the only way to have his revenge is for the judge's children to suffer for their father's sins....

Harlequin Intrigue introduces Patricia Rosemoor's QUID PRO QUO series: #161 PUSHED TO THE LIMIT (May 1991), #163 SQUARING ACCOUNTS (June 1991) and #165 NO HOLDS BARRED (July 1991).

Meet:

* *Sydney Raferty:* She is the first to feel the wrath of King Crawley's vengeance. Pushed to the brink of insanity, she must fight her way back to reality—with the help of Benno DeMartino in #161 PUSHED TO THE LIMIT.

* *Dakota Raferty:* The judge's only son, he is a man whose honest nature falls prey to the racketeer's madness. With Honor Bright, he becomes an unsuspecting pawn in a game of deadly revenge in #163 SQUARING ACCOUNTS.

* *Asia Raferty:* The youngest of the siblings, she is stalked by Crawley and must find a way to end the vendetta. Only one man can help—Dominic Crawley. But will the son join forces with his father's enemy in #165 NO HOLDS BARRED?

Don't miss a single title of Patricia Rosemoor's QUID PRO QUO trilogy coming to you from Harlequin Intrigue.

**THIS JULY, HARLEQUIN OFFERS YOU
THE PERFECT SUMMER READ!**

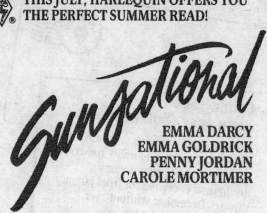

**EMMA DARCY
EMMA GOLDRICK
PENNY JORDAN
CAROLE MORTIMER**

From top authors of Harlequin Presents comes
HARLEQUIN SUNSATIONAL, a four-stories-in-one
book with 768 pages of romantic reading.

Written by such prolific Harlequin authors as Emma Darcy,
Emma Goldrick, Penny Jordan and Carole Mortimer,
HARLEQUIN SUNSATIONAL is the perfect summer
companion to take along to the beach, cottage, on your
dream destination or just for reading at home in the warm
sunshine!

Don't miss this unique reading opportunity.

Available wherever Harlequin books are sold.

Coming soon
to an easy chair near you.

FIRST CLASS is Harlequin's armchair travel plan for the incurably romantic. You'll visit a different dreamy destination every month from January through December without ever packing a bag. No jet lag, no expensive air fares and *no* lost luggage. Just First Class Harlequin Romance reading, featuring exotic settings from Tasmania to Thailand, from Egypt to Australia, and more.

FIRST CLASS romantic excursions guaranteed! Start your world tour in January. Look for the special **FIRST CLASS** destination on selected Harlequin Romance titles—there's a new one every month.

NEXT DESTINATION:
FLORENCE, ITALY

 Harlequin Books

JTR7